SPLIT DECISION

Carmen Capuano

Carmen Capuano Productions

ISBN-13: 9781916877108

Cover design by: selfpubbookcovers.com/Joetherasakdhi

Library of Congress Control Number: 2018675309
Printed in the United States of America

Dedication

This novel is dedicated to those I have loved and lost over the years, and to all the animals I didn't get to save.

It's dedicated to those who don't have a voice to speak up for themselves, to the oppressed, the exploited and the unloved.

It's a hope that together we can change this world into a better, brighter place; a plea that you'll help me in this; and a promise that if we work together, anything is possible.

Most of all, it's from me, to you. With love. X

Thanks

A heartfelt thanks to my children who never stopped believing in my writing and who are my greatest supporters. And to my partner who never once questioned why.

To friends who bought my books and told others about them.

And to you for buying this book to help me achieve my aim of helping animals in need.

Thank you all. X

Author's note

"Morality is herd instinct in the individual."
Nietzsche, Friedrich and Walter Kaufmann (Translator). The Gay Science. 1882.

I believe that the German philosopher was wrong. Morality isn't a set of rules to which we conform as a society, just because we have been told to do so. It is a choice we make every day and in every little aspect of our lives.

Morality is an invisible, indefinable muscle, which grows and strengthens with the exercise of giving and receiving love and respect. Or so I choose to believe…

Carmen Capuano.

FOREWORD

Everything significant in
life is in the timing....

SUNDAY APRIL 28TH

1:23 a.m.

Neon lights and siren wails slashed through the inky blackness of the night. The ambulance followed the police cars; screeched to a halt at the scene.

Paramedics leapt out, paying no attention to the actions of the police officers. Their attention was solely focused on the unconscious girl on the ground.

Carefully they picked her up and carried her to the ambulance.

Once more, they rushed into the night...

CHAPTER 1

Saturday April 27th 11 a.m.

"Well?"

Stacey took a long hard look, twisting her head to appraise all five foot two of me. Her black, bobbed hair curved around her face, outlining her cherub's lips and dark brown eyes. "They're very pink!" She grinned. "They're also really high! Can you walk in them?"

I took a couple of steps across the shop's stained, industrial carpet. "They're a lot higher than my other shoes but I guess I'll get used to them."

"Hmm, either get used to them or break your neck!" Stacey agreed. "Are they comfortable?"

"Since when has that ever been a consideration?" I laughed.

Stace shrugged. "I like the peep-toes and the little flowers above them," she said wistfully as I wiggled my toes inside the shoes, "kind of makes them look like little faces."

I pulled my dark blond hair behind my ears and tried to see what she meant.

"Look, the little flowers are the eyes and

the peep-toe is the mouth," she explained. She looked up at me, her face comically earnest. "You do know they're really sexy, don't you? They have a look that just screams *sex appeal*!" She widened her eyes as she said the words, running her tongue over her upper lip at the end, for added affect.

I giggled. "Well, the shoes can say anything they want 'cos I'm not going to be listening." But my head fretted over her words. Was I really up to wearing something so overtly sexy? A tight noose of apprehension wound itself around my heart.

"Ah, but the shoes just *scream* it, Nat! How can you *not* hear them?" She cupped a hand behind her ear as if listening. "Can't you hear their siren call?"

I pursed my lips and shook my head solemnly. "OK, I get the point – the shoes are sexy! The question is, do they look right on *me*?"

"What d'you mean?" she asked, brow furrowing as she re-examined them.

"Are you *having* the shoes or not?" a tetchy voice enquired, black kohl-rimmed eyes flickering over and dismissing me as unworthy of their regard. Barely eighteen, the sales assistant could have been any age under the thick mask of make-up she wore. Drawn-on eyebrows, higher than their natural lines, and over-painted lips obscured her features, making her look like an older

3

sister of the girl who had been only a year ahead of Stace and me in school.

"That's what we are just deciding, Suzie. If you need to go help someone else, that's fine," I said, expecting her to move away to deal with other customers in the shop. Instead she stood her ground, fingernails of one hand worrying at a ragged nail on the other.

"Manager says I have to *attend* to you." She succeeded in making it sound like she had been put on guard duty; as if Stace and I were known shoplifters and troublemakers. She pulled off the little strip of nail and dropped it to the floor before sliding one foot over it, crushing it into the pile.

"What manager?" Stacey challenged, looking around as though she expected to find someone watching us from the shadows. I followed her gaze. No one paid us the slightest bit of interest in the crowded shop.

Suzie shrugged. "*The manager,*" she repeated, as if that should put an end to it. She brought her brightly painted fingernails to her face and examined them for imperfections. Finding none, she folded her arms across her chest with a sigh, an exhalation of terminal boredom.

"If you want my opinion, I agree with Stacey. The shoes are too sexy for you." The unsolicited judgment added to the cursory glance over me with half-closed eyes, made me feel that a plastic bag would be too sexy for me. "Perhaps you should try something with a lower heel. Something more *sensible*..."

"Actually I'm not interested in your opinion." I tried to sound unbothered but wasn't sure that I successfully pulled it off. "And don't worry, Suzie, I won't be wearing them to school. I'd never embarrass myself like that!"

For a moment I wished I'd held the barbed comment back. Her thick false eyelashes quivered and her mouth turned down spitefully at the corners. I wished too that we had come to the shop on her day off instead of today. Wished that I were anywhere other than the spot where I actually stood.

"Unlike *some* people who do much more shocking things at school..." Stacey butted in pointedly, eyes flashing fire at Suzie. I knew that Stace was only trying to fight my corner but I really wished she'd kept quiet. Instead I feared that she'd made things far worse. "And Nat, I never meant that the shoes were too sexy for you..." Big doe-eyes begged my understanding.

"Yes I know, Stace..." I replied, wishing Suzie would just go away. Perhaps she might have done before my comment; but now, with her arms still folded and a new coy expression lighting up her face, I knew she was intent on creating discord.

"Yes of course, you're both still at school!" she sneered in mock surprise, speaking very slowly, enunciating every syllable as if she spoke to a very young child. Her grin was acidic and cold ice glittered from under the fake lashes. Unfolding her arms, she placed her hands on her hips and tilted her head quizzically. "You know, I think Stacey could carry them off better than you, Natalie. She has a little more about her, if you know what I mean." Her eyes lingered on Stacey's long, toned legs and narrow hips, before they moved back to me, giving the impression that the comparison had not been at all in my favour.

"Still it's your call," she said flatly. "So are you having them or not?" Icy gaze flitted nervously towards the shop door as if she really did think I might be planning to run off in them.

"Yes, I'm having them," I chirped brightly, refusing to acknowledge her attitude and my own relief when I slipped my feet out the shoes. They were more than a little high and I was rather uncomfortable with the battle Suzie had picked. But I was not of a mind to back down.

She lifted them reluctantly, handling them as if they were radioactive, contaminated by the short contact with my skin and flounced off in a huff of rustling uniform and prickling attitude, shoes held stiffly out in front of her. Watching her go, I was filled with a strange sadness, as if the day had already peaked and begun to wane.

"Why has she always hated me?" I asked, unsure whether I was talking to myself or Stacey.

"It's 'cos you're prettier than her," Stace said without the slightest hint of comedy.

"I'm not prettier than her. Just different." I looked at my friend. "And if she hated anyone for their looks, it should be you, Stacey Papadopolous, Greek Goddess!" I bowed down at her reverently. Her cupid's bow lips parted to reveal two rows of even white teeth as she laughed.

"OK, so maybe it's not the looks then," she said mischievously. "In that case, I have no idea why she hates you, Nat. But she definitely does!" Whilst I had been trying on the shoes she'd held my bag; she passed it back to me now. "Do you think your mum is going to be alright with them? The shoes I mean."

"Why wouldn't she be?" I asked, genuinely surprised.

"Because they're so sexy!" Stacey breathed, as if afraid to say the words too loudly, now that I had claimed the shoes as mine.

I laughed again. "Well, I'll be sixteen tomorrow so I guess she won't mind too much. Not so sure about my dad though!" I grimaced. A thought ran through my head and although I didn't want to voice it, I knew I had to. "She was right, you know."

"Who was? About what?"

"Suzie. She was right when she said the shoes would suit you better than they suited me..." The admission of truth stung. "You know if you wanted to get a pair in a different colour…" I held my breath, hoping that she wouldn't take me up on it.

"Well, the red looked great too…and they would go with…" in her excitement she didn't hesitate, eyes flying to the crimson heels on the shelf. But then suddenly she stopped. "Is that too awful?" She looked at me and then back at the shoes once more. "No, you saw them first. Therefore you get them." Her voice was longing and although her face was turned away from me, I was sure it mirrored that sentiment. She tore her eyes away from the rack, wrinkling her nose at me as if determined to stick to her promise.

"Do you think those rumours were true?" she asked, changing the subject. She looked pointedly at Suzie who was waiting for me at the till.

"Is some of that stuff even possible?" I shrugged. My head automatically followed Stacey's gaze to find that Suzie stood watching us from behind the counter. I knew that she could see we were talking about her.

"All those guys…they couldn't *all* have been lying…" Stacey mused.

I was suddenly suffused with guilt. Whatever had happened had happened. None of it had anything to do with me or Stacey. It was none of our business. "Well, whatever the truth, she's certainly paying for it now." I indicated the less than up-market shop.

"Yeah well, that's her own fault, isn't it!" Stacey replied without the slightest trace of empathy. "She deserves everything she gets!" Despite her vitriolic words, Stacey's face remained impassive and she shifted her gaze to something else in the shop. Judgement given, she had already moved on.

For some reason I knew I didn't want Stacey at my side when I went to pay for the shoes. "Why don't you have a look, see if there's something you like?" I suggested.

"Hmm, that's not going to happen! You've already snagged the best shoes in the shop!" There was a hardness to her voice that surprised me, a remnant perhaps of the conflict with Suzie. Involuntarily I flinched. Completely unaware of this, she wandered off, leaving me to walk to the till alone, as I had hoped.

With the counter between us, I watched Suzie ring up the sale, fingers jerky and tight as if she used the machine to vent her anger. Using only the tips of her fingers, she snatched the money from my hand and dropped my change into it from a height, reluctant to let her flesh suffer the slightest contact with mine. She ripped a bag from somewhere below the counter and stuffed the shoes into a box and the box into the open bag, each movement an act of warfare, an invitation to conflict. Her movements were stilted, seemingly so automatically performed without emotion or significance that they stood out as exactly the opposite.

The receipt emerged from its slot like a white flag waved from a rampart and was ripped off with trembling hands and thrust towards me. Not a word was spoken by either of us and I almost turned away without looking once more at her face. But that tremble mesmerised me. It captured my attention and forced me to follow its line of wrist to shoulder and upwards to her face. And for just a moment, in that second of unguarded expression, what I saw there, surprised me.

Underneath the thick make-up and the attitude, I saw the schoolgirl that she had been - right up until she had a baby in the girls' locker room in the middle of lunch.

CHAPTER 2

11:30 a.m.

I swallowed the lump which sat uncomfortably in my throat; it was easy to see how Suzie had perceived Stacey and me talking together.

"It wasn't about you, Suzie," I said quietly, searching for the right words to say and unable to find them, knowing that I was lying.

"It's not like anything you said hasn't been said before." Suzie shrugged indifferently, but her eyes would not meet mine and her face maintained a hard set. I remained where I was for a moment, hoping that the force of my presence would make her look up at me, make her see how genuinely sorry I was. And a deep shameful part of me ached to ask what the truth really was.

"I didn't sleep with half the neighbourhood though, if that's what you were thinking. Not even a quarter of it." Behind the sarcasm her eyes betrayed a deep hurt before they became cloudy with malice once more. She thrust her chin out defiantly. "Not that I actually care what *you* think; what anyone thinks."

Something about her vicious tone dragged

a half-truth from me. "That wasn't what I was thinking at all, Suzie. What I really wondered was what I'd ever done to you, to make you hate me so much."

My feelings of hurt and injustice bounced off her, leaving no indication she'd even noticed them. "You really don't know, do you?" she snorted, as if my question singled me out as an imbecile. "Miss Perfect Little-Girl-Next-Door!" The words were bitten out, each one a fired missile.

I stood dumbfounded, no idea of what to do or say.

"Are you quite finished?" From the queue behind me, a woman impatiently elbowed me aside and thumped a pair of black school shoes onto the counter. "Just these please," she said to Suzie, trying to fish her purse out of her bag.

"But I like the other ones!" A child pulled desperately on her arm.

"And I already told you, Maggie, that the heel on the other pair is too high!" the mother snapped.

"Yes, *schoolgirls* need to wear low shoes!" Suzie said pointedly and I knew her words were for me and not the little girl.

I was too unaccountably embarrassed to counter the remark; too ashamed to walk away. Perhaps I would have stood that way forever if the spell hadn't been broken by the little girl trying to snatch away the unwanted shoes before her mother could purchase them. There followed a slight tussle between mother and child, mother reigning victorious and daughter reduced to tears. The shoes were once more slapped onto the counter with the payment held out, demanding action.

I saw Suzie's hand reach forward and take the money. And although I knew the petulant shrieks which rent the air were those of the child, my mind fabricated the image that it was Suzie who uttered them. The sound scraped along the edges of my nerves until I thought my eardrums might shatter.

She completed the sale without once looking in my direction, without once acknowledging that I remained where I stood. A sick feeling settled in my stomach and I was forced to shuffle back to Stace, eyes downcast and colour flooding my face.

"Let's get out of here!" I urged, pulling her towards the exit.

"What did she say to you?" Stace enquired, dropping a pair of trainers back onto the shelf they had come from.

"Nothing really." That was the truth. She hadn't said anything directly. It was what she had *implied* beyond the words themselves. "Come on, let's get out of here!" I repeated, dragging her towards the door.

The morning air was crisp with a brittle not-quite-there tang. A heady promise of summer. I drank it in greedily, seeking its sharp cleansing nature to rid myself of what had just happened.

Inhaling great lungfuls of oxygen whilst Stace prattled on about everything and nothing, soothed my soul and my conscience. It wasn't exactly that I was *not* listening, more that I had become adept at tuning her out ever-so-slightly when the need arose.

Birds perched on rooftops and flew overhead and I had such a feeling of anticipation, as if the world were holding its breath for something – waiting for some momentous event to occur, that it was almost as if the whole planet existed within a glass dome. I saw the universe in a microcosm. My life, my *essence* reduced to a particle of dust – so insignificant to the rest of the world, to the function of the universe. And yet inside me bubbled the thought that in twenty-four hours, I would be sixteen!

"Nat. NATALIE," Stacey shook me into awareness. "Look! Rhys is over there!" she exclaimed, pointing one short-taloned finger in his direction.

I focused on the fingernail instead of the boy. "Your dad will go mad when he sees you with nail varnish on!" I warned.

"Hmmf!" she brandished bright red-lacquered nails in front of my face. "I'll take it off before he sees it," she conceded. "But I'm not going to be serving fish and chips forever!" She looked at me shrewdly, "Are you trying to change the subject?"

I had no answer for her and none for myself.

"Let's go and say hello," she said excitedly.

Rhys hadn't seen us yet. Head bent over his phone, he seemed oblivious to everything around him. It was entirely possible that we could just walk past.

Stacey grabbed my arm and pulled me across the road. "You've known him forever," she said breathlessly. I noticed how brightly her eyes shone as she flicked them towards Rhys and back to me.

"Hmm, not for a while really..." but she wasn't listening.

"He's been gone a year, Nat. Not a decade."

"Thirteen months actually," I corrected.

"Not that you're counting." She arched her eyebrows at me. "He was gone thirteen months - so now you don't know him?" Her eyebrows stayed dramatically high, lips pursed in that 'I'm right and you know it' look I knew so well.

I reasoned that it was entirely possible that she was right. "When we were little, he was my best friend. But he's kind of different now." I forced out.

"Yeah!" She slapped her forehead as if I were an idiot. "He's older now, isn't he? Seventeen?

Eighteen? He's grown up." There was an admiring quality to her voice that despite my reservations, I found appealing. One step ahead of me, she continued to pull me in her wake.

We approached him. Way too close for comfort, I watched his pulse throb through a vein in his neck, the line and angle of his jaw turned in my direction. He remained completely unaware of our presence, still fully focused on his phone.

"Hi Rhys, what' you up to?" enquired Stacey too-brightly, shattering the stillness around us. For a golden second her words faded to nothing and eternity hung in the balance before us. A moment when anything was possible and the future was open. I felt it shimmer in the air expectantly, entranced by the sheer possibilities that were contained within it. I could not speak. I *dared* not speak.

"Hi Stacey...oh um...Nat! I didn't see you there. I'm just picking up a few things." His eyes shifted towards the shoe shop we had just exited and I wondered briefly if he was lying, if he had seen us after all and had been avoiding us for some reason. Maybe I was right, maybe his thirteen months away was too long, after all.

"Hi Rhys," I replied in a voice that seemed too loud and strangulated, as if Stace had tight hold of my throat rather than my arm. I'd never felt this awkward talking to him before; all the summer nights that we had played out together or sat on walls and discussed our innermost fears and secrets. Things had been easy between us. We'd always been able to count on each other back then. Now a strange tension hung over us. But in those days, we hadn't had an audience.

It seemed that Rhys had had the same thought. "Sorry Stacey, could you give us a minute?" he asked, flashing her a winning smile.

"Yeah, sure…um…what for?" she stuttered, frowning at this apparently unexpected development. "I mean, what d'you wanna do…oh…oh, I get it!" Her eagerness seemed to fade a little as she turned her gaze to me and I got a strange but distinct impression that she was disappointed in some way. "I'll be over there, looking at the dress in that window, if you need me," she smiled conspiratorially and for a second I thought I saw her force a wink at Rhys. Clearly I had been mistaken about her reaction.

We watched her leave as if that had been the sole purpose of the request. My mouth was bone dry and my head empty. I couldn't think of a single thing to say or do.

Rhys turned to me, slowly and deliberately. I was struck by how well-defined and precise his movements were. The sun caught his ash-blond hair and lit it up like a halo. But it was his Adams' apple I focused on, which bobbed up and down in a fascinating way as he stammered, "Nat, um - there's something I want to ask you…" He swallowed hard as I stared at him, his impossibly blue eyes for once not smiling or joking.

Still in his hand, the phone emitted a loud bleep and he shoved it dismissively into a pocket. Another beep followed and another, but he ignored them all. Minutes seemed to be measured only by the faint noises issued by the unseen phone, the bleeps and pings testament to the world progressing through space and time around us as we stood immobile.

Hand lingering on the pocket where his phone lay concealed, he lifted his face up, his eyes drawing and pulling mine into their depths.

"I was thinking…would you come out with me?" He exhaled in a rush.

In an instant, everything between us had altered. I saw him appraise the physical changes the thirteen months had wrought in me; the lengthening of limbs and filling of curves. A mild tingling sensation started somewhere near my stomach and radiated outwards, unnerving me - scorching my body with a growing intensity that made my breath catch in my throat and my heart accelerate. I hadn't ever felt like *that* before.

I hadn't ever been looked at in quite that way either – like he was looking both *at* me and *through* me.

Memories stored as pictures flitted through my head, racing faster and faster after each other. Rhys and I outside in his back garden, laughing as we watched my shot just miss the hoop, yet again; him chasing me at the park, longer and more muscled legs finally outstripping my smaller frame; me being unceremoniously hauled up by him and thrown into the small pond. And that last night before he went away, both of us huddled on my back step, pledging eternal friendship through time and distance.

And I remembered too, how the weekly phone calls, so initially bright, became tainted with perceived loss and the news of new and more relevant friendships formed. An old hurt in my heart made a feeble pang...a memory of its own, flickering around like an unwanted ghost.

We'd been friends. We had drifted apart. And now he wanted more than friendship. It felt strange. Would I be able to handle it? Could I really turn him down?

"Yes, Rhys, I would love to go out with you." Somewhere in the back of my brain I was surprised at how calm and quiet and *formal* I sounded, like one of those women from old black and white films.

Rhys merely smiled, the grin extending all the way up to those sky-blue eyes, in a way that I remembered from old. I traced the smile back down to where it originated from, and lingered there, focusing on the minute lines which defined the shape and form of his lips. Would I really kiss those lips? Only in my peripheral vision did I see

19

the slow smile that carved itself upon his face and which sparked in me a tingling flush, suffusing my face with unwanted colour and laying bare my intimate thoughts.

A sudden breeze ruffled his hair and seemed to leave him reluctantly, brushing gently across my face with its cooling essence. I would have sworn that it carried the scent of honey. Perhaps it was only my imagination.

Once again, time seemed to stand impossibly still and when reality reasserted itself, it did so with a *whoosh*, like someone had stopped spinning the world for a few seconds, only to start it up again, speeding it faster and faster until it regained its full momentum.

I glanced over at Stace who was pretending to be interested in a shop display. She stood sideways to the window, leaning towards us. I was amazed that she was able to maintain the pose without toppling over. Even from a distance I could see that her eyes were slanted in our direction and for a moment I thought I could see her ears wiggle with the effort of straining to overhear.

Rhys followed my gaze and when we turned back to look at each other, we were both grinning. "Hmm." I pursed my lips dramatically. "OK! Looks like I'd better get back to Stacey and fill her in," I giggled, turning away and concluding the conversation.

"Guess so," he laughed. Then suddenly serious, "Will you meet me tonight, Nat?" he asked, once again seeming hesitant and unsure. His apparent lack of confidence boosted mine, as if unconsciously he had given me the upper hand in the burgeoning relationship.

"Yeah. Sure. Tonight. I'll meet you by the school gates. 7.30pm. OK?" My voice was more clipped and assertive than I'd intended and I watched surprise flit briefly over his face.

"Great, see you there," he responded, with a grin. "Text me if you're going to be late."

I nodded and turned away, knowing that there was no way I'd be late. Even though I could no longer see him, I felt his eyes burning into my back as inside me a bright flame of anticipation flared.

I was going on a date!

CHAPTER 3

2.30 p.m.

I couldn't concentrate on Stacey or anywhere she led me. Everything seemed to be merely a distraction until half seven - an easy way to kill time. I looked through shop windows at clothes I didn't see, jewellery I didn't notice. Instead of shining displays of coloured glass and trinkets, I saw images of me on my date, bright kaleidoscopes of Rhys and me, laughing and having fun.

"Nat? NAT!"

"Hmm? What?" I looked at Stacey properly for the first time since Rhys had asked me out. Hands on her hips and an impatient glare on her face, she was a strange and probably unintentional parody of Suzie earlier.

"I said," she repeated pointedly, "do you like that ring?" she pointed to a gaudy looking metal band which sported several different coloured pieces of glass in a geometric shape. I shrugged. She sighed.

"Come inside with me so I can have a proper look. You know you haven't paid the slightest bit of attention to anything I have said since Rhys..." she said petulantly, shooting her eyebrows up disdainfully.

I tried to sound apologetic. "Sorry, Stace, you're right." I hung my head sheepishly and held the shop door open for her to pass through ahead of me.

"So will you be wearing *the shoes* tonight?" she said, as if they were endowed with magical qualities. Clearly she had decided to forgive me.

"Hmm. Toto, I have a feeling we're not in Kansas anymore," I dead-panned.

Rooting through a basket of bangles, Stace slid two of them onto her wrist and held a third up to compare. She worked her arm up and down, causing the thin metal to make a satisfying jangle when they collided against one another. Then she slipped the third on to see if it was an improvement.

"Tap your heels together three times. And think to yourself – there's no place like home. There's no place like home." She finished by clicking her heels together just as we'd done when we'd been younger, watching *The Wizard Of Oz*, side by side, a huge bowl of popcorn between us. There was a strange unfathomable melancholy in her eyes.

"It's been a while," I said. I couldn't quite keep the wistfulness from my voice and hoped that she didn't laugh and shatter the memory.

She didn't. "It's been *too* long. You know me Nat, never could get enough of that Tin Man." She laughed softly, a subtle sadness that was almost imperceptible. Things were changing. *We* were changing.

For a long moment I considered the unknown future, what bright joy and untold misery it might contain. A thin spindle of excitement curdled into uncertainty in my soul, seeming to taint the very air around me. I struggled to shake it off.

"Never did know what you saw in him anyway. Care to share?" I winked half-heartedly.

Stacey seemed not to notice my changed mood. "I ain't gonna share any man, not even with you!" she stated mock indignantly, eyes twinkling and deliberately misunderstanding me. Her giggle was contagious and I couldn't help but join in. Maybe the future wouldn't be a constant beacon of shining brightness but we would always have each other.

"Well, it's just…he's got no heart…" she pulled a sad face and it was so genuine that even though I laughed, I was haunted by the hollowness of the sound which seemed to echo through my soul. An uneasiness assailed me, a foreboding of future events as yet unknown and therefore unavoidable.

A silence descended between us and I wondered if Stacey felt the uncertainty too. Unwilling to mention it, in case like a demon, its voicing summoned it into being, I stared fixedly at her arm where the three bangles lay silent and still on her wrist. I was strangely afraid that she would jangle them again, bizarrely concerned that the noise would summon some *thing* which would wreak havoc in an unknown way...but to my great relief she slid them off without further testing and reached for her purse.

Eyes lowered and appearing to avoid me, she offered what was on her mind. "At least you get to go out with a guy!"

"Yes, and you will too!"

She snorted derisively. "You think? What with my dad and Theo acting as bodyguards? Wow, what fun that will be!" she rolled her eyes theatrically.

"Hmm," I empathised, unsure how to continue. "You don't know that's what will happen..." I tried to sound convincing but Stace was having none of it and cut over me with an attempt at her older brother's voice.

"Ain't no little sis of mine gonna be mauled over by some worthless piece of..."

"What if you arranged to go out on a night when you knew Theo was going out? Maybe that's the answer!" Assuming that anyone was brave or stupid enough to risk the wrath of Theo in the first place, I thought.

"Oh Nat, you are a twit sometimes! That's even worse! Then Theo the Dope will insist on a double date." The use of his school nickname was a clear indication of how intolerable it all was to her.

"So? Maybe that'll be easier? Maybe he'll be so caught up in his own date, he won't pay any attention to yours."

"Do I have to spell it out to you?" She stopped in front of a mirror set above a cosmetics display. A bright pink nail varnish the exact colour of the new shoes caught my eye. I found myself reaching for it without even thinking. It wasn't that I didn't sympathise with Stacey's problem but it wasn't the first time we'd discussed it, and I was annoyed that it had been raised again, today of all days.

In silence we walked over to the till. I noticed that she still had the three bangles clutched in her hand. Clearly she'd not given up *completely* on the idea of being glamorous.

"Have you forgotten that Theo is three years older than us?" she asked pointedly as she handed over her cash to the assistant.

"He's had three years to figure out what goes on and he's probably just about able to hold himself back for one night. Just long enough to make sure that whatever *goes down* normally between him and his girlfriend, isn't going to be *going down* on mine!"

I looked at her sharply. There were things implied in her words that we had never discussed before. I'd always thought that she feared she wouldn't be allowed to date, not that she was concerned about activities being curtailed *during* it.

"But Stace...you wouldn't go that far, would you?" An odd image flooded my brain...Stace and the Tin Man locked in a passionate embrace. Bizarre as the image was, I was unable to shake it off. And unable to dismiss too, that idea of him being without a heart.

She laughed, bright jangling sounds that reminded me of how the bracelets had collided together. It was a fraction too late to have been spontaneous and I got the distinct impression that the sound was faked.

"Well, no, of *course* not!" She tilted her head slightly to one side. "But you know what? I'd like at least to be given the *option*!"

I laughed, thinking that I was being dumb, mistaking her frustration and concern for something else, something more fundamental...

"And you've already had a date. Tell me about it again," she begged, sounding like a small girl requesting a favourite bedtime story. I hesitated briefly, worried that our comfortable familiarity would revert back to the edgy uneasiness of a few moments before.

"What, so now you don't want to tell me the details?" she said, a peevish note spiking her voice.

"It's not that I hid anything from you then or

that I'm hiding anything now. It's just that there isn't anything to tell really." I looked at the tight set of her lips and the way she was standing, body tense and rigid. "One previous date in my whole life doesn't make me a date guru, does it?" I was annoyed that once again I was on the defensive. Didn't she understand that I just wanted to float through the rest of the afternoon, thinking about what I was going to wear and where we would go? And whether he would kiss me? And whether I would kiss him back? Didn't she get any of that?

But Stace wasn't deterred in the least, hanging on grimly to her anger like a dog with a bone. "It's still one more date than I've ever had!" She looked at me slyly and for a moment the old Stace humour was back in evidence. "Even if it was with Josh Cooper," she finished, smirking.

"Oh please, don't remind me!" I pleaded, grimacing and giggling at the same time. "Perhaps it would have been more mysterious, to have dated a boy who didn't sit behind me in biology for the previous two years, flicking his pencil at me every time Mr Baum looked away."

"Ya gotta give the guy credit for effort," she sniggered. I wondered exactly why she wanted to hear the tale all over again. Was it just something to lighten the mood? Or did she think there was some tiny bit of information I hadn't yet disclosed to her, that I might this time be persuaded to divulge?

"Yes, well, perhaps he should have saved the effort for the date!" The words came out sharper than I'd intended. I really didn't want to be examining the parallels between then and now.

"It was really just Josh and me hanging out. Wasn't anything special...apart from the odd kiss." I suddenly realised what an appropriate choice of vocabulary I'd used. "You know, the kiss *was* odd. I mean, actually peculiar."

Stace looked at me questioningly as if perhaps I had disclosed something new after all. "Well, it's got to be strange...your first kiss, hasn't it?" She slid her purchased bracelets onto one wrist, making them jangle, reminding me of that false laughter.

"Maybe. But it was more than that." I realised that despite what I'd thought earlier, I actually hadn't told her everything. I hadn't even admitted how it had been, to myself. "How did you know?" I asked her. "How did you know that I hadn't told you everything?"

"Because I've *never* been kissed, never been on a date...but you *have*. And never once did you tell me how wonderful, how exciting, how *sexy* it was. And I kinda figured it had to be at least one of those things. Because if it wasn't..." her arms dropped to her sides in a dramatic jangle of bracelets. Refusing to break stride, using my forward motion as a way to unravel my thoughts, I stepped past her.

There was a sudden crowd around us, people exiting and entering the store and bunching up around the narrow doorway. Deliberately, I let the tide of customers swirl around me, separating me from Stacey for the short time that it took to push my way out and leave the store behind.

I found a spot in the street where she would find me and where we would not be automatically overheard by every passing stranger, and waited for her. I couldn't tell whether her curiosity had been appeased or she was just giving me space. Either way she said nothing as she approached and I was relieved. I needed to tell her what was in my head without interruption.

"There was this kind of awkward anticipation. I didn't know if he wanted to kiss me or not, or even if he did, how I would react. Then he just leaned towards me and I tried to do the same… but I was too far away!" I remembered that for a moment I had feared I might actually topple over. "We were both stretching over so far that we kind of stumbled into each other…and he had to grab onto me to stop us both from falling. It didn't seem funny or sweet – just dumb."

"Romantic!"

I couldn't tell if she was being sarcastic or dreamy.

"It was more like a football tackle than anything else…and then we kissed. And it felt…like nothing." Both at the time and in the retelling I was peculiarly devoid of emotion, as if the whole experience had happened to someone else.

"Oh!" Stacey sounded a bit put out.

"Exactly! It wasn't much of an experience, I have to say."

"I liked him."

It was said so quietly I nearly didn't hear and had to ask to make sure I had heard right. "You like him? Josh Cooper?" I looked at her, astonishment banging a big drum loudly in my head. "You *like* Josh Cooper?"

"Correction – I *liked* him!"

"Oh Stace, I didn't know. Why didn't you say? I would never have gone out with him if I'd known!" I wailed.

"No, I know you wouldn't. But he didn't ask *me*, he asked you."

I had no option but to say what we were both thinking. "But he couldn't ask you, could he? Not with Theo to have to answer to," unintentionally I echoed her earlier worry. "If you do still like him, you could always ask *him* out," I offered. It was met with a withering stare. I guessed it was not quite the same as us both liking the same shoes.

"I don't fancy him anymore."

I detected something unusual in her voice, a note that was there but almost wasn't - like it was deliberately disguised. I wondered if it was hurt, or loss of pride, that almost petulant quality which wasn't quite fully described by her words. Whatever it was, it was gone as quickly as it appeared, replaced by a wry smile.

"Well, if there's one consolation, I guess it's that I don't risk getting anyone else's germs!"

"EUCK!" We grinned at each other, our friendship back onto mutually calm waters. But because of the revelations, I felt the need to continue the discussion. Although from a different perspective. "It wasn't what I expected." My voice was small, reflective.

"No, it doesn't sound much like I would have expected either!"

I realised her misunderstanding. "No, not the kissing! I mean the actual date."

Stace remained silent, waiting for me to continue.

"It was boring."

She turned her head so sharply to look at me that I could almost hear the tendons in her neck popping.

"There was nothing to say. I mean anything remotely interesting that had happened at school, he already knew about. We were the same age, at the same school and lived in the same neighbourhood...what was there to talk about?"

"So how is it going to be different with Rhys?" she asked.

"The weird thing is that I just think it will. I have known him for so long...surely we won't just run out of things to talk about? Or be awkward with one another?"

"You mean like you were earlier, when you refused to see him, across the street?"

She had a point.

"Yeah well, we've reconnected now," I countered.

"Hmm, sounds to me like you've been watching too many slushy movies!" Stace laughed but it was soft and genuine.

"Well…" I laughed too, relieved that the awkwardness between *us* had completely gone. "There was one on the other night." I admitted.

"I knew it! Let me think what it was." She raised a bangled hand to her forehead as if it helped her remember.

"Jennifer Lopez and Matthew McConaughey," I supplied helpfully. Even as I said it, it was not lost on me that Stacey was more J Lo than I could ever be.

"Oh yes. The one where he suddenly realises the perfect girl-next-door, right in front of his eyes?"

And just like, that Suzie's words echoed painfully in my head. *Miss Perfect Little-Girl-Next-Door*. Hadn't those been her exact words? I wondered if it was just coincidence or if fate was moving in mysterious ways after all.

CHAPTER 4

4 p.m.

By mid-afternoon I was all shopped out. Unfortunately Stace was not all talked out.

"And when he kisses you, make sure you open your eyes just to check that *his* are closed," she ordered.

I laughed, surprised. "Why?"

"Because if he means it, his eyes will be closed," she informed me as if she were the one who had been kissed before and not me.

"You mean like he might have kissed me by accident?" It was a ludicrous idea and I was finding it hard to concentrate over the empty gurgling of my stomach.

She didn't even break stride as she pulled me up. "Look I know you have been kissed before but guys…well…"

"Guys well, what?"

"Theo says that guys sometimes act a certain way just to get girls…*interested*…"

I found it hard to imagine even the dumbest girl being that interested in The Dope. *Least said, soonest mended*, I reminded myself.

"Not that I'm suggesting that Rhys would…"

Stace bit her lip, seeming to realise that she was digging herself into a hole. She shrugged her shoulders and changed course, dragging me in her wake. "Wanna go get some chips?" she smiled, proffering up her peace offering. "I could get Dad to throw in some fish too, if you fancy it?"

I sighed. Her dad's fish and chips were legendary, but I didn't want to risk the bloating. "I don't know...fish and chips might not be the best thing to eat before a date!"

"Don't stuff yourself then, just have a few chips!" Stace's tone was dismissive as only those who can eat whatever and whenever they want, can be.

"OK, just a few chips. As long as your dad doesn't mind, that is."

She flipped me a smirk. We both knew how she could twist her dad round her finger...unless it was about the one thing she really wanted – some freedom.

The thought of chips made my stomach clench ravenously. "Now that you have mentioned chips, I can actually smell them," I teased, clamping my jaw to keep from giggling as she pulled her top away from her body to sniff at the fabric before sweeping each sleeve under her nose for inspection.

"Really?" she asked, her usual self-confidence gone. Until she saw the stifled laughter on my face. "And I believed you!" She thumped me good naturedly on the arm.

"I'd better call my mum and let her know not to do any tea for me," I said, already dialling. No one picked up. I thought briefly about phoning Mum's mobile but decided against it. It was just as easy to leave a brief message on the answerphone.

"Your mum is so cool! Mine would still insist I ate the dolmades that she had 'lovingly prepared', even if I had stuffed myself silly elsewhere. Do you know that the Greek language doesn't have a word for 'full'?" she prattled on.

"Really? No word for 'full'? So how do they explain..." I was cut off by the look of sweet revenge on her face.

"Oh Nat! You believed me, didn't you? You really are a ninny sometimes! As if there really isn't a word for 'full'!"

It was my turn to slap her playfully on the arm. But my smile faded and was replaced with a nervousness I didn't like. "What do you think my mum will say when I tell her about Rhys?"

Stace was quiet a moment, giving the question her full consideration. "I think she'll be pleased. She knows Rhys and she also knows that you have to start dating properly sometime...unlike *my* mother!"

I headed her off and back to my own problems. "Yes, but I don't know for a fact that it is a proper date..."

"It IS a proper date," she insisted and propelled me onwards, refusing to slow even when she saw the queue which stretched outside the shop and snaked along the street. Gathering pace, she edged around the customers and towards the congested doorway which led inside.

Always busy, the shop seemed more hectic and its customers more diverse than usual, underlining my own emotional turmoil.

On the narrow pavement, gangs of teenagers jostled for space and position with swarms of pre-teens. Here and there an adult waited patiently, out of place in a sea of youthful faces; cast adrift like a piece of flotsam, awaiting their chance to be served; their pass to chip heaven.

As if on this special day people had been placed in my path as a sort of celestial warning from on high, I caught a glance of one particular customer and could not look away.

Chas Davies slouched in the outdoor queue and regarded nothing in particular with a vacant stare. If Suzie was the head of their particular flipped coin, Chas was the tails. At least Suzie was working and presumably looking after her kid.

Not yet out of her teens, Chas's hair hung limp and bedraggled around her face in a tangled mess. Cavernous hollows at her cheeks and a soulless emptiness in her eyes marked out her addictions better than any words could have.

But it wasn't her my eyes lingered upon, it

was the little boy who clutched at the dirty and frayed leg of her jeans. Tousled hair and wide eyes looked out from a face that was cherubic, despite the river of snot which ran unchecked from his nose. From behind his mother's twig-thin legs, he peered out at me, hesitant yet curious, afraid and yet hungry for affection.

Was this just another coincidence? Coming face to face with both Suzie and Chas - in one day? The same day when I had been asked out on my first proper date? No, I was being ridiculous. Rhys was a good guy. I would never be anything other than safe with him.

The stream of snot had reached the child's upper lip and I watched horrified as it pooled for an instant on the ridge, before running down and into the creases where top lip met bottom.

Revulsion and gut instinct made me reach for a clean tissue for the kid but stilled my hand before I stretched out to wipe his nose. Neither cowardice nor self-preservation halted me, but rather a sudden shaft of knowledge which made me hesitate. How could one lousy tissue help this kid with the problems his mother would accrue? With the problems she would heap upon his for-mative years?

My heart swelled with rough pity and anger. But the tissue was all I had to offer. It wasn't much but that didn't make it worthless. I held it out to the boy but he just looked at the little white rectangle of paper.

With a magician's flourish, I shook out the soft paper folds. Laying it flat in one hand I held it up to my face and mimed a comical sneeze. Then I offered it again. This time the boy took it and copied my actions, clutching the used tissue in one hand and grinning at me.

His lively, animated face was so at odds with his mother's dead expression that I couldn't bring myself to smile back, regardless of how I tried. An ache clutched at my heart and I almost wanted to snatch him away from his lamentable excuse for a parent. Feeling both guilty and impotent, I moved away, striving to keep my eyes focused on the pavement under my feet.

Stace stood waiting for me at the entrance to the shop, a resigned look on her face. "You can't help those who won't help themselves, Nat. Chas is a lost cause," she said quietly.

"I know that…but her little kid…it's not *his* fault." There wasn't any more to say but I said it anyway. "He doesn't stand a chance in life, does he?" My throat was sorely constricted and it hurt to force the words out on vocal chords that were tight and strained.

"Look, if it makes you feel better, I'll get Dad to throw in some chicken for free with his chips. OK? How's that for a good idea?" she watched as I swallowed and nodded, eyes brimming with unshed tears. If she wondered why my emotions were so close to the surface, she gave no indication. But I wondered how she had remained so *unaffected*. "That's settled then. Now come on, I'm starving!" she said as if we had found a solution to global hunger.

I managed a wan smile, knowing that she would keep her word and that her dad would honour it.

"Now stay close and stay focused," she joked as she began to fight her way through the crowd to the front of the shop. The throng swallowed her up in its midst; a sea of people before me surging this way and that as she jostled and 'excuse me'd' her way through and around them.

I followed in her wake but neither as nimble as her nor as forceful, I was left slightly behind. The crowd closed in around me and I was effectively trapped.

And then I saw him. The new boy from school. Nathan Bridges.

Flanked by boys either side of him, boys I recognised from around school but had no names for, he stood out like a raven amongst ducks, black hooded jacket and dark hair combining to make him appear to be lurking within his own shadow. It was almost as if the colour leached from his hair and clothing to the air around him, lending it a feeling of darkly expectant malevolence. Despite the warmth of the vinegary air, I shivered, spine tingling as the hairs on the nape of my neck pricked up.

Coolly aware of my gaze, he stared intently back at me, unworried about who might notice. Was it my imagination that he regarded me with such interest or was he merely examining my flaws, my plainness and ordinariness, my unworthiness of his attention?

There was no doubt that he and I were polar opposites. He was cool, witty, and according to Stacey's dad, 'Trouble', with a capital T. I was - even by my own admission - 'uncool' and therefore did not warrant his attention unless it was a set-up for a cruel yet witty anecdote he would laugh with his friends over - how plain, boring Natalie had thought for even a second that he could be interested in her!

My face flushed with imagined embarrassment and I stumbled over someone's unseen foot, causing me to crash into the person ahead of me. Had the shop been less busy I would more than likely have fallen on my face.

Forced to turn away from his gaze, I was sure that when I glanced back at him I would find him deep in conversation with his mates, already laughing cruelly about me. I risked another quick look.

He was still staring at me, his eyes following my movements as I awkwardly shuffled past a couple in their twenties, squeezing between them, so that they had to drop each other's hands to make way for me. "Sorry," I muttered apologetically, as I felt their glares on the back of my neck.

Refusing to look up from the forest of torsos and legs which surrounded me, I imagined Nathan's cool and unkind smile, the way his mouth would curl up contemptuously at my awkwardness; I could feel the heat of his amusement burning on my skin and his unwanted focus on my ungainliness. I pushed harder through the crowd.

I seemed to be moving without getting anywhere. How long was the queue? Perhaps I was adrift in some sort of weird space/time continuum, destined to spend eternity pushing through a throng which spun out to infinity!

My head whirled with irrepressible thoughts. Why should his opinion matter to me anyway? What did it matter that I had just confirmed myself as uncool as he had no doubt already labelled me? Why was I giving it a second thought? Angry at myself for even entertaining such ideas, I pushed through the queue with renewed vigour. And as if this were the behaviour the crowd expected, perhaps even *revered*, it parted in front of me.

Suddenly I was there at the front of the line. Still angry at myself, I didn't even consider that trying to emulate Stacey's graceful swing under and up the other side of the counter would be in vain, that the likelihood that I would half-brain myself on the Formica was too high to risk the action. I just did it. Just swung down and under and up. Confronted with this unforeseen and unlikely triumph I stood there, almost expecting a round of applause before I realised that no one was paying me the slightest bit of attention. No one in general. And Nathan Bridges in particular.

For some stupid reason I felt that I had lost something. Something I had never even had.

CHAPTER 5

4:15 p.m.

"It's busy today, Mr Papadopoulos!" I hid my embarrassment and sense of loss and focused instead on Stacey's dad. I tried to avoid looking at Theo, in case it made him think I wanted to start a conversation with him. Not that I disliked Theo, he was just incredibly boring. For all I knew, he probably felt the same about me.

"Lots o' those 'Trouble' kids!" He kept his voice low but inclined his head towards where Nathan's gang stood in the queue. I managed to notice who he was indicating without looking directly. There was a strangely *torn* feeling inside of me, almost a desire to protest at the label he had applied to them.

As far as I knew, Nathan Bridges and his friends had done nothing wrong, even if they did look like they were about to light a flame under the world. Something flickered at the edge of my consciousness and flapped there discordantly, awaiting my attention. I mentally flicked a tongue around it, teasing it out and unravelling it for consideration.

Shaken flat on the landscape of my mind, I

traced the curvature of the memory. A lesson in school. A hypothetical conundrum that had been put to us in class. Something like this: If we were capable of time travel and could go back to pre-Nazi Germany, just before Hitler came to power, would we sanction his assassination? Pull the trigger and eradicate him from history?

There had been no hesitation or equivocation necessary for me. Of course I would! The Second World War would be prevented and millions of lives saved! But Stacey had shook her head. "Hitler hadn't done anything wrong at that point…he was an innocent man. If you killed him then *you* would be the murderer!" she had proclaimed.

"But he would kill millions of Jews and people who were not-" I'd protested.

"He hadn't done it *yet*…he was still innocent."

I'd been flummoxed. "The rules of the question state the only time we can travel back to, is *before* he's done anything…and we know he killed millions…"

"But at that point he was still innocent!" She'd been unrelenting and I hadn't been able to change her mind.

Now I stood before her father who had appointed a label to someone else for crimes that had not yet been committed and I suddenly understood with crystal clarity the nuances that had evaded me that day. Not every moment makes a memory but some do. I wondered if this day would reappear in my future, dredged up from a past where Nathan was still innocent of the heinous crimes that Mr Papadopoulos was convinced he would one day perpetrate.

But why did any of this matter to me? I tried to pick the lock to the little room where my thoughts were so guardedly stored, finessing my movements, refining them with every click of a chamber unlocked, every *thunk* of a tumbler falling...

My confusion was all about the comparison between Nathan and Rhys. They were in the same school year, perhaps even some of the same classes and yet they couldn't be more different. Brooding with a dark mystery to him, Nathan was undoubtedly more intense, more dramatic and surely infinitely more dangerous. Safe within my fantasy world, where thoughts could never become reality, I wondered what it would feel like to be kissed by him, to feel his arms around me, his lips pressed onto mine...

I liked Rhys, I always had, and I was excited about our date. But Nathan...Nathan's eyes burned into my soul with an intensity that was matched only by the quickening pace of my heart, his proximity causing it to flutter almost painfully. Though I hated to admit it to myself, I was more than slightly in awe of him. I wanted Nathan to notice me, for him to wonder what it would be like to hold me, to kiss me...

Only belatedly did I realise that a warmth had infused my body which had nothing at all to do with the heat of the fryers and everything to do with my musings. I bent my head to hide my confusion and ignored Mr Papadopoulos's mutterings.

"Stace, did you ask your dad..." I used the question to focus my thoughts away from further self-analysis and to bring myself back to the real world. Yet I was reluctant to mention the promise she'd made, in case mentioning it or the little boy in the queue would sully my other thoughts; as if deep down I didn't really want to consign the delicious fantasy to dust.

Stace nodded towards a golden bubbling of oil in one of the deep fryers. "Already popped a couple in for him," she said, presuming that I would know she meant chicken pieces. I tried to smile but wasn't sure I pulled it off.

"Got no business to be bringing up little scraps of kids," Mr Papadopoulos mumbled under his breath as he slung another load of chips into the already full compartment.

The combined smell of vinegar and hot oil was almost claustrophobic and seemed to replace the air rather than scent it. My breathing quickened as my lungs demanded more oxygen. I sucked at the vacuum around me, desperate for relief but willing to expire behind the counter rather than admit to how I was feeling and why.

"Trouble kids. Up to a-no-good!" Stacey's dad muttered, his native accent accentuated in his worry over the fate of the world. "In Greece – none of this unmarried mothers…"

I felt like a fish in a waterless tank, suffocating, looking outward from within and powerless to change anything.

"Papa! None of our business!" Theo warned, loading chips onto the paper he held stretched out before him, wrapping and thrusting it into the customer's hands and accepting payment in return.

"That's why these Trouble kids do as they please. Everyone say, 'it no my business – it no my problem!'" Mr Papadopoulos heaved steaming piles of fresh chips into the draining compartment where fat ran from them in sizzling golden rivers.

I found myself considering the difference between the fat on the surface of the chips and how it looked as it congealed cold and used in the drip trays below. My stomach clenched and a large part of my hunger evaporated. Was what lay beneath the surface, always infinitely less desirable than what lay above?

With dwindling enthusiasm I watched Stace wrap my portion of chips, enclosing one end whilst leaving the other open, just how I liked it. Did all best friends know each other so well?

I wondered if she had any idea how Nathan had affected me.

Like me, Stacey's dad had focused on her actions, although for a different reason entirely. "What you wanna be wearin' that stuff on your fingers for?" he asked, eyes fixed firmly on the varnish highlighted by the nimble sweep of her fingers over the white paper.

"Oh Dad, don't start!" Stace rolled her eyes at the ceiling, "it's not like I'm serving customers!" She realised her mistake immediately. "I just couldn't resist it Papa...just like I can't resist your chips!" She threw back her head and tossed a chip into her mouth like a trained circus performer, grinning and winking simultaneously.

Mr Papadopoulos beamed. "See, load-a rubbish chips make you fat!" he exclaimed loudly. "Load-a rubbish they bad for you. They give you good energy, good life. See my Stacey here," he gestured in her direction with a Shakespearean flourish, "chips every day. Chips with fish, chips with chicken, chips with chips..." He stopped to laugh at his own joke, captive audience waiting expectantly.

Stace rolled her eyes again but gamely played her cameo role. "Yes, chips and chips and chips!" She reached up to give him a hurried kiss on the cheek and a whispered reminder about the chicken for the little boy.

But instead of alleviating my conscience I

49

found the opposite happened. What would tomorrow bring for the child? And the next day and the next? I tried to tell myself that all of his days were beyond my control but the words sat greasy and cold in my stomach.

I wished I could be more like Stacey, able to accept that there were only some things I could change. There was a prayer about it, about changing the things that you could and having the wisdom and graciousness to accept that which couldn't be changed. Whether it was wisdom or graciousness that I lacked was irrelevant, my ineffectiveness was its own curse.

I took the chips Stacey handed me, wondering how on earth I was going to choke them down my throat. If I was slow in closing my hands over the hot, damp paper, Stacey didn't seem to notice and I was relieved. To have been ungrateful would have been both wasteful and churlish.

Dodging back under the counter Stace emerged on the other side, a playful glint in her eye. "Bye, Pops!" she called, "see ya laters!" moving through the crowd which parted before her as if she were royalty.

Her father was as peeved as she had intended him to be. "No Americanisms here, Stacey Papadopoulos! Is disrespectful! I am your father not your *pop*!" As ever, Stace knew exactly where to hit the nerve.

I followed in her wake, trying to move neatly

into the spaces that she had just vacated but it was almost impossible as the crowd closed ranks once more, unwilling to step aside for a lowly courtier such as me.

Pushed one way and then another by the sinuous queue, I suddenly found myself face to face with Nathan. Having tried to avoid this at all costs, I realised too late that I had made it an inevitability. In purposely not looking towards him, I had been unable to prevent myself being forced in that very direction.

I watched his lips curve into a slow grin so wide I thought I could see every tooth. His eyes dipped down from my face and hovered at the level of my chest. Breath pulled hard and sharp into my lungs, I tried not to think what had captured his attention. Heat flared in my face and I wanted to look anywhere, everywhere other than at him, but my eyes were drawn there and held against my will.

Deliberately and excruciatingly slowly, he reached towards me. For the briefest of moments I was convinced that he intended to brush my hair away from my face, but at the very last minute his hand darted lower, disappearing out of my line of sight. The fire in my face flared a hotter red, a conflagration that threatened to extinguish me to the depths of my soul.

But his hand never once touched me. Long, slim fingers dipped into my chips and emerged with a steaming sliver of potato which he tossed to the enamel sharks between his lips.

"Have you ever wondered Natalie - Nat - why our names are the same? Have you?" he asked me in a half-whisper I was sure that no one else in the crowded shop had heard. My mouth was suddenly dry and my brain seemed to have forgotten how words were constructed. Strangely though, I was aware of every fibre of my clothing, how it lay against my skin, where it touched and where it billowed out away from me. I was aware of the tightness of my jeans and how the fabric had moulded itself to my body, fusing itself to curves and hollows like a warm caress.

The fire on my face spread with too much alacrity for my comfort, suffusing my form with a burning desire I had no knowledge of how to quell. More than the rest of me, my arm burned intensely and stupidly I wondered if the hot chips were scorching me through the paper they were wrapped in. But when I glanced down, I realised that the chips were in the other hand. The fiery sensation came from where Nathan had grabbed my arm, the heat generated from that mere touch, such was the effect he had.

A deep shudder coursed through me and I had a strange sensation of tingling in my upper thighs. Close enough that we were standing face to face, I somehow could not focus the image as my eyes flitted from his eyes to his mouth, his hair and his chin and back to his eyes again. I still couldn't speak and had lost the will to even try.

"Have you Natalie, Nat?" he continued, either not caring that I hadn't answered, or having not expected an answer. "Natalie and Nathan, Nat and Nate. Works well, doesn't it?" he explained, perhaps thinking I was too stupid to grasp what he was talking about.

"Come out with me tonight, Natalie Nat and I'll show you just how alike we really are. Meet me on the corner outside at 7.30. Don't be late!"

I was aware he wasn't asking. It was a challenge – a dare! Did he think I would be scared? Be shocked? Or didn't he care either way? He didn't seek an answer and I didn't offer one. I wasn't even sure whether I thought it was a joke or not.

But before he let go of my arm he had scribbled something there – a string of numbers. "Just in case you're going to be late…you can text me," he said, letting go of my arm. Released from his hold it dropped to my side. I could still feel the pressure of his fingers on my flesh, as though he had pressed so hard that he had left an imprint.

On the upward movement of the nod I found myself drawn into those searing eyes again and I was once more lost within them. My mind whirred with confusion. How could I meet him? Even if I wanted to…*did* I want to? I had already agreed to go out with Rhys and on *the same night at the very same time.*

I had to get away to think clearly. I backed up and pressed through the crowd, only at the last minute able to sever my gaze from his.

Stace was waiting for me outside. On seeing me she stopped mid-flow, a single chip frozen in time, halfway on the journey to her mouth, her lips still shaped in a perfect 'O' ready to receive it. "What's up with you? What have I missed?"

I led her around the corner of the shop and away from any curious eyes before I could bring myself to spit the words out. In those few moments I worried how she would take the news that I had been asked out for the second time in one day. I wondered too if she would think I had encouraged Nathan somehow.

"Nathan Bridges! He just asked me out! Tonight. 7.30!" I noticed my voice had assumed a staccato effect. I was anxious to give her the facts without any embellishment.

I took a gulp and a breath before continuing. "He didn't actually *ask* me out…he sort of told me," I said honestly, hoping she would understand. I didn't want her to think I had encouraged him or that I was gloating.

"Did you say yes?" she asked, eyes wide and with a hint of breathlessness.

I had to think about it for a moment. What *had* I said? "I didn't *actually say* yes…but…well, I nodded."

She looked at me gravely as if she couldn't

quite believe I was so stupid. And maybe she couldn't. "Oh, Nat, trust you! What a dumb thing to do! You can't go out with both of them at the same time! What are you gonna do?"

"I don't know! What *can* I do? Guess I'm gonna have to go out with one and cancel the other! But which one?" My mind was completely fogged and confused. "I've known Rhys forever…"

"It's like those films where the girl has to choose from the boy-next-door and some other bloke. You know she *always* chooses the other bloke first…" Stacey chewed down contemplatively on a chip. "Then when she discovers he's a dirt bag, she goes for the right one! And of course he's always still waiting for her," she finished.

"So I should stick to Rhys?" I asked anxiously.

"I dunno, it's your choice. Rhys is nice, but Nathan…well, he's got that dangerous thing going on. I mean, you know how the girls at school talk about him! He's hot, Nat. And he's asked *you*! They'd all be *soo* jealous if they knew! But you *know* he's trouble! You go out with him – anything could happen!" Stace's voice held a mixture of awe and trepidation, and possibly the slightest tinge of envy.

"I know that's what people say but as far as I can tell he hasn't done anything to deserve that reputation," I answered uneasily.

"So what you gonna do?" Stacey asked.

"I don't know! You're right - Rhys is great and

he's good fun and good-looking. But Nathan is ..."
My throat constricted as I thought about him,
about the effect he had on me. "Well, Nathan's
sexy!"

Stacey popped another chip into her mouth
as she considered my words. "Actually Natalie,
they're both sexy but in different ways. Rhys is
more than good-looking. And Nathan, well, as I
said before, he's *dangerous*. What you have to ask
yourself, is which one you are more likely to have
a proper relationship with."

I looked back at her blankly. She sighed, irritated that in my confused state she had to spell
everything out to me. "Which one do you think
you could go out long term with?" She looked me
straight in the eye. "'Cos whichever one that is,
well, that's the one you should choose!"

Rhys or Nathan? Nathan or Rhys? The boy I
had always been closest to, the one I had looked
up to for years, trusted, admired and had even
had a secret crush on, or the boy I didn't know,
who looked like he was so excitingly fast he
would leave me in his dust - which should I
chose? It was an impossible choice, surely. And
yet I suddenly knew beyond question who I
would be meeting later and who I wouldn't.

"I have to tell him I won't be going!"

"Who? Which one?" Stacey asked eagerly,
pupils dilating.

I didn't answer her; instead, I reached for my

phone. It was then that I remembered my credit was low and this wasn't exactly an emergency.

"Can I use your phone?" I asked sheepishly. "I can't face telling him face to face... but over the 'phone ..."

She sighed but handed it over.

I keyed in the number.

CHAPTER 6A

7 p.m.

I brushed my hair into a smooth mane and popped a band around it, securing it into a high ponytail. A few strands hung loose, curling around my face and softening the effect. It made me look pretty and kind of laid back, as if I hadn't tried *too* hard. Even though I had.

I had taken over an hour to get ready and half of that had been used in showering and lathering myself in every kind of scented lotion and cream until my room smelled like a perfume shop and a heady aroma settled around me.

My newest jeans had been plucked from the wardrobe and paired with an amazing top. It was a swirly mix of colours - more pink than anything else - with barely-there shoestring straps and little diamantés which caught the light and glimmered enticingly.

The jeans gripped me across the hips and cupped my bottom into a smooth curve whilst the top pulled in tight around my waist and boobs. It wasn't exactly low-cut but it certainly showed enough to leave no doubt that I wasn't a kid anymore.

In the mirror I examined myself from every angle, turning this way and that, checking how I looked from all sides, fidgeting with the straps on the top, pulling them up at the front and down at the back and then reversing the procedure until I found a level that I was happy with. Low, but not too low.

From the back my bum looked perfectly proportioned to the rest of me, shapely and big enough to catch attention. The new shoes peeped out from under the hem of my jeans like shy puppies seeking approval and I wiggled my toes excitedly.

What would he think when he saw me? Where would his eyes focus, his gaze linger? Would he want to kiss me? And if he did? Would I still want him to...or would I panic and pull away? My breath caught in my throat at the thought of his lips on mine, his mouth pressed onto mine, bodies so close we could feel one another's heart beating.

Hurriedly I pulled my thoughts away from the image, confused by the feelings that surged up in me. Was I ready for this? Was I ready to be kissed in a way that would no doubt alter me forever? Was I prepared for the confusion and heartbreak that seemed to be a part of every relationship, if movies and books were to be believed?

I locked gazes with my reflection, surprised at how different I looked. Like a cover girl on a glossy magazine. I looked smooth and perfect, almost too perfect to be real. And I wondered how the real me felt about this facsimile of me…it was me without being me somehow…like wearing a mask and a costume; as if I were free to act differently than I otherwise would have done.

Chin raised, I scrutinised my face, looking for gaps or unevenness in my makeup. Layer upon layer of colour had been painstakingly built up to achieve a fresh and dewy complexion with large, emphasised eyes and well-defined features, yet in a very natural way. No hard lines of eyeliner rimmed my eyes although they were accentuated, making me look older and more knowing. I smoothed a hand over my hair once more, fingers quivering in anticipation.

The clock on my bedside table flashed its red glowing numbers at me as if urging me onwards, beating out a response in my veins, a quickening of purpose. And yet I hesitated. I had made the right choice, hadn't I?

I remembered the curt texts and how bad I'd felt. *Can't make it 2nite,* I had sent to the guy I'd decided to cancel on. I hadn't wanted to give an explanation, hadn't been brave enough to.

OK. Maybe another time, he'd texted back. I either meant nothing to him or he was hurt by my rejection. A sick feeling lingered in my stomach at the thought and I wasn't entirely sure how I felt about his response but the decision had been made and there was no going back. And perhaps there *would* be another time, I consoled myself. Who could say how things would turn out? Maybe I'd made the right choice, maybe not, but it was hardly a life-or-death decision and nothing was irreversible, was it? Well, not during the course of the first date!

I grabbed my bag and slung it over my shoulder, took a deep breath and prepared myself. My heart hammered with anticipation and I seemed to have to think about inhaling and exhaling, as if it no longer came naturally to me.

Mum and Dad were in the lounge watching TV. For a moment I stood unnoticed in the doorway, able to watch them whilst they remained completely unaware of my presence, able to observe them as a stranger might; as if for the very first time.

I had seen them like this many times but never before had I understood the depth of love that I was witnessing, the particular shade and hue of the deepest emotion. At once I understood what they meant to one another and by extension, what I meant to them both. A blade of excitement quivered through me. Could I be on the verge of finding something remotely similar for myself?

Dad stroked Mum's hair as she sat next to him, her body entwined with his, arms linked and torsos leaning towards one-another. They were

61

such a perfect vision that I hesitated to shatter it with my appearance before them. Like strangers to me, they were complete without me in a way that made me feel suddenly insignificant and small. What if I never found a love like theirs? Not just tonight or next week, but ever? What if there was no one special person for me? What if in the vastness of space and time, there really was only one true love for each and every person?

A minute spun into eternity before Mum saw me from the corner of her eye and nudged my dad, turning away from him towards me, giving me the benefit of her full attention. Dad followed her gaze.

"You look fantastic, Natalie. Have a great time and be back by eleven, OK?" he said a little too briskly, betraying a quiet and unspoken worry.

My mother focused on the practicalities. "Have you got money and your mobile?" She seemed to be racking her brain to think of anything else I might need, face struggling to not look concerned and failing dismally.

I nodded. "And I've just put some credit on my phone," I said, hoping to allay at least some of her fears.

I'd told her the story of the two potential dates. She'd listened quietly and without interruption until I got to the part where I had made my decision. Even then she hadn't questioned me too much but focused on why I'd made the choice I had. I guessed that the idea was as new and strange to her as it was to me. I couldn't have possibly felt more awkward and embarrassed at the idea of them thinking about me out with a date than I already did, if I'd tried.

Having confronted them, I was eager to be away. "Bye, Mum, Dad." I moved into the lounge to kiss them both. "I'd better hurry or I'll never get there on time." My keenness to leave was as much due to embarrassment as it was to eagerness but my mum caught my hand in hers as I moved to turn away, pulling me back towards her and into the spotlight of her gaze. But it was my dad who spoke.

"If there is any change of plan, or if anything happens you're uncomfortable about, phone us and we'll come get you, Natalie," he stated, looking me straight in the eye with 'the LOOK' as mum and I called it. I felt a pressure in my hand as mum gave it a secret squeeze. 'And have a good time', I took that to mean.

But my dad's words hung in the air and there was a moment of uncomfortable silence. A slow flush crept onto my cheeks and there was a sudden lump at the back of my throat. Could I honestly say I hoped that the guy I was about to go on a date with wouldn't try anything on? That I would be so unappealing to him that he would merely talk all night long? That he wouldn't even try to kiss me?

At the thought my heart skipped a little beat and there was a vague burning sensation in the pit of my stomach. I had to get out and get some air!

"Don't worry, Dad, I'll be fine!" I chirped brightly, belying the thoughts which circled around my head. Very deliberately I didn't cast a backward glance as I flitted from the room and out the front door, pulling it shut behind me with a solid thump.

The time on my phone showed 7:30. Tottering on the heels as much as walking on them, I made my way to the rendezvous.

CHAPTER 6B

7 p.m.

I brushed my hair until it shone, styling it so that it fluttered around my face and over my shoulders. Then I blasted it with hairspray. Posing in the mirror, I leaned forward to see how it would move to partially obscure my face, then turned to look over my shoulder through the curtain of hair that glimmered there. Both effects were sultry, tantalisingly sexy.

A shiver of anticipation ran up my spine, a tingling that radiated both outwards and inwards at the same time and for a moment I saw myself as others would; a young woman who oozed sophistication and confidence.

I'd got ready at a leisurely rate, bathing and scenting myself, letting the steam and the water carry me into fantasies of romance and seduction. My eyes had been closed in the bath, feeling the hot water slosh over me, imagining how I would feel during that first kiss, how his eyes would meet mine and how my heart would ache.

After much deliberation, I was wearing the dress I'd bought a couple of weeks before. Purchased apprehensively, aware that I would have to get Mum's approval before I wore it, I'd been reluctant to get her verdict.

"It's a bit revealing," she had stated flatly when I'd first shown it to her, eyebrows raised so high that they were almost in danger of disappearing into her hairline.

"Not really!" I'd protested, adding what I hoped would be the selling point, "and I can always wear a little cardigan over the top." Mum's face had relaxed then into an 'oh, OK then' sort of look and I knew that I had won. I wondered suddenly if I had won the battle or the war. What would she say when she saw me in it ready for a date, face made up and hair styled?

There was no doubt it was a lovely dress, pale pink with a neckline cut just low enough to make it demurely sexy, and dainty little straps. The cut was flattering, cinching me in at the waist and boobs and flaring softly over my hips and bottom.

In the mirror, I examined myself from every angle, twisting this way and that, bending over to look down my cleavage. Upright, my silhouette was good; my boobs were high and protruded enough to be noticed but this was toned down by the modest cut of the material which gave only a hint of the shapely curve of my bottom. Below the dress, finely turned calves and ankles were set off beautifully by the new shoes.

The make-up effect I wanted to achieve had been much harder. Colours had been smoothed on, one after another until I looked like a completely different person.

In the mirror, chiselled cheekbones and glistening red lips caught my attention whilst smoky-grey eyes, rimmed thickly in black eyeliner and mascara looked back at me haughtily. I could have been any one of those models who graced the covers of glossy magazines. The real 'me' was hidden somewhere inside, buried under make-up and fantasy.

I remembered something I had watched once, that claimed primitive tribes were afraid when they saw photographs, believing that the camera had somehow captured their soul. For the first time I understood that fear – this girl in the mirror was me without being me; looking different was she also free to act differently?

How would he feel when he saw me? Would there be a tingle somewhere deep inside of him? In his heart? Or lower? And if he tried to kiss me? What then? Would it be Nat who responded to his kiss? Or this unknown vamp from the mirror?

My breath caught in my throat at the thought of his lips on mine, his mouth pressed onto mine, bodies so close we could feel one another's heart beating. Hurriedly I pulled my thoughts away from the image, confused by the feelings that surged up in me. Was I ready for this? Was I ready to be kissed in a way that would no doubt alter me forever? Was I prepared for the confusion and heartbreak that seemed to be a part of every relationship, if movies and books were to be believed?

My heart hammered at the thought of what might lie ahead. The evening stretched out empty and yet full of promise. How different would I be by the end of it? I wondered.

But time was flying and I would soon have answers to all my questions. Only a small quiet voice nagged me from inside my head. I should have been less abrupt with the text I'd sent to cancel the other date. I could have made some excuse, given some explanation, and then perhaps I wouldn't have had a response that sounded like he couldn't care less, that hadn't sounded as if he'd already made alternative arrangements.

I picked up my bag and riffled through its contents, ensuring I had everything I needed. Sounds from the blaring TV directed me to where my parents sat, curled up against one another. On the point of entering the room, I suddenly saw them as I had my own reflection in the mirror – they were my Mum and Dad and yet they were unknown to me.

Was that what it was like? Becoming part of a couple, losing your own identity as an individual and merging into someone else? How would it feel to be loved like that? To *love* that deeply? For there to no longer be just a *me*, to be instead part of an *us*?

Mum smiled up at Dad and the love that shone forth from her eyes was so obvious, so palpable and *real* that it took my breath away. Almost twenty years of marriage hadn't diminished her feelings in the slightest. Would I ever feel that way about anyone? Would anyone feel that way about me? I hoped so, but there was no guarantee.

I stood in the doorway, reluctant to step forward. For the briefest of moments I was scared... not just to shatter the image before me but to consign myself to my decision, to take the next step in growing up. Then Mum saw me from the corner of her eye and beckoned me forward. Nudging my dad, she turned away from him towards me, giving me the benefit of her full attention. But it was my dad who spoke first, following her gaze.

"I haven't seen that dress before," he frowned. "And it's a little low cut, isn't it?" He turned to Mum, expecting and receiving her back-up.

"I thought you said you were going to wear a cardigan over it?" she asked, moving away from Dad and sitting bolt upright, a mirror-image of my dad's frown on her face.

I knew why she was concerned but I was unwilling to answer, lest my own worries and concerns be revealed in doing so. She waited me out, aware that I could not leave until I had their approval.

"Um…it's in the wash," I stuttered, knowing that there were plenty other ones in a drawer in my room.

"Then perhaps you should go get another one before you go out…" Dad spoke quietly, always a bad sign. Mum flicked her eyes over me and sighed.

I'd already told her the full story of the two potential dates and she'd listened quietly and without interruption until I got to the part where I had made my decision. Even then she hadn't questioned me too much, but focused on why I had made the choice I had. I guessed that the idea was as new and strange to her as it was to me. I couldn't have possibly felt more awkward and embarrassed at the idea of them thinking about me out with a date than I already did, if I had tried. But I still didn't want to go out wearing a cardigan over my dress. I beseeched her with my eyes, hoping she would understand.

She turned to Dad with a rueful look. "If she takes one, she will only take it off once she's out of the house anyway." I was only half surprised that she knew what had gone through my head. She placed a hand over Dad's. "Do you remember the ridiculous things I used to wear when we were dating…my dad used to go ballistic when he saw me…"

"But Karen, you were older then than Natalie is..." Dad protested, his eyes still convinced he was right and fixed on my face.

A slow burning flush had crept its way up my neck and now began to suffuse my face with colour. I had worn the dress for a very particular reason. I wanted my date to look at me with desire and interest. I wanted him to want to hold me, caress me, smell the skin on my neck and feel the warmth of my body. And in that one glance, my dad had known and recognised all of that.

Suddenly I felt naked standing there in front of him, as if he could see all of these disturbing thoughts coursing through my head. Shame bit into my throat and robbed me of any words I might have uttered and there was a stinging burning behind my eyes. I took one step backwards, ready to admit defeat, ready to return to my room in disgrace and be made to change into something less alluring, when my mother spoke once more.

"They grow up faster these days." She smiled at me but it was tainted with her fear for my future. "Let her go, Matt. She's a smart girl and she's sensible."

Dad sighed, knowing when he was beaten. "If there's any change of plan in what you're doing, or if anything happens you're uncomfortable about, phone us and we'll come get you, Natalie," he stated, looking me straight in the eye with 'the LOOK' as Mum and I called it. "Have you got credit on your phone?"

I nodded. "I have just put some on," I said, hoping to allay at least some of their fears. "Don't worry, I'll be fine!" I stuttered, not believing my luck that they were not making me change clothes - or plans - and desperate to be gone from there, gone from the interrogation that was too piercing, too embarrassing. I fled the situation as if bats from Hell were on my heels, not even casting a backward glance as I flitted from the room and out the front door, pulling it shut behind me with a solid thump.

The numerals on my phone showed 7:30.

CHAPTER 7A

7:35 p.m.

It was only just after half seven but he was already waiting for me, a grin on his face like he was ready to eat me up. I almost hoped that he would.

He was wearing jeans almost the same shade of mid-blue as the ones I wore, and a tee-shirt that seemed to have been made exclusively for him. His eyes shone as he looked at me and I realised he hadn't been sure that I would actually turn up. The realisation made me feel incredibly powerful and infinitely important, as if his whole world had turned on that one thing. But if I could so easily lift his world, then I could just as surely cause it to come crashing down, displaced by a crushing sense of disappointment if the evening proved to be less than he had imagined.

"I'm sorry I'm a little late," I blurted as I rushed towards him, hoping he wasn't annoyed at having to wait. He shrugged like it didn't matter, like it wouldn't have mattered if I had been an hour late, he would still have been standing there, patiently waiting.

With my heart banging in my chest and a sick

excitement churning in my stomach, I stopped close to him. The tension between us was palpable. I wanted to kiss him; a throwaway kiss, delivered to his cheek as if we had met many, many times before like this, but I wasn't brave enough.

"You have a little bug on you," he said, brushing one hand against my bare shoulder, making the skin there tingle, wiping the insect away with the lightest of touches. His hand lingered and I saw his eyes move to my mouth.

I was painfully aware of my bare skin under his palm and of the empty space between our bodies. Feeling as if the gap between us was a gulf that spanned a thousand lightyears, I took a step forward. Close enough that I could feel his heartbeat, I marvelled at the speed it careered, beating an extra note against my own. He leaned forward and his lips brushed against my cheek. I soaked up the smell of his skin, the nearness of him, his quiet strength, before he took a step backwards, away from me.

He didn't kiss me properly. Mouth so close that a kiss would have been the most natural thing in the world, he held back awkwardly, pulling his head away so that I was left with only the memory of the warmth of his breath on my cheek, and the sweet minty tang of it. A light flush had spread across his cheeks and his eyes avoided mine.

"You look great!" he breathed, letting go of

me as suddenly as he had held me, leaving me tingling deliriously and wanting - no, *needing* - more of him. I ached to be back in his arms, to stay there forever and the feeling of loss was too sudden and too deep to bear. I felt infinitely bereft, like a small child who has been promised a prize that never materialises.

Without his support, having given my body over to his control for that one brief moment, I struggled to stand alone. My jeans felt as if they were glued to me and I could feel the material of my top where it lay against my skin, as if I suddenly had some hyper-sensitivity never experienced before.

"I thought we could take a walk into town and grab a drink and maybe some pizza later," he said.

"I...um...," I stuttered stupidly. I didn't want to share him with a bunch of strangers. Didn't want the distraction. But it was a date and a prerequisite for that was to go somewhere. Then a more mundane worry assaulted me. Would I be refused admission at a pub? I tried to think if I looked eighteen rather than almost sixteen. Would the doorman put his arm across the entrance when he saw me? If he did, I would die of embarrassment! "I don't know if..."

He cut me off. "You look older than your age and with the way you're dressed, you'll be fine. And if there are any problems, I have this,"

75

he brandished something from his pocket and passed it to me. "As long as the guy has ID, they don't usually ask for the girl's. So we should be fine."

A moment of doubt entered my head. How adept he was at this! Had he taken other under-age girls into bars and plied them with alcohol? A thread of misgiving sneaked into my conscious-ness but I dismissed it as both unkind and irrele-vant. This was a date and what else was there to do? And if he had taken other girls out before, so what? He clearly wasn't with them now. He was with me!

"You do drink alcohol, don't you?" he asked almost as an afterthought as if it was unheard of that I didn't.

I hesitated. Did a glass of champagne at Christmas and my birthday count? I suspected not. Then again it wasn't as if alcohol had never touched my lips.

"Yes. Of course!" I hoped I sounded surprised at the question.

He nodded as if accepting the answer at face value, unquestioningly believing me. And I should have been happy with that, should have stopped there...but then I went and ruined it by being over-effusive.

"I drink all the time. Wine with dinner and sometimes brandy afterwards." It was a ridicu-lous thing to claim and we both knew it, but he didn't contest it and we left it hanging there between us like a bridge that we were both afraid to cross. I didn't see how I could retract the statement without looking even more stupid than I already did. He probably thought I was an idiot and wished he had never asked!

"OK, great!" He smiled but I thought I could see a strain in his eyes. Was he already tired and bored of me, a girl more than a year younger than him and more than a little naïve?

He held out his hand. Afraid that I would clasp it too tightly or not tightly enough, I took it tentatively. His grasp was warm and firm and perfectly right. For a moment, the only sound to be heard was the clicking of my heels against the tarmac of the pavement. It was as if we were the only two people out on this warm evening and the sexual tension between us was almost unbearable.

I desperately wanted him to stop and draw me into his arms again and this time kiss me... kiss me in a way that fused our bodies together, melded us into one and broke the uncomfortable newness of this situation. I racked my brain to say something, anything, to break the silence.

"Which pub are we going to?"

"All of them!" He looked at me appraisingly. "After all you are a girl who likes a good drink." He smiled, either intent on having me on and doing a great job of it, or entirely serious. I genuinely couldn't tell which.

"Oh OK!" I said lamely, unable to think of what else to say. What was the natural rejoinder? "Do you go to pubs a lot?" I asked, slowing my stride down a little, partly delaying tactics and partly because the new shoes were killing me, pinching on my toes and heels. Stace had been right – they had never been meant for walking in, only for posing!

"Don't you?" he responded. "Or do you do all your heavy drinking at home? Or perhaps at the park?"

This time I caught the irony and the subtle humour in his voice. He knew damned well, that I wasn't a drinker. I decided to play him at his own game.

"I usually go further afield. This town is full of kids – I prefer the city pubs." If I could've instantly bitten back the words, I would have done so. Not only had I insulted him and his choice of pubs but I had made myself look snobbish and shallow.

He snorted with laughter. "Well, that told me!" But instead of being angry and offended, he stopped walking and pulled me towards him again. This time I forced my pelvis to meet his, jeans to jeans, muscle to muscle.

I could feel the heat of him burning through my clothes and where his hands rested on the backside of my jeans, they seemed to sear a handprint through the material and onto my skin.

He pulled his face close to mine and in the instant before our lips met in a kiss, there was a tingling sensation inside my jeans, at the junction where thigh met groin.

The kiss might have lasted a minute or ten, there was no way of knowing. Inside my open mouth, his tongue stroked my lips and tongue and flitted tantalisingly towards teeth and cheeks. I felt the urge to push my tongue ferociously into his mouth, demanding to taste him as he tasted me but I was too weak and swept away in the moment to be able to summon the energy.

His tongue pushed and probed and for every millimetre that it conquered we edged another fraction closer, until thrust exquisitely together, there was no space left between us, nowhere else to go.

This heady thought swam into my brain, swirling images and ideas around, causing my heart to beat a painful lament. Just what was happening here? Unwilling to let him stop this intoxicating madness, I wrapped my arms around him and pressed in even closer.

Were his eyes closed as mine were? Slowly I opened mine to see. His eyes were tightly shut, long lashes dusting the cheekbones below. I wanted to close my own eyes again but the proximity of his face held my attention and I felt my heart try to memorise every tiny detail of his face. As if he felt my scrutiny, his eyes flickered open, pupils dilated- huge pools within which I could easily have lost my soul.

He pulled away and took a step back.

"Whoa Nat!" he said shakily and I knew that it was not just me who had felt the deep desire we shared. "If I didn't need a drink before, I do now!" He laughed, breaking the tension between us. "Come on, let's get on with this date!"

Not offering me his hand again, he wrapped his arm around my waist instead. Once more my heels resumed their *click-clack* on the tarmac as we walked towards town.

CHAPTER 7B

7:35 p.m.

He was late. Was he going to stand me up? Had I chosen the wrong guy after all? I fidgeted with the straps of my dress, feeling uncomfortable and stupid. What would I do if he didn't turn up at all? I imagined how it would feel to trudge home, to let myself in and have to explain that I'd been stood up…and then suddenly he was there beside me and my concerns were forgotten.

"Sorry, I had some stuff I needed to do and it took longer than I thought it would," he said, sounding cool and not particularly regretful, despite what his words claimed. He didn't volunteer what the stuff was and I didn't ask. It was of no importance, he was there! Everything else was irrelevant.

Suddenly I was self-conscious, there in my very grown-up dress and with my cleavage on show. Perhaps I should have brought a cardigan after all? Even though I was covered more than I would have been in a swimming costume on the beach, I felt bare and vulnerable. Yet it was a tantalising sensation – exciting and frightening at the same time.

He took a step backwards, using the space to

look me up and down. A slow smile flitted across his face and his eyes widened in what I thought was appreciation. I didn't know how the date would go and what the evening would hold, but in that instant I wanted the night to have reached its conclusion, just so that he would hold me and kiss me and I would feel his body hard against mine, lips pressed to lips and arms entwined. A heat rose in me that had nothing to do with the temperature of the evening air and everything to do with my imagination.

Wearing a pair of dark jeans and a casual shirt he looked smarter than he'd been earlier. His eyes met mine in a frank stare and I realised he had never had a moment's doubt that I would be here waiting for him, that I would stand and wait for as long as it took him to turn up. I wondered what he would've thought if he'd known I'd turned down another offer to be with him.

"You look nice," I said awkwardly to break the silence which had grown between us and for want of something better to say.

"No, not really," he smiled. "But you on the other hand, look fantastic. And incredibly sexy!" He grinned and a delicious shiver ran down my spine. No images or words flitted across my mind other than 'desire' and my limbs seemed to resonate with a sense of urgent need. My head was an absolute blank, like someone had wiped it clean and my mouth was paper dry. I waited for him to kiss me and when he made no move to do so, I was infinitely disappointed. I thought about reaching forward but was not sure enough of myself to initiate the action.

"I was thinking we could go to the cinema if you fancy it." It seemed to be more of a statement than a question, as if the matter had already been decided and the posing of it to me was more a point of politeness than anything else. I wondered how long he had thought about asking me out. Had it been a spur of the moment thing? Or had he been thinking about it for some time? Planning and awaiting the right opportunity?

I had no idea what was showing at the cinema but it seemed as good an idea as any. I nodded. There was a cinema in town and although not a multiplex, I had always found it nice enough.

"OK, great! That's a great dress by the way," he commented, looking me up and down again as if once hadn't been enough. "Where's the rest of it?" he joked, his eyes lingering on the patches of bare skin where the dress did not cling yet still accentuated.

Smiling at his cheekiness, I felt his gaze linger on my breasts and a tingle ran through my flesh, piercing through to the core of me, heart quickening and breath catching in my throat. Without knowing how I got there, I was suddenly in his arms, pulled tight against him. His lips were open and the tip of his tongue protruded into my mouth, darting in and out, causing delicious sensations to run up and down my spine. I felt his hands on my waist, fingers drawing tantalising circles on my back but then without warning they moved lower...and lower still, until they cupped my bottom! My eyes flew open at the unexpected grope to find his eyes wide and staring fixedly at my face. I pulled away, uncomfortable and embarrassed.

"Don't..." I said, thinking that he would understand things were moving too fast for me. He gave no indication whether he had understood or not but he didn't reach forward for me again.

"If we don't hurry, we're going to miss it!" he simply said, holding out his hand for me to take. "There'll be plenty opportunity for snogging later."

I was put out not just by his words but by his attitude. This was not how I'd envisaged things at all! Then again what would I know of dates? My one previous experience had been neither illuminating nor extensive. What had just happened was surely a misunderstanding, it would not do to put too much undue emphasis on it and ruin the night, I decided.

My dress billowed around me slightly as I hastened to match his speed and the new shoes clip-clopped brightly on the pavement.

"What are we going to see?" I asked, slightly

out of breath and desperate to slow down. My shoes were already causing me pain around the toes and the heels. Stacey had been right; they were not made for walking, only for posing. I thought of how she would nod her 'I told you so' when I related the night back to her. I hoped she was having at least a reasonable evening at home and her dad hadn't made her work to add insult to injury.

"Not sure yet but there's a crowd of us going and we have to meet them to get a lift."

I was suddenly confused. Was this not a proper date after all? But that couldn't be right, not after the kiss we'd just shared! So who were the other people in the crowd and why did we need a lift? I decided to address the last question first.

"Why do we need a lift? Town is only a few minutes' walk away…"

"*Our* town. But we are not going to our town…" he said mysteriously, refusing to give much away.

"Oh!" A pinprick of anxiety assailed my conscience. Mum and Dad thought I was staying close by. *I* thought I was staying close by! Now I'd learned I was going to a different town somewhere undisclosed and further away, I was a little unsettled.

I dismissed the thought. I was being silly! Of course I was. My date was merely trying to impress me with his experience and I was acting like a stupid, naïve kid! I put a smile on my face and tried to pull off a nonchalance I didn't feel.

"Who are we going with?" I asked instead.

He thought for a moment, not slowing his pace. If he went much faster he would be pulling me off my feet, I thought. "They are a little older than you, so I doubt you'll know them. Maybe one or two, but that would be all, I guess."

One or two? How many of them were there? And even if they were older why would I not know them? Our town was hardly noted for its extensive population.

"Anyway, you'll know soon enough," he said as we rounded a corner.

An old battered but painted-over car stood by the kerb, engine idling and driver waiting for something or someone. I veered around behind it, checking that no other cars were coming, preparing to cross the road. But before I could step onto the road, I realised that my date had stopped next to the car as if we had already reached our destination.

I looked with horror and incredulity at the car. Were these the friends he had mentioned; the lift we were getting? Surely he wasn't intending for us to travel in something that looked as if it were only fit for the scrap heap? A clang of uncertainty sounded in my head. Was this car even in a roadworthy condition?

"Milady, your carriage awaits," he said, opening up the rear door and ushering me inside, apparently unable to read the expression on my face.

For a moment I stood undecided and then the reality of the situation hit home. His friend had probably only just passed his driving test. This old banger was probably the best that he could afford and to turn it down would put an immediate stop to the date and embarrass both of us forever. It would make him look foolish in front of his friends and would make me look like a snob.

I gathered up my misgivings and stuffed them into a sealed compartment in my brain and took a step towards the open door. Immediately a dank smell wafted out of the interior of the car and engulfed me. Half recognisable and half not, the fumes were both strong and intoxicating. Unprepared to be met by such a noxious malodour, I'd choked on a breath before I even knew what was happening and struggled to breathe through the vapour.

"Put those out for now, you're going to suffocate her with the smell in this car!" my guy said laughing, still holding the car door open and waiting for me to get in.

I hesitated once more, unsure about this decision. There was something so wrong about the situation, the smell, the seeming unplannedness of it all, the fact that without even bending down I could tell that there were already enough people in the car to fill it, as three pairs of legs shuffled over to make space for us to get in. And yet I still feared that I was over-reacting.

I waited until two guys and a girl whose face I couldn't see, squeezed themselves to the far side of the back seat before I reluctantly climbed into the space they had vacated, crammed up too close and personal when my date also got in next to me. Busy trying to make myself as small as possible, I didn't take a moment to look at the other passengers and it was only when the girl shuffled herself onto the lap of the man sitting at the side of me, that I got a look at her. It was Suzie! Suzie from the shoe shop who had served me earlier!

"Hmm, it's you," she drawled, sounding thoroughly unimpressed. "Move your arse onto his lap so we can all have a bit of room!" she instructed, nodding at my date.

I was not inclined to follow her advice but it would be impossible to shut the door otherwise and my hips already felt as if my bones were being slowly pulverised! There was no real choice in the matter and it wasn't as if we were naked or alone. In fact the opposite was true - there were plenty of chaperones here in the car with us.

I tried to manoeuvre myself into the correct position but it was awkward within the narrow confines of the back seat. Reluctantly, I half-clambered, was half-dragged onto my date's lap and sat there awkwardly, head bent at an angle against the interior roof of the car. I could only hope that the journey would prove to be brief.

Two men sat in the front, cigarettes hanging out of their mouths. I didn't recognise them and thought that they looked not just older but rougher than I'd imagined they might be. They were certainly not the sort of guys I was used to hanging around with and I was glad they were in the front and not the back.

Although I now sat on top of my date, there was no sexual frisson for me the way there had been earlier. Perhaps it was the presence of the others which made desire so unlikely or perhaps it was the situation itself. But to my slowly dawning horror I realised the feeling was not mutual. I could feel a new and unwelcome hardness grow from him.

Embarrassed and uncomfortable, I tried to wriggle away from him and his rigid anatomy but with every movement, I seemed to only make the situation worse.

"Looks like your girl isn't too comfy there," the guy next to me sniggered. I looked away from him, from all of them but there was nowhere else to look. Unable to see out of the windows I shut my eyes in horror at the situation I was forced to endure.

"Maybe she would enjoy the ride better on my lap," he continued in a slimy tone. Expecting my date to defend my honour, I was upset and alarmed when his body shook with laughter. "Dream on and get your own shag!" he scoffed.

Shocked by both the words and the tone they were delivered in, I felt my heart quicken in anxiety. I kept my eyes firmly shut and prayed that I had misheard, even though I knew I hadn't. Peals of laughter boomed in the car but none of it was mine. Belatedly, it occurred to me that there was a danger in keeping my eyes pressed closed. Who knew what innuendos and silent signals I was missing?

I forced myself to open them and look. One of the guys in the front had taken the cigarette from his mouth and had passed it to the back, where it had been received by the guy Suzie sat on. Up close it didn't resemble a cigarette so much and I realised that they were smoking grass or some other drug. I didn't know enough about it to even identify what they were inhaling.

What on earth had I got myself into?

CHAPTER 8A

7:45 p.m.

The doorman didn't look too impressed until my date showed him his ID. Rather than just glance at it, the bouncer took the card in his beefy hands, flipped it over, scrutinised both sides and finally handed it back. I wondered if everyone got this level of inspection before they were allowed in.

"On you go, but I'll be keeping an eye on you." He waved us into the pub and turned to examine his next victims. I wondered whether the comment was addressed to me, my date or both of us. I figured it didn't much matter – it amounted to the same thing. I watched, openly curious as the next couple were waived in without any display of ID. Perhaps it *was* just us then?

"What are you having? Wine? Beer? Or are you going to branch out and have a shot?" my guy shouted above the din, almost grinning from ear to ear.

In truth I wasn't sure. I quite liked wine. From the few times I'd tried it, I'd found it to be sweet and easy to drink - but looking around no one else seemed to have chosen it. Glasses and bottles of all shapes, sizes and colours were lifted from chest height to lips and back again and it was almost impossible to count the bewildering variety on display.

Inspiration struck me. "Whatever you're having!" I yelled back, copying his grin. With a chaste peck on the cheek he left me to force his way to the bar, elbowing through couples and groups with what seemed like a dangerously wild abandon. I watched the crowd swallow him up and then he was gone and I was adrift in a wide sea of unknown faces.

Standing alone in the crowd, I was glad I was wearing jeans, they sort of cushioned me from the stares of the horde of strangers. Even though they were probably just as unknown to one another as they were to me, they seemed to close ranks around me, as if aware that I was not a frequenter of such places. I had the strangest feeling of paranoia that they wanted to oust me as an imposter.

Where had all they come from? They surely didn't all live in this little town did they? I didn't recognise a single face! I tried to focus on the practicalities of the situation.

People jostled against me from all sides and I was relieved when after what seemed like an interminably long time, my guy arrived back at my side, identical looking glasses held in each hand. I dragged my gaze away from the crowd which seemed to shrink back as my date approached, much like a pack of hyenas would relinquish the gazelle to the stronger and more ferocious tiger. An unaccountable surge of pride that I was his chosen one suffused me and I struggled to hold it in check.

He smiled as I took the glass he proffered and sniffed at its contents. It was dark and had a sweet scent to it, only slightly reminiscent of coffee. "What is it?" I asked.

"What do you think it is? With your vast experience you should be able to tell straight off," he teased.

I shook my head. I had no idea. The smell was strange and I wondered for a moment if it was some sort of alcoholic iced coffee. I took a sip. "Coke and...Bacardi?" I guessed, plucking the name from thin air.

He shook his head. "Try again."

"Vodka?" A wild guess, it could have been anything from whiskey to tequila as far as I knew.

"Hmm, not bad. Half right!" He laughed. "It's called a Black Russian. Coke, Vodka and Tia Maria." He took a glug from his glass and I sipped from mine. It was a good choice, really lovely – sweet and tangy without too much kick.

Unexpectedly, he drained his glass in two large swallows and turned his attention back to me. He didn't have to lean far to press his lips to mine but I shuffled closer into the kiss anyway.

The heat from his body suffused mine, growing the tingling in my upper thighs until it was almost unbearable. And yet the thought of pulling away was even more unbearable. His lips were sweeter than before but there was something else too – a forcefulness that hadn't been there previously. I wanted to dissolve myself in his mouth, be lost for all eternity in him.

"Ready for another?" He pulled away without warning and I was almost lost, cast adrift without his arms around me. My breathing was shallow and rapid, and a coolness washed over me where once his heat had warmed.

I was forced to move aside a little as someone squeezed past, making their own way to the crowded bar and I used the time to drain the last of the drink and to think. Was it normal that a guy's kiss could have affected me so much? Or was it the alcohol that was enhancing my emotions? The drink had been sweet but hadn't tasted particularly strong. Surely another would be fine?

"I'll get them," I offered.

"You got in. But getting served at the bar? That's pushing your luck," he said.

He was right. I fumbled for my purse. "Then I'll give you the money."

"I asked you out, remember?" he said. "I'll pay. You can pay another night. Fair?"

My heart pounded with the confirmation

that this was to be the first of many dates. I tried to appear nonchalant. "Yes, fine!" I answered, handing him my empty glass. He laughed but he took it anyway, holding it next to his own empty one with one hand. With the other, he took my arm and pulled me alongside him.

To my surprise he headed towards the exit rather than the bar, dragging me behind him and handing the empty glasses to the doorman who set them on a table by the door.

"That's handy!" I said to the bouncer, meaning the position of the table but it came across as stupid and I could have kicked myself when he looked at me as if he had never quite encountered anyone as dumb as me before. I coughed to hide my embarrassment but to my horror the cough turned into a real one which hacked my chest, making me sound like a heehawing donkey. Eyes watering and spluttering loudly, I couldn't decide whether I looked or sounded more ridiculous. I tried desperately to catch my breath and halt the coughing. My guy stopped and rubbed my back whilst the coughing subsided. "Thought I was on a date with Dolores for a moment," he said.

Lungs sore and highly embarrassed I was further upset that he'd compared me to a previous date. "I don't need to know the names of your ex-girlfriends," I said haughtily, recovering my composure and striding out ahead of him. Only the sound of his guffaws halted me in my stride.

"Dolores the donkey! The kids' programme on TV?" he clarified, laughing even harder at my consternation and embarrassment until I started laughing with him. Arm in arm, we giggled our way across the high street to the next pub. Even though we were laughing, the sexual tension that I'd felt between us had grown rather than abated. I was tantalisingly aware of how his body moved when he walked.

Like the bar before, music blared from the open door into the night beyond, a mating call for the ranks of young adults I was not quite eligible to join. This time I went with him to the bar. I wondered whether he thought it was braver of me to fight through the crowd or whether he realised my reluctance to stand alone in the throng once again. Without him. Or perhaps he didn't care why I went with him. Perhaps he was just glad I was there. I hoped that was the case.

"Two Jager Bombs!" I heard him shout to the barman over the music. I turned away to survey the crowd which looked no different to the previous one. Again I wondered where all these people had come from. When I turned back to my date I found him looking at me with a smile which lit up the corners of his eyes. I wanted to ask what he was thinking but held myself back.

"What's *that*?" I asked as I accepted a large glass from him.

"Just try it."

It didn't look or smell as appealing as the last drink but I wasn't about to offend him by refusing to at least try it. Besides, I had put myself in his hands hadn't I? It would be both churlish and immature to change my mind after he'd paid. I lifted the glass to my lips.

Even a small sip of the fiery liquid had my brain and tongue in a contest as to which was the most fazed! It was like nothing I had ever tasted before but there was an intensity of flavour and effect that grabbed my attention. This time I finished my drink first! I don't know who was more surprised, him or me. I presented him with the empty glass like it was a trophy. Then I leaned over and kissed him. It was a new tradition – a kiss for every drink, but one I was establishing eagerly. This time I took control. With his hands holding our glasses he felt somehow at my mercy. I wrapped my arms around his shoulders and pulled myself close to him.

Our lips were ablaze together. I ran my tongue across the opening of his mouth, flicking slowly at that chasm without yet daring to enter it. He sighed, a long, drawn-out breath and I swallowed it down greedily. This time I pulled away first.

"Where to next?" I asked breathlessly, gulping back my emotions and trying to get myself under control. I watched him drain the dregs of his own drink, wondering if he felt the same. My eyes felt slightly glassy but it wasn't an unpleasant feeling and there was a warmth in my stomach that hadn't been there before.

He laughed. "Look at you, Miss Party-Girl! he teased, eyes dancing merrily.

I laughed along with him. It was easy to do and he was easy to be with and it didn't matter anymore what we were laughing at, as long as we were laughing together. It was also a welcome relief from the steadily increasing intensity between us, which threatened to shatter me into a million pieces.

A guy stumbled towards me, ricocheting from someone who had stumbled into him, and like human dominoes I was pushed up close to my date once more. The same feelings that I'd had moments before assailed me again, but this time they were amplified even without his touch, as if the alcohol in my bloodstream had cranked up the desire, cranked up the *need* in me.

I wanted to run my fingers through his hair and leave a trail of kisses across his neck. Vaguely I heard the guy behind me apologise but my focus remained on my date and I didn't even acknowledge the apology. If anything, I was grateful for the guy's loss of footing.

There was a charge running through my body, an undercurrent of electricity which flowed outwards, snaring my date and drawing him towards me. I could feel it pulsing through the core of me, silently crackling with a palpable energy, a heat of attraction...I held my breath, not daring to exhale unless that slightest waft of air between us shattered the spell...

Until someone pushed roughly between us on their way to the bar and the moment was lost.

"It got pretty intense there," he said quietly, smiling to lighten the remark. So I hadn't been imagining that he had felt it too, this thing between us. I nodded, not trusting myself to speak.

"I have to say, Nat, this date is turning out nothing like I'd expected!"

I didn't want to know what his expectations had been. It was enough to know that they were different to how things had become. And he was right – things were different to what I'd thought they would be too.

"So where to next?" I repeated, hoping that it would involve moving on, getting out into the night air and allowing my head to clear.

"I thought we could go bowling...it's probably not your sort of thing but..."

I broke in. "That sounds great!"

I couldn't tell whether he looked more surprised or relieved but either way he seemed pleased.

"Great! Let's go then."

The night had grown a little cooler since we had come out but it was still warm enough to make the journey to the multibowl a pleasant stroll. Even though it wasn't late, it was too dark to see my new shoes peeping out from under my jeans but I could still hear the *clack-clack* they made on the pavement.

"You could never creep up on anyone wearing those shoes," he commented.

I laughed. "I don't tend to go around creeping up on people!"

"You kinda crept up on me though," he said mysteriously. I wondered if he meant that there had been a sudden change in his feelings towards me. He was quiet for a moment as if he were thinking about his own comment. "Look," he said hesitantly, "there's stuff you need to know."

I smiled back at him. "I already know everything I need to know about you, about us," I said, hoping that I didn't sound cocky.

"People make decisions about other people all the time." His voice had a more far-away quality than it'd had before and I wasn't sure if these words were related to the idea that I had crept up on him, or if he had moved onto an entirely different topic. I waited for him to continue in his own time. Even in the near darkness, with only the streetlights to illuminate us, I could see the passion in his face.

"They make decisions for you and about you, about where you should be and how you should act…they change your whole life with their decisions and they don't even ask your opinion."

Intuitively I understood that he was thinking about how he had moved houses and schools, how his whole life had been turned upside down and there had been nothing he could do about it.

"I guess that must be hard," I agreed. I had lived in one place my whole life. I'd started school with the same kids that I had gone to nursery with and had the same friends I'd had since then. Even though I had made new friends over the years, my old friends were still there, still around, should I have wanted to see them. To have to move to a new house and make all new friends...that would be tough, especially if you didn't want to move in the first place. It struck me then that both Nathan and Rhys had been uprooted, moved from their homes, their schools and their friends. I wondered how I would feel if it were me.

"Do you like living here?" I asked, suddenly shy, aware that it was important to me that he said yes. What would I say, how would I feel if he said he liked it better somewhere else?

He nodded. "It's not that I'm not happy here... it's just that I'd like some say in what happens in my own life. Do you know what I mean?"

I nodded again and we carried on walking but there was an uncomfortable silence between us. Something inside of me jangled discordantly at the idea that perhaps he was not settled permanently in our town. That I would lose him.

At the entrance to the bowling hall he turned once more to me. The light from the neon sign overhead was reflected in his face, giving it an almost eerie glow and an intensity that drew me deeper to him. "But if it means anything to you at all, I'm glad that I'm here with you right now." He pulled me to him and under the illumination of the sign, it felt as if we were cast adrift on a red sea, just him and I alone. A delicious shiver ran the course of my body and left me feeling physically weak.

This kiss was different to the ones before, softer and gentler, with a tenderness that caused an echoing ache in my heart. A light feathery touch of lips upon lips, it was a promise of strawberries and sunshine and a guy at my side to share it all with.

CHAPTER 8B

7:45 p.m.

"Pass the spliff back!" the driver ordered brusquely. The joint which had been passed around was duly returned to his lips where he took a huge drag of it, holding the smoke inside his mouth for an impossibly long time before breathing it out in a long flume that swirled around his head.

The exhaled cannabis smoke came towards me like a rolling fog across a lawn and I tried to turn my face away to avoid breathing it in. The combined drug fumes and stranger's exhaled breath made my stomach recoil in revulsion.

"You squirm much more in his lap and you're gonna have a very wet pair of knickers," Suzie drawled with a smirk. The others laughed and I felt myself go bright red in embarrassment. I was not so naïve that I didn't know what she meant or failed to hear the truth in her words.

And even though I had never been in a situation remotely like this before, I sensed the overtness of the threat in it. Like a rabbit sniffing the air outside its warren, I smelled the ripe scents of exposure and peril. It didn't matter whether the risks were small or whether I was over-reacting, I intuitively knew that I needed to call home. My stomach was tense with anxiety and I felt duped and foolish.

But how would they react if I pulled out my phone? Would they just think me dull and boring? Or would they be angry? Would they be irritated that I had messed up their plans? Would they be livid enough to stop me? I knew I had to test the waters first.

"I have to be back by eleven." Even to my own ears my voice sounded ineffectual, weak and strained like a little mouse's would be. It was hardly the sort of voice that would make them change their plans.

"You'll be back by then, Nat, don't stress," my date said easily as if he expected that to put an end to the conversation. He reached around and slid a hand onto my thigh and I felt something inside me wither and die in fear. I thought it might have been my hopes.

His hand sat there unmoving but threatening me with its presence. I tried not to look but my eyes seemed inexorably drawn towards it as if without an observer to arrest its progress, it would begin to take liberties.

There was something very primal about that thought and my heart quivered in lament. I recognised it without even really being aware of it. If I paid his hand no attention I was convinced I would be providing a licence to move on.

What should I do? Remove his hand? Or cover it with my own and keep it fixed safely in place? As the quandary hurled itself through my brain, my eyes lost focus and the hand moved slightly higher up my thigh. I had been right. Without my constant attention, all would be lost!

"I ought to call home and tell them I'm going out of town!" I blurted, trying for nonchalance and failing dismally.

"God, you are such a prissy pants!" Suzie spat out in disgust.

"Are you wearing 'prissy pants' then? Let's all have a look!" Suzie's guy, clearly the self-styled comedian of the group guffawed. Before his words had lodged in my head and quicker than I would have thought possible, the guy next to me grabbed the hem of my dress and pulled it upwards, intent on revealing my underwear. Conversely, it was the weight and position of my date's hand on my thigh which prevented anything from being revealed and the dress just folded over the back of his arm.

Horrified, I pulled the hem back down and placed my hands over my knees, holding it firmly in place.

"Spoilsport," Suzie's guy laughed. He laughed even more when Suzie took his hand and placed it firmly on her top, directly above her breast.

"You wanna cop a feel of something, then feel

this," she teased, arching her back and pushing herself more firmly into his lap and hands.

"You can keep Miss Prissy-Pants to yourself, mate," her bloke sniggered. "I got me a better deal right here," he said, grubby hands squeezing the soft flesh. On half-closed eyes Suzie glared at me – a challenge and something else I wasn't quite sure of. The guy who sat between us was also transfixed on the mauling of Suzie's breasts and I wondered if my date was similarly fascinated. I tried to pull further back and away from them.

Embarrassment washed over me and it was only partly due to what I had witnessed. Some of it was for their belief that Suzie was a better catch than I. Although I wasn't interested in what they thought, I bristled. Logically it didn't make sense. I pushed the stupid thought from my brain and tried to focus on how I could extract myself from the situation.

"Suzie knows how to show a guy a good time. Isn't that right, Suzie?" my date asked, but before waiting for her answer he carried on. "Do you know how to do that, Nat?"

The atmosphere in the car was suddenly thick with sexual tension. I could feel all of them straining to hear my answer, listening with their groins rather than their brains.

A primitive fear coursed through me again, riding a tidal wave of doom. There was no right answer here, only a series of wrong ones. My heart pounded at the steel cage it was entrapped within, banged itself into the padded walls around it and no one heard it scream. No one but me. Whatever I answered, I was damned if I did and damned if I didn't! It was a circular route to Hell.

"I...I..." At first I didn't notice the car swerve but when it swung back the opposite way, I was thrown roughly against the side of the car door, banging my shoulder hard on the front seat head-rest. "Ow!" I hissed in pain as a barrage of complaints went up from everyone.

"Steady on, Tyler! We're not going to get any action from a hospital bed!" the front seat passenger exclaimed. Everyone laughed. Apart from me.

"You never know. Maybe a fit nurse will come along who has a liking for skinny acidheads and she'll fuck your brains out," the driver responded.

"He'd have to have brains to begin with, for that," Suzie drawled. They all laughed.

I was grateful for the near miss on the road, whatever had caused it. It had taken the focus away from me and given me a little time to think. And in that time I had formulated a plan. As soon as we got to the cinema, I would go to the toilet, and then in the privacy of that space, I would phone home.

The mobile which rested silently inside my

bag suddenly took on the weight of the world. I prayed that no one would text or phone me, alerting them to the fact I had a phone. Survival instinct had set in and overtaken other thinking which reflected my civilised and sheltered upbringing. A small but insistent voice inside my head told me in no uncertain terms that if these guys were reminded that I had a lifeline to home they would remove it from me. I got the distinct feeling that these were not guys who were easily thwarted.

Focusing on *not* thinking about my phone was almost impossible. Pushing its image away only brought the feel and particular weight of it to my mind, as if I already held it in my hand. A fine sweat broke out across my body and my dress stuck to me as if it had been applied with glue. And yet I dared not move in any way, in case I attracted the full attention of my date again.

Luckily since the near miss, he'd been involved in relating anecdotes of other near misses to his companions. Even though I still perched on his lap, he seemed to have almost forgotten about me and that suited me just fine.

But with my attention so deliberately *not* focused on my phone I suffered that strange fear of making it happen exactly by willing it not to. It was akin to trying too hard to *not* look at someone only to turn and catch them staring at you. Like speaking too long and too hard of the Devil, inviting him in.

That made me think of my gran who had always insisted that the Devil wore many guises and that he was harder to spot than a person would think. At that moment I knew exactly what she'd meant.

Then again perhaps I was over-reacting. They were smoking pot and they had made lewd comments but it wasn't like they had ram-raided a store or knocked anyone over. Perhaps I was being a little too melodramatic?

I wasn't the same as them. Wasn't the same as Suzie. But perhaps they just didn't realise that? Perhaps once we got to the cinema I could explain to my date how uncomfortable I felt and we could separate from the rest of the group and get back on an even footing. Perhaps it was all just one big misunderstanding.

I was so wrapped up in my thoughts, I didn't immediately realise that the car had stopped. I clambered out, mindful not to bump my head on exiting and for a moment was too caught up in assuring myself that I still held my bag, to really take any notice of where we were.

But when I raised my eyes, I didn't find the cinema I expected before me. Instead a run down and grubby façade proclaimed itself to be 'The Very Best In Adult Cinema'.

I didn't need to say anything, the look on my face must have said it all. But perhaps it was misinterpreted.

"Don't say I don't know how to give a girl a good time," my date laughed, brandishing a huge bottle of cider in each hand. His friends slapped him on the back and lined up to forage around in the car boot after him.

"Did you only get us two bottles each?" someone asked querulously.

Unexpectedly it was Suzie who answered. "It was all the cash I had, you ungrateful pieces of shit!" but she was laughing as she spoke, clearly intending no malice and receiving none in return.

The guy whose lap she had sat on for the journey gave her a fierce slap across her rump. "Don't be dissin me, Bitch!" he said in a mock American accent.

Not to be outdone, Suzie hit straight back. "And what you gonna do 'bout that anyways?" she said in her own mock ghetto dialect, making a grab at his genitals and squeezing slightly in pretence of a threat.

I watched the play-acting in horror but with my face as tightly closed to my emotions as I could. "I don't think I want to see this sort of film," I attempted to extricate myself. Perhaps if my date knew how I felt, he would change his mind. But my protest was ignored as if it had never been voiced.

"Come on, Sexy, let's get you inside," he said,

taking my elbow as if gallantly escorting me to the prom instead of this sleazy porn palace.

"I think you got your words mixed-up there... shouldn't that have been 'come on, Sexy, let's get inside you'?" one of the guys sniggered and yet again everyone laughed. Except me.

I hadn't thought it possible, but my heart sank even lower. Until I could get to the toilets, there was nothing I could do to extract myself from the situation.

With one hand on my arm and another on my back I was propelled into the foyer.

CHAPTER 9A

8:30 p.m.

"Hey! You're rubbish at this!" I jeered play-fully, as yet another of his carefully bowled balls veered off course and into the trench at the side of the lane. All ten pins stood resolutely straight on their marks, not a single one knocked down in spite of his efforts.

"Maybe I'm trying too hard?" he asked, turning back to me whilst the mechanism at the end of the lane ensured the pins were set up correctly for my turn.

"Perhaps you're not trying hard *enough*?" I queried. A thought came to me. Was he deliberately messing up so that my shots looked good by comparison? Letting me win? I wasn't as bad as him but I wasn't that great either and my hits tended to be down to good luck rather than judgement.

"Or am I luring you in? Letting you get confident before I smash your score?" His face was completely straight before it softened into a smile. "No, trust me, I really am this terrible! I don't know why I didn't suggest a movie in-stead!" He threw a puppy-dog look in my direction.

"Perhaps you should have," I joked back but seeing him standing there with mock indignation on his face, I knew that he had absolutely made the right decision. "But we couldn't have talked like this during a film and I'm having such a good time," I threw my ball with abandon, as if I had such skill I could afford to be nonchalant about the accuracy of my aim.

The ball rolled squarely down the middle of the aisle. Neither speedy nor languorous, it travelled with a seeming certainty that it was dead on course. One after another, every single pin went down! I held my hands up like a champion seeking acknowledgement and laughed when he dragged his hands down his face in despair.

"That's it, rub it in!" He looked at me, head cocked to one side. "Now de truth," he stage-whispered in a phoney Russian accent, "you have done this before Miss Natalie...you come here every night after the rest of the town has gone to bed and practise and practise until you are perfect. No?" He had stepped closer as he spoke. The Russian dialect and the proximity of his body made me feel woozy with desire and I focused on his mouth and the way his lips were moving.

"I shall torture you until you give me the answer I seek," he drawled, eyes narrowed and fixed on my lips.

I waited expectantly, both of us in bowling

shoes and in the middle of a noisy, dank, raucous place which rang with the laughter and triumphant cries of other players, other lanes – but none of that mattered. All that concerned me, all that made a difference in the world, was how I felt right then. My body pushed against the fabric of my clothes, arching towards him, *yearning* to be close, held tight against him.

There was a tingling sensation in my heart and it was echoed in other parts of my body, a longing for something more than perhaps what was on offer. I leant towards him, drawn inwards by the curve of his mouth and the way his eyes sought mine. There was something about those eyes, some unfathomable darkness that touched my soul and anchored me there.

Our lips met. There was a new depth to the kiss, as if our hearts had recognised one another… as if they had been separated in another time and place and had spent countless lifetimes searching for one another. Until this one perfect moment.

My breath came quick in my throat and was exhaled in a flurry, pushed from my lungs as if it were no longer required, as if the kiss would provide everything I needed.

I let myself inhale his breath, drawing it into my body, using it as a magical elixir; miniscule fragments of his DNA which could be stored forever within me.

There was a physical ache in my heart, a

longing somewhere inside which called to him voicelessly as I felt his body respond to mine. He pressed up against me, hard and firm and I moulded myself to him. I could feel his desire, his rigidity as his tongue tasted mine, *drew* mine into the mysterious depths of his mouth.

"Ahem, guys, there are other people waiting for this lane when you are done here!"

Shocked to discover that we were not alone, I pulled away, but my breathing was impossible to control. My chest heaved and there was such desolation in our parting it almost brought me to my knees.

An attendant stood to one side of us. Visibly uncomfortable, his eyes flitted between the floor and the ceiling, avoiding us at all costs. Embarrassment and shame flared hot and red into my face. Whatever had I been thinking? Except that I hadn't been thinking at all. I had been reacting.

"I...um...sorry!" I stuttered as he moved away.

"Guess we had better get on with the game!" my date said, laughing at my discomfort, stepping away from me and leaving me feeling confused and awkward.

"You know, I don't go around kissing guys all the time," I said, an intense need to explain how he affected me catching the words in my throat.

"So you *do* take time off?" he teased, hoisting a new ball into his hand, feeling the size and weight of it.

I laughed, caught off-guard. "No, I mean... I meant that this," I gestured at the empty air between us as if there was an invisible cord that drew us together, "this sort of thing...this kissing...I haven't done it before." I was self-conscious and yet also proud of my novice state.

"I already know that," he smiled.

I was intrigued. "Really?"

"You don't think I would have asked you out if I thought that you were that sort of girl, do you?" He bent to roll the ball down the aisle and winced a little, favouring one side as if he had pulled a muscle. "Then again people aren't always what they appear, are they?" His voice was sharper than before. He took a controlled swing and rolled the ball accurately towards the pins, hitting several of them dead on.

For a moment I wondered if he had been lying to me before. But it was my imagination surely? What reason could he possibly have had for lying? I let him take his second turn before I spoke again.

"So if I'm not the sort of girl who goes around kissing random boys," I turned away to select my ball, taking longer than I needed, hoping to wipe the confusion from my face before turning back to him. "What sort of girl am I?"

"You're a nice girl."

I felt myself smart a little from the comment.

"A *nice* girl? Who *are* you, my granddad?" I didn't mean to sound nasty but that was how it came out. His eyes took on a wounded look and I realised that I had surprised him with the ferocity of my words.

"Ok, I take it back, you're *not* nice," he only half-joked.

"Look it's just that word 'nice'. It's so...so..." I searched for what I meant. "How would you like it if I said you were sweet?" I shoved my fingers into the ball I had chosen and lifted it up, supporting its weight with my other hand. I swung forcefully, perhaps a little too much, and felt it leave my fingers on a forward thrust which saw it bounce its way down the lane before crashing into the pins on the left-hand side and knocking them flying.

He winced, whether at the temper-thrown ball or at my words, I wasn't sure which. "Yeah, point taken. I definitely wouldn't want to be thought of as *sweet*." He took a swig of his beer and set it back down. "Let's try again. You are the sort of girl who is more discerning about who you hang out with."

"Obviously! Because I chose to hang out with you!" I laughed but the mirth was short lived and I felt the smile curve down at the corners of my mouth. Did he realise that I'd had a choice of two dates to go on? Did he know that he was not the only guy who had asked me out tonight?

117

But of course not! I was being overly dramatic, I cautioned myself. And anyway, what if he *had* known? What did it matter? I had chosen him. In fact if anything, it would surely be a compliment, wouldn't it? I dismissed the thought as of no consequence.

"Well, hanging out with me was not really a choice." He took a swig of his drink and turned away to choose another ball. I wasn't sure if it were a ploy for information – perhaps he did know that he'd had a rival for my affection – or whether I was reading too much into it. "It's more like a compulsion than a choice," he winked and grinned.

He threw his ball and was rewarded with a perfect strike.

CHAPTER 9B

8:30 p.m.

The adult cinema was as dismal inside as I would have expected from a seedy establishment. Faded, stained flock wallpaper lined the walls and here and there patches of it had peeled off to reveal the damp and decayed plaster beneath. It was reminiscent of the people who frequented the place I imagined, people who were grubby and shabby and had vital pieces missing from their lives and personalities.

My heart thudded in my chest, apprehension sliding into genuine fear.

What would my dad say when he picked me up from here? I knew he would believe my explanation that I was brought against my will and I knew that once I phoned him he would come straight away...but what would it mean when I was asked out on another date at some point in the future? Would he refuse to allow me to go? Would he insist on dropping me off or on picking me up – or both?

But none of these worries were reasons not to call him. Things were getting increasingly out of control and I didn't even want to think how they would progress.

"I...I need to visit the Ladies," I stuttered, turning towards my date with a false smile plastered on my face. I worried that he would see through the lie but he merely sniggered. "Don't know if any 'ladies' have ever been in this joint but the toilets are that way. I'll wait here for you."

I nodded. I had hoped that he'd say that he would wait by the ticket counter. If he had said that there would have been a possibility that I could have sneaked past him. But waiting at the entrance to the building, there was no chance of that happening.

My hopes were crushed further when Suzie piped up, "I could do with visiting the loo too." Her gaze flicked coldly over me.

I tried to smile again but my face would not work properly.

"Now don't you girls be getting too friendly in there and forgetting about us horny guys!" Suzie's bloke sniggered, making me want to punch him where it hurt.

Suzie shrugged, "Girl-on-girl ain't no substitute in my eyes for some real-man action," she laughed. Her words were directed at her guy and yet I had the strangest sensation that her eyes lingered on my date a little too long. Not for the first time tonight, I wondered if there was history there.

"Anyway once you've had a real man, there's no looking back!" she reiterated and this time I *knew* there was something else going on, some undercurrent I couldn't quite grasp.

My guy laughed and poked the other guy in the ribs. "Do you hear that, Shaun? Suzie's *had* a real man and you just ain't up to the job!" he sniggered. Shaun's eyes blazed with a brief hatred before clouding over into their usual blankness.

Suzie's laughter lasted a little too long before she turned and walked away, sashaying her hips like a siren from an old movie. I followed dumbly, trying my hardest to look as unappealing as possible.

"You shut your mouth," I heard someone mutter behind me. It sounded like Shaun's voice but I didn't dare turn around to see. I had my own concerns to worry about.

Suzie pushed through the toilet door to the area where six cubicles were laid out in a row, not bothering to hold the door open for me. The smell was somewhere between nauseating and repulsive and made me wish that I had the ability to hold my breath indefinitely.

Was there any advantage in appealing to her and asking her for help? Perhaps it was worth a try. I stopped in front of one of the grimy cubicle doors. Suzie was examining her face in the dirty mirror glued to the wall above the equally grubby sinks, squeezing and prodding at her skin with bare fingertips and dirty nails. The taps looked rusted shut and I wondered if anyone ever washed their hands after using this facility, or indeed whether the sort of patrons who came here, washed their hands *ever*. There were no paper towel dispensers and no hot-air hand driers either.

"I didn't think it was going to be like this…" I began nervously.

"You mean you though it was going to be just you and him, all loved up?" Suzie barked a harsh laugh and I realised there was probably less than a slim chance that I could get her on my side. That she would be on anyone but Susie's side. Ever.

"What I mean is…" I tried another tack. "I didn't think we would come out of town and I didn't think…"

She cut me off. "What you mean is you wanted to stay where it was nice and safe! You really are a Miss Prissy-Knickers!" She laughed in my face and once more I saw beyond the make-up and the cool attitude to the nasty girl below. I was a fool to think that I would get any help from her, I realised.

I turned away dejected.

"He gets fed up with them quickly, just so you know!" she turned her face in the mirror, eyes still fixed on her own image. Her words caught me unawares and I halted, the cubicle door only half-closed between us.

"He likes to toy with new girls but he gets bored with them fast, bored with their crying, bored with their stuck-up ways. None of them hold his interest for very long. You won't be any different!" she mocked dismissively, pulling a lipstick from her bag and reapplying it over already shiny lips. She reminded me of a viper preparing to pounce.

Some half-hidden element in her tone of voice set off alarm bells in my head and there was something else too – a gut instinct I couldn't quite put my finger on. And then in a blinding flash of intuition I knew what it was – without any shadow of a doubt.

"He's the father of your child, isn't he?" Even as I spoke the words aloud, I marvelled at how ridiculous they were. Suzie was clearly with Shaun, not my date.

Like someone had thrown a switch, shutters came down over her eyes and her face took on a guarded look. "If five minutes shoved up against the wall at the back of the supermarket counts, then yeah, he's Jakey's father. But it would be more accurate to say that he's his sperm donor!"

Although shocked to the core, a brave insight snared me in its grip and like a runaway train I had no ability to stop myself from uttering the next words.

"And now you are with Shaun. But you still have feelings for-"

"Doesn't matter who I have feelings for! Feelings aren't worth the price of a Valentine's card. And what would you know about it anyway, Prissy Knickers?"

I ignored her insult and focused on the bigger picture. "You still have feelings for him but you're with Shaun." I knew I was pushing my luck but if I could get through to her in some way, make her acknowledge that he'd done her wrong, then maybe I stood a better chance of gaining her help. Winning her trust.

"I'm with Shaun...then I'm not, if you know what I mean." She looked at me knowingly and when my face failed to register the understanding she sought, she was obliged to spell it out for me. "I'm with Shaun until *you* get boring. When you bore him he'll throw you aside and come back to me. Like he *always* does." Her face was incredibly smug.

"And Shaun, where does he fit in then?" I asked, not really caring or wanting to know but because we were on this confessional track and maybe at the end of it, there would be a safe place for me to disembark.

"Shaun fits in wherever I let him." She gave that knowing laugh again and tilted her chin upwards in defiance. "He knows his place. And sometimes it's more exciting when things get a little cosy..."

I wasn't sure if I was catching her implications correctly. "You mean all three of you...?" My stomach churned at the thought. Primal, bestial images ran through my head and I felt physically sick. Suddenly the noxious smell of the toilets rose upwards, thickening and cloying in my throat, bringing with it the taste of acid bile.

"Sometimes three, sometimes more," she laughed, aware of my discomfort and enjoying the sick power it gave her over me. There was no chance she would help me. She would die before even trying. Silently I slipped into the cubicle, her words ringing in my ears as painfully as a physical assault. I elbowed shut the door and latched it securely, touching it as little as possible. I felt as cold as ice.

My phone was in credit and fully charged but how could I make a call with her standing there? What would she do? Would she call the guys in to take care of me? And if she did, what would that mean for my safety? As it was, my date thought that I was playing along but if I got caught phoning, that would be the end of that. I just knew it.

I would have to text rather than try to whisper. Quickly, I pulled my phone out of my bag and into the palm of my hand. Its slight weight and warm solidity were comforting. But as I unlocked it, it gave a single tell-tale solitary bleep. Hoping and praying that the sound had not been overheard, I held my breath.

Already I was out of luck.

"What was that?" she enquired, voice sharp enough to cut steel.

"What was what?" I called back, knowing that I was fooling no one. Hastily I pulled down my pants and squatted above the filthy toilet. If I could urinate forcefully enough, I could perhaps cover the few bleeps the phone would make as I turned it to silent. Then I could text freely.

I pushed the pee out with all my might and fumbled with the phone buttons, fingers numbed by fear. There was a banging on the cubicle door.

The door juddered in its frame but the lock held.

"What are you up to in there?" Suzie demanded.

"N...nothing," I stammered, cursing the slowness of the phone to respond and the wavering signal strength which seemed to flutter from three bars to one in an instant then back again. "I'm just having a pee!" I said desperately.

She didn't respond and I thought that maybe I was safe after all. Pulling my pants up I picked out my dad's number from the scrolled list. But before I could type a single letter, I felt the phone roughly snatched from my hand and my head jerked violently upwards.

Suzie held my phone in one hand and a good fistful of my hair in another. Unless she had taken an Alice-In-Wonderland pill and was now incredibly tall, she must have been standing on something in the adjoining cubicle – presumably the edge of the toilet bowl. Unfortunately, the way the cubicles were constructed, there was just enough room for her to manoeuvre the top half of her body through the gap between the dividing wall and the ceiling, so that she dangled above me.

She looked at the number listed and the one tell-tale word next to it. "Phoning Daddy to come rescue you? Phoning home to ask him to pick little Princess up?" she sneered. "You are such a stupid, predictable little bitch!" She yanked once more on my hair, making my eyes smart with tears. "And you won't be needing this again!" From her additional height she dropped my phone into the dirty toilet pan, where it sank to the bottom like sunken treasure in a sea of pee. "Not even worth flogging, it's such an old model. Couldn't Mummy and Daddy stretch to anything better?"

My heart sank with the phone. It had been my lifeline home. Now I had no hope at all.

Suzie laughed. The sound was hard and brittle and filled with loathing.

"Flush it!" she instructed, watching as I pulled the lever which sent jets of water streaming into the bowl. My phone disappeared from sight taking my last hopes with it! "Now out!" she bellowed, waiting for me to unlatch my door before she climbed down and exited her own stall.

For a moment I considered relocking the door but it was not a failsafe plan. Suzie would either just climb in here herself or call in the guys.

Frantically, I tried to think of some way to get her back on my side. Only one thought sprang to mind.

"What if he got bored of me more quickly than he had with the others?" I spoke directly to her, held her gaze and matched it eye to eye as if I were unafraid. My pulse was doing a polka with my heartbeat, both of them racing to compete with one another and I felt as if I would collapse at any minute. But I held my nerve.

"What if I became so unappealing to him that he decided he wanted you back?" I could see from the new distant look in her eyes that she was considering the possibility. "What if I could get him to see the advantages of being with someone who is..." I struggled for the right words, "fun-loving and spontaneous like he is – get him to see that you're right together?" I pushed with all my might.

"Why would you do that?" she eyed me shrewdly, head tilted to one side and appearing suddenly younger than before, as if the mask had been torn away from her face to reveal the disillusioned girl underneath.

Caught up in her own delusions she had forgotten that I was not a willing participant in any of this. Caution told me not to remind her too much of that, it would force too many comparisons between us and maybe, just maybe, shatter my last chance. I tried to tread carefully.

"We could be friends, you and I..." immediately the words were out of my mouth, I knew I had made a gross miscalculation. By the hair, she swung me towards the door that led back into the foyer where the object of her affections waited...and Shaun.

"Miss Prissy-Pants has returned...and she's full of excitement for some action!" Letting go of my hair, she pushed me forward so that I stumbled into the guys. "And she's been having quite an exciting time of it already, haven't you?" Suzie said.

All eyes turned towards me.

CHAPTER 10A

8:45 p.m.

"I know what you mean but I'm not sure college would be any different." He tried to attract the attention of the girl behind the bar who had just finished serving a large group of bowlers. They were laughing at one another's scores and jostling each other playfully. I turned my attention towards them whilst I thought about the answer he had given me.

"You don't think I would be treated more like an adult there than at school?" For some reason his opinion on the matter was very relevant. Perhaps because I wanted him to see me as older. Older and more worldly wise.

"Well, when the college lecturers came round school taking about what they 'could offer us'," he put on a dry adult voice and I laughed, "they certainly seemed to look at us like adults...but man, they were so uptight. I actually wondered what they were hiding."

"Why would they be hiding anything?" I asked.

He shrugged. "Just a feeling I got."

I wondered why he was so distrustful of everything.

"You know, Nat. Once you are an adult, that's it," he said thoughtfully. "There's no going back. Perhaps you shouldn't want to just rush in. Enjoy the here and now and let the future have the time it needs, to sort itself out."

I recognised the wisdom of his words and yet something within them rankled me. "But you said yourself that you hated people making decisions for you..." I didn't get to finish before he was nodding his head in agreement.

He swallowed the sip of beer he had taken and put the bottle back on the counter. We were still wearing ugly bowling shoes, unsure whether we would play another game or not. I hid my feet under my bar stool as he stuttered his seat closer to mine across the wooden flooring.

A fleeting grunt as he bent made me wonder what was wrong with him, but the thought was as transient as the sound, and soon forgotten in the warm proximity of him. I felt the breath of every word he spoke brush gently across my face, and I leaned forward, eagerly inhaling his essence.

"Do you think that stops - people making decisions for you - when you become an adult?" He looked at my quizzical expression and tried to explain. "I see my dad go to work every day. One eye on his watch and another on his phone, he hurries off in the car every morning. And every time, he's nervous. What if the traffic is bad? What if they've called an earlier meeting and no one told him? What if his boss decides that my dad needs to go to Japan next week and oversee the new plant they're building there? What if his boss decides that my dad has to be out there for a few *years* to oversee things...I don't want to be just like him when I'm older."

I cut in. "You mean you might have to move again?" I was almost distraught at the idea. I tried to shake myself out of it and stop being ridiculous. One date did not a relationship make, I told myself. But the few short hours that we had been out seemed like a lifetime and I couldn't imagine *not* sitting here with him again. I couldn't envisage not talking as freely as we were doing - and for the life of me, I couldn't imagine not kissing him every single day of my life, until we were both old and grey. The ache in my heart amplified, cutting me a thousand times with my own fears.

"I don't know," he replied with a searing honesty. "I hope we don't and I'd do anything to avoid being like my dad...but who knows." His gaze shifted away from mine for a moment. "See, that's my point. Decisions still get made for you, even when you are an adult. Sometimes it's just circumstances. Just a continuation of the life you know." He took another swig of beer but this time when he put the drink down he did so a little too heavily. The bottle thumped onto the bar.

I noticed a couple of the guys in the big group look over, perhaps expecting trouble. One of them looked me up and down but not in a lascivious way; I felt more like he was making sure that I was alright. I flashed him a brief smile to let him know that everything was cool. He turned back to his friends and his drink.

"All that stress, a boss who is always on his back, it makes him nervous and when he's like that he's not pleasant to be around." He took another swig of his beer.

I noticed how white the knuckles which clenched the bottle were. "My dad can be a jerk sometimes too, when work gets him down," I empathised. "Mum says that's when he needs his cave," I laughed but my mouth turned down with the fear in my next words. "I really hope you don't have to move again." I brushed my hand lightly over his arm, feeling the muscles there tense briefly, as if that fleeting contact had stirred something within him. A quickening of my heartbeat seemed in direct response to the touch and I raised my eyes to his, to find him looking at me with such depth of passion that it took my breath away.

"I've had a good time tonight, Nat," he breathed. The pause was so long that for a moment I didn't think he would follow the statement up with anything else. Was he waiting for me to respond? But before I could reply, he carried on.

"To be honest I've had a *great* time and I'd like to keep on having great times with you. But I don't know how long I'll be here and it's unfair to not tell you that at the start." He looked crestfallen.

For a moment I wondered if this was what older kids referred to as 'the brush-off' but one look at his face told me otherwise. His eyes met mine and there was such pain evident there, I wanted to look away, but I didn't.

I placed a finger across his mouth to silence him before following it with a light touch of my mouth to his. There was a sharp but not unpleasant tang of beer on his lips and tongue and I wondered how I tasted to him. Did he taste the sweetness of the wine I had been drinking or did his beer overpower other tastes, just as he overpowered me?

"Look, what I'm trying to say, is that you shouldn't get too involved with me..." Reluctantly he pulled away.

I shrugged. It was already too late for that, I thought. "Let's enjoy the here and now and let the future sort itself out," I paraphrased his wisdom back at him.

He laughed. "Wow, you are a fast learner, Natalie!" He leaned forward once more but instead of kissing me again on the mouth as I had expected and hoped for, his kiss landed on my cheek.

I looked at him, suddenly worried that his interest was based more in friendship than in romance after all. Had I got this all wrong? My eyes must have spoken volumes, because without me saying a word, he seemed to understand the thoughts which raced through my mind.

"That was just for being understanding, for you being you." He smiled at me and I smiled back in return, relieved and deliriously happy. So that he could not see how focused on him I was, I turned towards my half-full glass on the counter. The pink wine was clear enough that I could see through the coloured liquid to the bottles racked up on shelves behind the bar. A range of alcoholic drinks clustered together there, clear liquids side by side with darker, less translucent ones. There were brightly coloured jewels of intoxication and thicker more viscous potions of libation but I knew in that instant that none of them could make me feel at heady as I did at that moment - as drunk with pleasure just by being in his company.

"So, shall we play another game? Or are you too focused on this *very minute* to think up more strategies for winning against me?" he teased, sliding off the stool and holding his hand out to me, even though the bowling shoes meant that I didn't really need the help.

"After that last game, I honestly don't think I need any strategies, do I? Besides, does there need to be a winner and a loser? We could just be first and second," I suggested.

"Second is for wimps!" he declared. "There is one winner – and everyone else is a loser. That's just how it is in life. The sharks eat up all the little fish." There was a new glint in his eye which made me a little nervous. Was he still talking about bowling? I dismissed my concerns as fanciful worryings and followed him back to the booking desk. There was only one group in front of us and they were soon on their way.

"Do you have a lane free?" he asked the girl behind the counter.

"Yes, number 12," she responded, clicking her fingers rapidly over the keyboard in front of her. "How many for?"

He didn't miss a heartbeat in the answer. "Just me and my girlfriend," he said casually, unaware of how the word 'girlfriend' shot a quivering arrow through my heart.

I watched him pay the charge and collect the receipt, all the while wanting to frolic around, shouting at the top of my voice that I was his chosen one!

I was his *girlfriend*!

CHAPTER 10B

8:45 p.m.

All eyes turned to me and my breath caught painfully in my throat. What was Suzie going to say? What was she going to tell them? And more importantly, how would they react? Panic bit into my brain and heart so far that I thought I might drop down dead onto the floor. Perhaps if I did, it would be the lesser evil, to have died before they did whatever they were intending to do with me.

My date looked from Suzie to me and back again. "Tell me more," he said in a voice that was full of expectation.

Suzie laughed but the sound was devoid of humour. It reminded me of a graveyard full of clattering bones. What was she going to say? Desperate to head her off, I stuttered something out, not thinking it through before letting it tumble out of my mouth but trusting to an instinct that to stay safe, I had to put *her* on guard too. If I couldn't get her on my side then putting her on edge had to be the next best thing. Because whilst she was trying to watch her own back, she would have less time to think about stabbing the metaphorical knife into mine!

"Suzie was telling me what good friends you all are!" I shot out, watching the pupils of her eyes contract in surprise. A wariness crept over her face and I felt her regard me with a new respect. It was the sort of respect I never wanted to have bestowed on me again. It made me feel unclean.

Shaun guffawed, clearly missing the finer points of my insinuation but it was not lost on my date, as I had suspected it would not be.

"Yes, we're all good friends here. Isn't that right, Shaunie?" he slapped the still laughing Shaun on the back but his eyes lingered on Suzie a little too long. We stood there the four of us, as if we were set pieces on a chessboard and I had such a hollow feeling inside, I could easily have truly believed that I was made of spun glass – a hard, brittle exterior with absolutely no internal substance. The feeling was so strange that I half expected some loud voice to hail from the heavens 'knight to queen's bishop 3' and for some otherworldly force to propel me forwards or backwards as desired.

Instead the call came in the rather more earthly tones of the guy behind the cashier's desk. "You goin' in or what? Movie's about to start!" He slavered in our direction, eyes darting over Suzie and me, finally resting on the point where my breasts jutted out the most. I could feel the heat of his gaze and when he ran the tip of a white-furred tongue over his lips, I felt my stomach clench in revulsion.

"Yes, yes, of course we are!" Suzie snapped back and started forward, seemingly eager to end the discussion which she had begun; postpone the revelations that she feared. I wondered what it was that she was avoiding. Did she think he would be angry if he found out that she had admitted he was the father of her child? It was a possibility but I dismissed it as of no consequence. It didn't seem to be something he would be worried about. No, it was something else, I was sure of it.

As we walked past the ticket desk, I saw the cashier's eyes follow my every step. Dressed casually, he wouldn't have looked out of place in a homeless shelter or hostel. Only his name badge, pinned haphazardly on his shirt proclaimed him to be someone with a vestige of responsibility. 'Barry,' the badge announced, as if any of the clientele of this joint would be interested. But perhaps I was wrong. Perhaps the people who frequented this fleapit visited so often that they wanted to know Barry's name. I planned to never have to remember it.

He lowered his hand below the grubby desk and for a moment I feared that I was about to see a bit more of Barry than I already had, but when his filthy paw emerged, it was holding out a garishly printed flyer depicting a naked woman with masked off areas where the photograph had been deemed too explicit for publication.

'Extreme adult erotica!' the flyer announced in bold letters. Barry passed it to Shaun. "You don't want to miss this one! Starts next Monday!" he said in reverential tones as if discussing a tour of the greatest works of art. "She does things you wouldn't even think was possible!" He spoke as one who knew his topic well, but I doubted the validity of his opinion. Barry looked to me as if he had much experience with the celluloid variety of women and none at all with real life versions.

Susie whipped the flyer from Shaun's hand before he had a chance to deposit it in his pocket for later contemplation. "We won't be needing this, thanks," she said, tossing the flyer back onto the desk. "He's got as much as he can handle!" It was said in an off-the-cuff manner and yet I felt it was probably an accurate statement. If I hadn't been so terrified at what I had got myself into, I might actually have laughed at Shaun's crestfallen demeanour.

"Ain't nothin' you don't already get from Suzie, I suspect!" my date agreed, although whether it was in consolation to Shaun or to anger Suzie, I was no longer sure. There were dangerous undercurrents here and I was afraid that at any moment I was about to lose my footing in them.

I was hustled into the cinema.

Even from the entrance, the smell was a hundred times more rank than it had been in the foyer. It was too dark to see where the other guys from the car were seated but no one seemed bothered about that since the alcohol had already been distributed.

The cinema was warmer than the foyer and that combined with the darkness, only served to make the stench more ominous. There was a melange of aromas mixed together I thought, one of which had the strong muskiness of human body odour. The pervading scent of damp and decay seemed to issue not only from the building and its furnishings but from the bodies of the audience.

Traces of air freshener could also be detected but overlying all of this was a smell of what I could only think of as a saltiness. Not quite the briny scent of the sea, that clean sharp tang of air that blows away the cobwebs in your lungs but a more earthy odour, the source of which flummoxed me.

In single file we shuffled into a row of seats and I tried one last time to dissuade my date from keeping me here. "I really don't think this is my kind of movie," I said to his back as he walked slightly ahead of me, selecting our seats. Ignoring me, he found one he liked and sat down on the filthy and torn cushion. He pulled down the seat next to him and patted it.

"You don't know that until you try," he said, waiting for me to sit, not taking me seriously. I wondered for a brief moment what would happen if I started to scream and holler. Would anyone here come to my rescue? Even without the covering of darkness I knew that these would be the sort of people to whom a scream would only lend another frisson and dimension of excitement.

I sat down and found that Shaun had been relegated to the end and that I was sandwiched between my date and Suzie. Although she hadn't chosen her seat to offer solidarity with me, at least it meant I would only have to contend with *one* pair of wandering hands, small comfort as that was.

The film credits began to roll but I paid little attention to these. What more horrors did the night have in store and how was I going to deal with them?

I passed along the bottles that were passed to me, handing them to Suzie who passed them to Shaun before accepting some for herself. The next bottles were clearly for me and I took them without fuss. If I held them to my mouth and pretended to drink, they would not know I was faking it. In the dim light I watched Suzie take a swig and copied her style, keeping my lips firmly closed in the hope that no-one would notice. I was wrong.

"Can't drink with your mouth shut!" Suzie stated dryly, deliberately dropping me in it. At that moment I hated her more than ever before, because I knew then that she would foil every attempt I made to stay safe. Regardless of whether there was anything in it for her, any benefit that might be wrought by my gratefulness to her for any aid, she was determined that I would suffer.

"Can't do very much with your mouth shut at all," sleazed Shaun which elicited laughter from everyone except me.

A tinny and rather tuneless music began and the film started. If this had been a normal cinema and a normal film I would have walked out after the first scene, the sets and acting were so dismal. But this was not a normal film, nor a normal cinema and it was not going to be my choice to leave or stay.

On the giant screen the scene cut abruptly from a bar where a very scantily clad woman was talking to a man about selling her house, to her showing him the living room. The set was not at all convincing and on at least two occasions I thought that I could see the huge microphone, the one they call the boom, protruding into the corner of the shot.

The male actor looked like he belonged in a time long gone; his facial hair and unfashionable hairstyle attesting to the fact that his youth was far behind him, although the much younger woman seemed too short-sighted to have noticed. When she led him up the stairs to 'show him the bedroom', despite my own fears, I couldn't help but be fascinated by the décor of the room and the bad acting.

But my unwanted companions were engrossed in the film for other reasons. Even before the man had ripped open the woman's blouse and hiked her skirt up, my date was breathing heavily and appearing to forget the alcohol at his feet, had turned to me and pulled me roughly towards him. Conveniently, there was no arm rest in his way to halt his progress. Either the seats had been manufactured like that or the arm rests had been removed to give the patrons better access to one another during film showings. I shuddered to think which. With an amplified breathing sounding out from the speakers above my head and a heavy breathing coming from my date, I felt surrounded, enclosed and trapped in a situation that was rapidly spiralling into decline.

Using one hand under my chin to turn my face towards him, he mashed his lips to mine. Alcohol fumes had mixed with something else, some remnant of exotic smoke perhaps, and were combined on his breath into a bitter and noxious smell. Instinctively I struggled to pull away, but as before in the car, I found that any struggling on my part only seemed to excite him more. Unwilling to stoke his fire further, I held my nerve and tried instead to sit still and suffer his kiss without protest.

The actress's breathing changed to a loud moaning and reluctantly he pulled away from me long enough to cast an eager glance at the film. Freed of his restraining hands and with a mounting horror, I too cast my gaze towards the screen.

What I saw there ripped away any remnants of naivety I may have held and I felt my soul sink deeper into a well of despair.

CHAPTER 11A

9:30 p.m.

"I won one game and you won the other... I guess that makes us even!" I declared happily. I liked the fact that neither of us had tried to smash the other into the dust. Despite his comments – there was something effortlessly romantic about it.

"So are we equally matched or is there another, more hidden game going on here?" He was smiling but there was a serious edge, a deeper meaning than the words themselves suggested, I suspected.

I took a swig of my drink, pure coke with no added alcohol. I'd had more than enough booze for one night, possibly even for two, and felt warm and pleasantly tipsy. I swished the dark liquid around in the glass for a moment, watching the bubbles form and subside as the drink was tilted first one way, then the other.

"I'm not trying to lose to you, to make you feel more macho, if that's what you mean," I said slowly. "To be honest, I had as much fun losing as I did winning."

He shot me a strange look, all tilted head

and raised eyebrows. "Trust me, losing a bowling game isn't going to make me feel less of a man, plenty other things in life have done that far more successfully." He took a swig of his drink and grimaced, as if it were suddenly and unexpectedly bitter.

"What do you mean?" A pinprick of worry penetrated my heart.

He laughed but there was a falseness to it, as if he forced the sound out of him. "Nothing. Ignore me. Too much booze probably." He laughed again and it was more genuine this time. "Are you still glad you came?" he asked shyly, leaning towards me on the bar stool, so that his words were quieter, more intimate.

The question took me so much by surprise, that I forgot about the straw I had been intending to raise to my lips and placed the glass back on the bar with a louder clatter than I had intended.

"Can't you tell my answer?" I felt my eyebrows shoot up . "Can't you tell that I'm having the best time *ever*?" The stupidity of my words stung me too late. Clearly he couldn't or he wouldn't have asked and as for saying it was the best time ever, how lame was that? I tried to shrink inside myself.

"So, if I was to ask you on a second date, you would say yes?" He looked away as he asked, refusing to meet my gaze. I reached out a hand to him, placing it on his arm and making him look at me.

"If you don't ask me on a second date, I'll never speak to you again!" I said in a voice that was pulled deliberately high and tight and sounded very much like one of the teachers at school.

I must have been more than a little accurate because his eyes widened and choking with laughter, he sprayed a large part of his drink over himself and the bar. "Hey, I didn't know you could do that!" he spluttered out between the thumps I landed on his back.

After a moment he was fine and yet I was reluctant to move from his side, even back to the close proximity of the stool. I left my hands resting on him, taking comfort from the heat of his skin through that subtle contact. I wondered what it would feel like to be able to run my hands over his bare back, to feel the muscles contract and relax under my open palms, to open myself to him entirely.

My breath came shorter and faster in my throat and I longed to taste his lips again, longed to have him taste mine, to feel his tongue deep inside my mouth once more.

"You OK there?" A new barman appeared behind the bar and began to mop up the spilled liquid. The moment was irrevocably shattered. I moved back to my own stool and yet a heat remained that pulsed inside of me.

"Yes, sure. Sorry about the mess. But was her fault," my date replied, grinning as he pinned the blame on me. The barman looked at me but said nothing and when the bar was clean again he moved away, leaving us alone once more.

I waited until he was out of sight before I said in a voice that was as close to the barman's as I could manage, "They don't give me extra wages for wiping up your spit, you know!"

Luckily, this time when he laughed there was no drink in his mouth.

"You're really good at that!" he said in awe.

"There was this one time," I ran my finger around the rim of my glass, wondering what he would think when I told him the story. I shrugged ruefully, "OK, truthfully, *two* times when I just didn't feel like going into school...and I phoned up..."

He cut me short, guessing ahead. "Oh my God! You pretended to be your mum! And you got away with it!" His eyes were as wide as dinner plates in disbelief.

I grinned. But only for a moment. "It was years ago. And I didn't get away with it."

He raised his eyebrows. "You got caught?" He waited for me to continue.

"When I phoned in, I knew I had to give a reason for 'my daughter' being off sick so I said that it was measles." I watched his face change, watched the tiny lines that appeared around his eyes as laughter caught him in its grip once more and then without even realising it, I was laughing at myself with him. "So when I went into school the next day with no spots and no idea that if I really had had measles I would have been off for at least a week..."

"You got caught!" he only just managed to get the words out before his breath was hijacked by another gale of laughter.

"I got caught!" I confirmed, nodding my head as the rest of my body shook with hilarity. I watched as he tried and failed to stop laughing. "I was grounded for a month!" I managed to choke out. "And my dad made me take out the bins for months afterwards." My face hurt with all the unaccustomed stretching but there was one final piece of the story I had yet to tell. I tried to draw in a serene breath but it was difficult.

"And every time I took the bins out I would say to myself under my breath, 'Natalie you have let your mum and I down'. I did it every time... until he caught me saying it in his voice and grounded me for *another* month!"

Real tears of mirth rolled down his cheeks and it was a while before either of us could talk sensibly again. "A talent like that's gotta come in handy though," he stuttered, trying to get over the comedic value of it. "You shouldn't keep it a secret."

"I guess," I said but I couldn't really think of

a way I could exploit it without getting myself into trouble.

"Can you do me?" he twisted his head to one side and I couldn't help but look at the firm line of his jaw and the Adam's apple that lay below.

I could feel his gaze on me even with my eyes shut. I focused on what we had already talked about. "I think everyone should have this much fun!" I said in a fair rendition of his voice. I opened my eyes to find him staring at me.

"Was it that bad?" I asked, strangely fearful. Had I insulted him in some way? I felt my innards clench and a cold sweat descend over me.

"That was fantastic!" The incredulity in his tone convinced me that he was being honest. "It was so like me. It was like listening to a recording of myself!" He stuttered his stool even closer to mine so that our knees were touching. "How do you do it and can you teach me?"

"I don't think it's something that can be taught," I said, relieved. "And I've never told anyone I can do it before. But what about you, do you have any hidden talents, anything I wouldn't already know about you?" Even as the words left my mouth I regretted them for the salacious way they sounded. I blushed from head to toe and hoped he wouldn't notice.

He did notice and laughed quietly. "Hidden talents...you are forward, Miss Natalie!" he mocked gently.

"I…I didn't mean anything like…like…" I floundered, not even clear any longer what I actually *had* meant.

"It's OK, really," he grinned, placing a hand on my knee, eliciting a shiver of desire from me that went unnoticed by him.

"So do you?" I pressed, wanting an answer and wondering why he hadn't for once picked up on how badly I needed his touch.

"Not like yours. But I see things…" he seemed reluctant to elaborate.

"You *see* things?" I felt my brow furrow.

"Do we have to talk about this?" he asked abruptly, turning away from me very slightly but enough that our legs no longer met. Instantly I missed the feel of his knee against mine. The warmth and comfort of the contact and the unspoken promise of what it meant - that we were an item.

"Not if you don't want to…I just thought…" I didn't know how to pull the situation around. At that moment I would have given anything to have taken the words back.

CHAPTER 11B

9:30 p.m.

The magnified woman on the screen wrapped her legs around the back of the man on top of her and heaved herself towards him. And at that moment I knew I would have given anything I owned, anything *I would ever own* to be somewhere other than this filthy cinema, being pawed by my filthy date.

The grunting on the screen was laborious and yet it was matched perfectly by the sounds emanating from my date to one side of me and Shaun on the other, beyond where Suzie sprawled in her seat.

I felt his hot breath on my neck; the foetid stench of it assaulted me as much as did the sheer proximity of the guy it issued from. And just as I clenched my teeth and relinquished all notion of being rescued, a further revulsion assailed me. Through the thin fabric of my dress I felt his clammy palm land on my stomach, just below my bra.

Like five squat slugs, I watched his fingers slither towards their ultimate goal...the peak of my breast. The heat emanating from his palm mixed with my own fear-induced body heat and I felt like I would explode at any moment. Perhaps like a damaged nuclear plant I would just get hotter and hotter until I obliterated everything in the vicinity. All that would be left would be a crater in the earth. It was a peculiarly peaceful thought. I didn't mind going nuclear, as long as I took these vile excuses for human beings with me.

Having found what they sought, the slugs began to squeeze my breast, shaping and forming it to their own desires, pinching the tissue and trying to pull it outwards. They weren't successful. Under his hand, my flesh withered from his touch. Acid on a rose.

I shrank from his touch, my nipple evading him and refusing to be drawn out. Did he not sense my revulsion? Or was he too fixated on his own thoughts and sordid needs?

What if I could get away from him? I feverishly speculated how I could escape. What if I squeezed past him, or even Suzie and Shaun at my other side, and made a run for it? Impossible in my new shoes! But if I kicked them off? Was it possible to get past them? Unlikely. They weren't going to just let me shuffle past…

I looked at the seat directly in front of me. It was empty. Would I be able to leap over the back of it and sprint away before he could catch me? Subtly I looked along the length of the row to where it met the aisle at the end. There were a couple of people sitting there. Not many, but enough to get in my way and prevent me from gaining clear access to the aisle. But the row in front of them had empty spaces. Could I jump into the next aisle and make my escape?

I had been so preoccupied with my plan that I had almost forgotten that his fingers still mauled my breast. But when his other hand landed in my lap I realised the plan would *have* to work. There were no ifs, buts or maybes. I couldn't sit impassively whilst he continued to assault me.

I felt his hand press into my groin through the material of my dress, pushing hard, bearing agonizingly down on me. Where my legs remained jammed shut he pressed more firmly, his other hand squeezing my breast painfully so that I would think twice before I denied him access.

Biting my lip against the searing pain I tried to kick off my shoes without moving my legs or opening them to his sick attentions. I got one shoe off with no problem but the other shoe seemed to be stuck fast. A combination of a slight difference in foot size, the heat of the cinema and my general terror seemed to have combined to swell my foot up enough that it was holding rigidly on to its shoe.

In desperation, I thrust my bare foot at the shod one once more, not caring as the sharp heel tore a little of the skin from the naked foot. It was nothing compared to the fate I knew I would suffer if I was forced to stay.

At my side he appeared to mistake my shuffling as signs of enjoyment. Perhaps he was surprised at this change in me, perhaps it was what he had expected all along. I neither knew nor cared. All I cared about was that the shoe came off…but still it would not budge.

"Knew there was a hidden little slut in you, Natalie…you can't pretend you're not enjoying this," he whispered salaciously to me, making my blood turn cold. *How could I ever have thought that I would be safe with him?* I berated myself internally for my own naïve stupidity. *What had I been thinking?* I had been too innocent to even realise what danger I was putting myself in.

I brought my shod foot up to my seat, uncaring in my panic as to how it left me momentarily exposed. Grasping the shoe firmly at the heel, I pulled with all my might. And unbidden, there came a voice, sharp and defined into my mind. 'Do whatever you have to do to get yourself out of there, girl!'

The memory of her was still clear and true, even four years after her death. 'Grandma,' I thought at her, 'what do I do?' But the image in my head was only a memory, not a visitation from the spirit world and there was no helpful answer. And yet instantly I *knew* what I would have to do.

I held the shoe by the heel and swung it up on a sharp arc, seeking flesh and muscle and skin with its razor-sharp heel. It caught him unawares but failed to do any real damage, glancing off his cheek and missing his eye by only a fraction. It was his lucky day, after all.

Knowing there was no going back, I dropped the shoe on the floor with a thump. Clutching my bag, I leapt over the back of the seat in front. I was one row ahead from where I had previously sat but there was no time to spare. I prepared to sprint up the row as far and as fast as I could, before leaping once more into the next row and then out into the aisle.

But as I leaned forward, legs ready to sprint, I realised something was holding me back. My dress! It was snagged on the seat back! Unwilling and unable to take the time to dislodge it, I renewed my efforts to pull free. The material strained and for a heart-stopping instant, refused to give, before finally tearing with a loud, wrenching rip. The sound was all but swallowed up by the noises coming from the film, where the actors appeared to be doing a whole lot of swallowing of their own! I dragged my horrified gaze away.

Reaching the people on that row who blocked my exit, I leapt once more over the back of a chair and into the row in front. I could hear a commotion behind me but whether it was from the audience or more specifically Suzie and the guys, I couldn't tell.

Fear bit at my heart and I desperately wanted to look back, wanted to be able to assure myself that they were still sitting where I had left them, even though every fibre of my body knew that would not be the case. Unable to stop myself, fear ravaging though me, sapping my energy whilst simultaneously filling me with adrenaline, I turned my head in the direction from which I had come.

The seats were empty! I swept my gaze towards the aisle behind me and found them hot on my heels. They were perhaps three full seconds behind and gaining fast!

I ran into the aisle, hair and ripped dress streaming out behind me, probably looking like a banshee fleeing Hell. The door which led from the room to the vestibule outside was heavy and damp to the touch but I wrenched it open, sinews and muscles straining with the effort and receiving no reprieve. I tore through the door and into the dingy hallway.

The front door was within sight! Even the sight of Barry, only half hidden behind his desk in the foyer could not dismay me. Escape was within my sight and once I reached those big glass doors; passed through them to the safety of the world outside, everything would be fine.

Feet thumping heavily on the worn foyer

flooring, I ran until I reached the smeared and soiled doors, their once shiny handles filmed over with grime and rust.

I reached a hand towards them, the dirty metal clean enough in places to show a reflection of my pale, panicked face...and the angry face of my date who stood behind me. With a slowness born of a surety that nothing could stand in his way, he reached in front of me, grasping the handle above where my hand rested.

In vain I tried to wrench the door open, kicking behind me with shoe-less feet, trying to ward him off. He simply reached his other hand in front of me, paying no attention at all to my attack on his legs and trapped my hand which held the handle, under his. He squeezed with all of his might, forcing my fingers to be squashed between the unyielding metal and his unyielding flesh. I watched my hand turn white as its blood flow was reduced; I felt the pain and I knew the answer to the question of what was about to happen next.

CHAPTER 12A

9:50 p.m.

He remained silent, reluctant to elaborate. I had a choice between pressing him on what he meant or moving on to another topic, drawing him out once more. The wise choice was to change subjects, as he obviously didn't want to continue our previous conversation. The wise choice was not the one I chose.

"What do you mean you see things?" I kept it light. I swear there was not an iota of intonation in my voice that he could have interpreted as disparaging, but even so, I saw him wince at the words.

"I shouldn't have said that," he mumbled.

I got the feeling he was trying to put me off. I held on tenaciously. "So what did you mean by it then?" I was determined to wait it out.

He shrugged as if it was nothing to be bothered about after all. "I guess I made it sound weirder than it is. It's not like I see ghosts." He tried to make a joke of it. "I don't see big white shapes floating around going *whooooo* or anything!"

I was confused. If forced to say what I thought

he'd meant it would probably have been exactly that! "So what then? What's the mystery?" I took a sip of my coke and watched as he took a sip from his drink before answering. His face was more serious than it had been all night and he looked older than before – no, not older – just troubled, like he had worries enough for the world.

"When you walk along the street what do you see?"

It was a curious question and I wasn't sure what sort of answer he required.

"I see the ground and the sky and whoever is there..."

"Close your eyes." He put a hand over them to make sure I couldn't cheat. "There are people sitting behind me, a man and a woman. Describe them."

Behind my eyelids I could only see dark red. I tried to bring the images of the man and woman to the forefront of my mind. I had glanced at them as we walked over to the bar but it had been a quick look, nothing more. And to be honest, I'd had eyes for no one other than the boy who currently covered my gaze, all night. "The man has short hair and the woman has shoulder-length blonde hair."

"What colour is his hair?"

I knew it wasn't blonde but was it brown, black or even grey? I had no idea. I remained silent, scrutinising my memory.

"OK then, the woman. Is her hair light blonde or darker? Pulled back in any way or left loose?"

"Um, it's medium blonde and she has something in it, a clasp but only on one side!"

"OK good. Now what is she wearing?"

"That's easy! I liked her top. It's silky, with sleeves which are quite floaty and a little shimmery."

"What colour?"

"Easy again. Blue with a hint of red in places."

He removed his hand, allowing my eyes to flicker open once more. "See, I'm not that bad, am I?" I grinned.

He grinned back. "Take another look."

The woman's top was green with a shot of orange running through it. I turned back to him, flummoxed. "I was wrong!"

"Behind me, at the far end of the bar there's a man sitting on his own. Can you see him?"

I looked over his shoulder to the man he mentioned. He was some distance away, past several other groups of people. "Yes."

"He's dressed wrong to be in here."

I looked again. The man was in clothing which would have been more suited to an office than to a bowling bar. I nodded.

"He has a battered old briefcase stuffed under his chair…"

I looked at my date. "You can't see that from here. Do you know this for a fact or are you surmising?"

He looked back at me, eyes boring intensely into mine. "Well, that's something you have to figure out for yourself, isn't it?" He carried on as if I had not interrupted him. "He has a battered briefcase stuffed under the chair but it doesn't look that full. He's wearing a watch but it's a cheap fake designer one. His shoes are clean and they were expensive but they are battered and worn now and where his wedding ring would be, there is a pale indent on his finger instead."

I laughed nervously. It was an interesting game but also a little too weird for my liking. "So did his wife leave him, Sherlock, or is she buried under the patio?"

There was a moment of perfect silence before he spoke. The noise of the bar seemed to fade out and I was caught in the timings between each breath he took. "She died. Drunk driver hit her from the side and overturned her car. She was killed instantly."

A chill descended my spine and leached into my heart. "You don't know that!" I whispered on a thin reedy voice I barely recognised as my own.

"Don't I, Nat?" His voice was full of pain, as if knowledge of the stranger's devastated life had by osmosis rubbed off on him. "I know more than you think."

It was the second time he had said this phrase during the evening and I began to get a little irritated. The evening, so pleasant before, had begun to take on a darker hue – a more ominous and sinister feel. I didn't like it one little bit.

"You are making it up as you go along," I said accusingly, witnessing the hurt my words had inflicted, flicker across his eyes.

"Go to the toilet, it's over by where he is. Walk close to him and on the way back, look at him. I mean *really look,* Nat, not just with your eyes, but with your soul!"

Uneasy, but needing to know the truth, I slid off the bar stool. He was right about where the toilets were located and it was easy enough to wind my way past the other customers and closer to the solitary man than it was actually necessary for me to be.

And then the strangeness of the situation took hold of me and I knew that I had to have some answers. Slowly and deliberately I walked up to the man as if seeking help. "I don't suppose you know where the Ladies is, do you?" I asked, ignoring the big neon sign which proclaimed the location of the toilets.

He didn't even look up at me, just nodded his head in the general direction. Perhaps he thought me an idiot although he gave no indication of it. I was still no wiser. I placed a hand on his arm and noticed that his hand displayed a pale ring of skin where perhaps a wedding band had sat until recently.

"Thank you," I muttered, mind whirling yet readying myself to move on. But before I had time to remove my hand, he had wrenched his arm out from under it as if it were on fire. More than his actions, it was the look on his face which seared me to the core. Unfathomable anguish filled his eyes and the lines on his face seemed carved in stone.

Even as I realised he was not much older than my own father, I saw the greyness of his skin and felt the sense of hopeless despair which clung to him, seeping out from every pore and infecting the air around him.

"I, I'm sorry!" I stuttered, not knowing whether I was apologising for the unwanted touch of my hand or for something more indefinable.

He looked at me for a moment and looked away, effectively dismissing me. Disheartened and feeling as if I had intruded into a very private situation I turned towards the toilets. Only then did I remember what I had been told about the briefcase and the shoes. I turned back and stole another glance, trying hard to be inconspicuous, as if I weren't actually looking.

The sunken briefcase silently accused me, as if in staring at it I was committing a cardinal sin. It had been stuffed between the legs of his stool, its sides squished together in a way that would not have been possible unless it was less than half full. Level with it on the rungs of the stool, rested his feet. Even battered and worn as his shoes were, there was a fineness of shape to them that pronounced their original worth. The leather had once been soft and exquisitely moulded – now it was pushed out of shape and dull with neglect.

I made my way to the toilet in contemplation.

CHAPTER 12B

9:50 p.m.

"That wasn't nice, what you did back there! You could've had my eye out!" he said, too calmly for it to be a real reflection of how he felt. I regarded him sullenly without bothering to respond. If my fate was sealed then I was not going to give him the satisfaction of seeing me crumble.

"Anyway, where are you going in such a hurry?" he asked in the voice that I had come to fear and hate in such a short time, "the party's only just getting started!"

There was no point in making excuses - it was too late for that. Neither was it any use trying to appeal to his better nature – I was no longer sure he had one.

There was perhaps one way out for me. It probably wouldn't work but it was about all that was left to me.

"Why are you being like this?" I twisted round to face him, hoping the accusation might shame him. "And why me? What have I ever done to upset you?"

To my surprise he laughed. "You don't get it at

167

all, do you, Nat? Life isn't fair...you don't always get what you think you're entitled to. Even when you work *really* hard for something, it doesn't always follow that it turns out well..."

"Look, I get it! I get it that you're angry that you got moved around, had to change schools, had to find new friends," I searched deep inside for an inkling of how he might feel, something that I could use in my favour. "I get it that none of it was your choice - but it's also not *my* fault." I tried not to make my voice whingey at the end but some of it leaked out, lending the words more self-sympathy than I intended.

"Never said it was your fault. You're just my consolation prize!" he declared. Teeth shining dangerously at me through a fog of alcohol vapour.

"And what about your son?" I threw at him, desperate for some hook to catch him up on. "Where does he fit into this?"

With a burst of temper that I swear I didn't even see coming, he released the door and turned to Suzie. With the back of one hand he slapped her hard across the face. I *felt* the sound as much as heard it. I also heard her sharp cry of pain as I grabbed my chance and wrenched open the heavy door and launched myself out into the cold evening air.

I felt the glass door close behind me, giving me a millisecond start. Whichever way I went, I would be clearly seen from where they stood.

Frantically I looked in every direction. A soft movement of air behind me indicated they were already opening the door. There was no time to choose.

The cinema lurked on a backstreet. No way out straight ahead, the route to the right led, I thought, mostly out of town. But the road to the left led back to the town centre, back to where normal, decent people were, back to bars and clubs and other streets to hide in. There was no real decision to be made. I fled to the left.

The hard concrete and tarmac punished my bare feet but I barely noticed. I ran as fast and as hard as I could, never minding how my knees jarred with every thud and the flesh of my feet ripped and bruised with each unmeasured step on the unforgiving road. There was a bursting pain in my heart and my lungs were on fire with the effort of drawing breath in and expelling it back out in a rush.

To my alarm I realised the streets were empty! There was no one around, no pub crawlers whom I might beg for help! Foot following foot without pause, ragged breath drawn sharply in on the back of a choked exhalation, with a sudden yet slowly dawning comprehension, I realised my mistake!

The road I had taken *did* lead to town. But it led firstly through a shopping area which at this late hour was closed and deserted. I kept going. The road split once again but this time there were three choices. Unthinkingly I chose. Each one was perhaps as good or as bad as the other. With no time to think it through, I was forced to rely on pure luck.

Heart hammering wildly in my chest, its fevered drumming was no match for the whirl of images and feelings and scenarios which descended upon my fraught brain. Desperate for breath, starved of oxygen and out of plans, I paused in a dark shop doorway, huddled over and trying to make myself as unnoticeable as possible. Perhaps I had lost them at the last turn I'd taken? I held my breath and prayed I was safe.

A distant sound of people running built to a crescendo, pulling at the frayed threads of my nerves until I wanted to scream, wanted almost to reveal myself, just to be done with it all…and then the rapid footsteps petered out. Had they gone past the turnoff to the street where I hid? Had they taken another road in their search for me?

I fought off the temptation to dash out, to run further up the road I was on and find another which branched off it. What if I did that and it led me by a more circuitous route straight into wherever they now searched? Wasn't it safer to stay in one place and wait it out?

Consciously, I thought about all the horror

movies I had ever seen. The guy or girl who got caught was always the one who sneaked around trying to get further away. Perhaps the best thing to do was to stay put? Then again how could I base that philosophy on a bunch of movies?

Heartbeat subsiding slowly, I tried to regulate my breathing too. All was quiet and still... except...what was that? I strained my ears to hear. Was it a gentle footfall? Some lone person strolling along past a row of closed shops? The anachronistic nature of the sound propelled a shudder up my spine.

The tread was closer now. Slow and deliberate, the footsteps echoed hollowly in the empty street and were reverberated in my heart. Icy cold fingers of dread clutched at my stomach and I thought I might vomit in fear. So unnerving and insufferable was the tension, that once more I had to fight the perverse impulse to leap out and shout, "Here I am!" at the top of my voice.

I felt the walker pause, hesitate as he passed some darkened doorway and I knew in the deepest part of my soul that it was *him*. Was he too expecting me to leap out with a flourish? Another thought assailed me. What if it wasn't him? What if this was some worse psychopath who now stalked me? What if all I had been about to be subjected to was a little unwanted groping but now that I had run away I had put myself in real danger? What if the person approaching so quietly, was a modern-day Jack-the-Ripper?

But before panic overcame my senses completely I remembered the look in his eyes…how he had leered at me and how he'd had no regard for the fact that his sexual advances were unwanted. He would never have stopped at a grope – sex and/or possibly rape had *always* been on his agenda. And so whether it was indeed him out there, or some other random predator, there would be no difference of outcome if I were to be caught.

One thing the reprieve in the chase had given me though, was my breath back. My lungs were almost back to normal, although my heart continued to beat a staccato rhythm of its own orchestrating. I concentrated on keeping my breaths even; keeping myself oxygenated…

He was close now. Any closer and he would find me. I could hear his ragged breathing; breaths rasping wet and deep as they were hauled in and out of his body. And yet like me, he had not been running for some minutes.

We were two sides of the same coin, fear and exertion had robbed me of breath; for him it was excitement. I could only conclude that its source was internal rather than external. For a split-second I wondered what thoughts rampaged through his brain, before I realised that there were things it couldn't possibly benefit me to know. This was probably one of them. Too much fear might prove incapacitating.

I wrestled with the best thing to do. Should I stay put and hope that in the darkness I was hidden from sight? Luckily, I'd picked a particularly deep doorway to hide in, where shadows colluded with one another to cloak me. But was it enough? Would he actually search *inside* the doorway or would he content himself with a quick look? Should I make a run for it while I could?

"She's gone! You are not gonna' find her now." Suzie's voice came as a surprise to me as I hadn't heard more than a single person approach. "Got you a souvenir, though!" She laughed harshly. "Stupid bitch came into the shop and bought these from me today."

The shoes. She must have brought my shoes from the cinema.

"Her and her bitch friend treated me like I was dirt!" I heard her hack up a gob of spittle and direct it somewhere, perhaps into the shoes themselves. I cared nothing about that, focusing only on willing her to dissuade him from continuing to search.

"I'm not so sure she's not hiding here somewhere," he said in response, ignoring her apparently hurt feelings.

"She's gone, I'm telling you!" For the first time I noticed that Suzie's voice sounded slightly different from before. Was that the result of a split-lip from when he had slapped her, I wondered.

"Get your hands off me!" he warned her in a stern voice. Despite myself I shuddered at the implied threat.

"Baby, let me make it better for you," she whispered huskily, "...let me make you happy again..."

His veiled threat was ignored at her peril and I heard her being smacked hard again, heard the pain in her cry and the fierceness of the contact of skin upon skin.

And I knew then that he had not, *would not* give up looking for me. I knew what I had to do once more. I took a huge breath. And I ran.

CHAPTER 13A

10:00 p.m.

I made use of the facilities in the washroom and took my time washing my hands. I felt cheapened by the contact I had instigated, as if I'd deliberately caused the stranger pain for some warped reason of my own; sullied as if I had performed it for a cheap thrill.

I balled up the paper towel and threw it in the bin. The other cubicles were empty but I had a perverse feeling of being watched. I raised my eyes to the mirror over the sink, surprised to find that the face which looked back at me showed no trace of the confusion that was inside my head.

I made my way back to the bar, avoiding the stranger who still sat alone, briefcase at his feet, wedding ring missing from his hand. All traces of hope missing from his face – perhaps from his life. I kept my gaze fixed on my date, sitting with his back to me. The short distance from the toilet to the bar seemed like a thousand miles.

"Well?"

"Well what?" I answered a little too brusquely, sliding back onto my stool but not yet reaching for my drink. I pulled my legs under the stool, preventing our knees from touching as they had before. I was disconcerted. And it showed.

"You spoke to him, didn't you?" He wasn't asking, merely confirming what he knew.

"Yes. You were watching?" My mouth felt dry at the thought.

"No."

"You must have been watching!" I exclaimed, unwilling to believe that he could just know things.

"No. Anyway, you talked to him and you looked. What did you see?"

"I saw the briefcase just like you said and I saw his shoes…and the space where his wedding ring used to be…but how can you know that his wife died? She might be at home baking cakes or she might have run off with a neighbour - it's all supposition!"

He laughed harshly. "I'm not claiming supernatural knowledge, Nat." Abruptly he stopped before his words had faded from the air. "His picture was in the paper a few months ago. He was the grieving guy whose wife had just been killed-"

"By a gang of kids in a stolen car!" I broke in, remembering now. "They never caught the kids, did they?"

"No, but they got the car which had been stolen…I guess they're still searching for the driver." He grimaced. "That's how quickly a life can be torn apart."

"But you remembered and recognised him..." I couldn't make up my mind if that meant he was more sensitive than me, or that I was of below-average sensitivity.

"I wondered what it would feel like to be him..." he blew his breath out explosively. "Wondered too what it would have been like to have been the other driver, the guy who caused this."

I didn't like the way the conversation was going but felt compelled to see it through. "You wondered about the driver?"

He nodded. "Did he feel guilty? Does he still feel ashamed with every breath he takes? Or did he just shrug it off, as nothing more than bad timing?" He took a long drink, his eyes focused on the bottles lined up neatly behind the bar. "Mostly I just wondered if it could have been me." He looked at me with such burning eyes I wished at once that he would look away, back to the bottles. "If I have badness like that in my soul."

I wanted to deny it but the conversation had made me extremely uncomfortable. I slanted the topic slightly, hoping he wouldn't notice. "What about the missing wedding ring though?" I asked perplexed.

"He was quoted as saying in the paper that every time he looked at it, he realised how much he had lost. It was a natural conclusion that he would have removed it. And I figured the way he was dressed, he had come straight here from work, to drink away his evening and forget. Hence the briefcase and the battered shoes." He wiped his hand over his face as if the ability he had to empathise had caused him pain.

"That was what I meant when I said that I saw things. I don't see things that aren't there…I just kind of see the connections between things. I see the detail that most people gloss over…like that woman over there." He nodded towards someone and I had to swivel in my chair to follow his gaze.

"The woman sitting with the man over in that booth?" I asked, fairly certain that I was looking at the right person. "What's wrong with her, then?" I was genuinely curious.

"She was alone when we came in but now she is sitting with a man."

"Maybe she was waiting for him?" I suggested.

He shook his head. "She was sitting in the middle of the bench. When someone is waiting for someone else, they generally sit at the far end, leaving enough room for the other person to sit down when they arrive."

I wasn't sure if that was always true but accepted it until it could be disproved. "Maybe she's a prostitute?" I asked, embarrassed to be even having the thought.

He shook his head again. "No, it's the wrong sort of place to ply a trade like that," he said making me wonder what knowledge he would have to enable him to make such a statement.

"So what then?" I said, out of suggestions.

"Pure and simple, it's a pick-up," he stated.

"He picked her up?" I asked.

"No. *She* picked *him* up. And he's younger than her by about eight years. She's worked at keeping her looks, but there are other tell-tale signs." He pointed. "Look at her neck just below the chin. You see that line, that stretch of sinew? Women over forty get those. And look at the line of her jaw. It's not as sharp as yours, not as smooth. There are a few little bumps there where the muscle has begun to go...only a full face-lift can fix that and she hasn't got the disposable income for that."

I laughed. "So you know her income too?"

"Roughly. It's more than a cashier at the supermarket and less than a bank manager's."

I giggled, my previous unease forgotten. "Now you are being ridiculous!"

"No, honestly. Look at what she's wearing. Her clothes are off the rack – they could have been bought from any average department store – but her coat is expensive and the rings on her fingers are good ones. It's like the cheap convenience things are fine if they are meant to be disposable but the things she wants or *needs* to last – the coat and the rings – they're better quality."

"You are so full of it!" I laughed, relieved that

this time our people observing was rather more jovial and light-hearted than the previous occasion.

"What, who, me?" he laughed with me. "As God's my witness it's the truth." He paused. "But there's a serious side to it too."

I waited for him to continue, knowing that he would in his own time.

"I see all the little things others often miss, the subtle acts of cruelty that people perpetrate on each other. The tiny wrong-doings and vague malices. The small deeds of kindness, the little acts of compassion and humanity that are sometimes shown to complete strangers, the little things that most people pass off as of no consequence, or maybe fate, or luck. I see that they are normally a result of someone, somewhere's actions."

He sighed. "But they don't balance each other on some great cosmic scale. The bad always outweighs the good."

I shook my head but he carried on.

"But most of all what I see is the indifference people show each other." He raised his beer to his lips and look a long swallow. I waited for him to continue but he didn't seem inclined to.

"You can't save the world." It was a lame response and I knew it but there was nothing else I could say.

"No, I can't save the world. But I can save

those I care about." His eyes blazed with passion. There was a hidden depth to his words that I wasn't ready to probe.

"Do you care about me?" It was a foolish question to ask on our first date but the words tumbled out of me with abandon. My heart constricted and pounded painfully at the thought that he might not.

His eyes took on a far-away hurt. "Very much. I care about you very much, Nat. That's why I am so worried about being with you."

CHAPTER 13B

10:00 p.m.

Only just ahead of him, I dashed out of the doorway and further up the empty street, legs pumping like pistons, dress wrapping around me, constricting my movements. Would I have been able to have run further - faster - in jeans? Or would they have hampered me more? It was a stupid question for my mind to focus on. But it was preferable to thinking about what would happen if he caught me.

When he caught me!

I tried to focus on the positives. I was ahead of him. But he was shod and I was not. He probably had Suzie trying to hold him back. For her own sake of course, not for mine. I had her vile image spurring me on. Perhaps he would get bored of the chase. Or grow more excited by it.

Soon I would get to streets that were busy – which had people in them...

And then I felt his hand close around my arm. All my hard-won positives vanished without a trace. I was left with only the negatives. My mum and dad knew who I had gone out with, but not that we were no longer in town. They didn't know my phone now lay at the bottom of a sewer. They wouldn't even be worried until it was past the time I was due home! And I had a pretty bad and explicit idea of what could happen between then and now. The negatives smashed the positives into dust!

"Bitch!" His fingers dug deliberately hard into my arm. Without premeditation I wilted under his cruel attention, watching as a sneer formed the corners of his mouth into a mask of derision. It was then I whirled around towards him, fear hammering in my heart so loud I couldn't hear the thoughts in my head. Thoughts of panic and desperation.

I kicked out hard at him and felt my battered and bruised right heel connect. I'd hoped to hit his groin but the kick had been unfocused and landed instead on the top of his thigh. But it was enough to catapult him from me, the unexpected blow forcing him to lose his footing and his grip on my arm.

I launched myself away from him, taking my chance to run...but a hand wrapped around my long hair and jerked me violently backwards. Forehead pulled taut towards the crown of my head, it was almost impossible to turn my face towards whoever held me. But it wasn't necessary to see my assailant to know that it was Suzie.

Just as she had earlier, in the toilets, she jerked on the rope of hair she held, making sure she had my full attention. Tears of pain sprang up in my eyes and I no longer had the courage to blink them back. Self-pity welled up inside of me but was tempered with a knowledge that at every step I'd made a bad decision. The *wrong* decision.

Even if I could have been excused for choosing this particular date out of the two I'd been offered, I had still thought it better to get in the car, rather than make a scene; better to have tried to phone from the toilets than from outside the cinema, when there had at least been other people around; better to have gone in quietly than to have appealed to Barry the ticket guy... Any one of those decisions, chosen differently might have avoided this moment...but it was all useless supposition.

The conversation I'd had with Stacey came back to haunt me. I'd been wrong. About everything. Just because it was the first date, didn't mean it wouldn't be life-or-death after all!

"Fucking bitch!"

This time his wrath was directed at me and not Suzie. I felt the back of his hand rip across the side of my face leaving a blazing trail of pain. Held immobile by my hair I couldn't even pull away as he came closer to me and thrust his body towards mine. I could feel his hardness, pressing at the area between my legs and I realised that I'd been right, the chase had only excited him more, worked him into a blood-rushing frenzy of adrenaline.

"You know what you need?"

I presumed it to be a rhetorical question and suffered his foul breath on my neck in silence. His tongue darted out between his lips but rather than lick them, he ran his saliva over my neck, from collarbone to ear, in a thick trail of viscous slobber. Like an animal, he'd marked his territory with his scent.

The spit seemed to defy the drying power of the night air. It felt wet and luminous on me as if possessed of some dark magic that allowed it to stay forever moist. Forever slick and repulsive.

Still pressing his groin against me, he peeled his upper torso away, enabling him to bring his hands up to my breasts. Taking a breast in each hand, he squeezed hard, bringing further tears to my eyes. Pain and humiliation. His triumph was my degradation.

"Why so uptight, Nat?" he asked in an almost conversational tone as if we were sitting, having tea in the garden. I hated him with my eyes but kept my mouth shut. I wondered what would happen if I screamed. Probably nothing. There were no houses or dwellings nearby and no one around.

"Don't you like me doing this? What about this then?" He released my left breast and pushed his free hand roughly between my legs, to that soft private area. I could feel the flat of his hand digging into me, prevented only from entering by the thin cotton panties I wore. "You like this don't you?"

Like I was a marionette, Suzie pushed my head roughly forwards before cruelly jerking it back by my hair, making a rough likeness of a nod. I could think of only one thing which might make him stop. "My parents know I'm out with you." Delivered as a warning, I hoped it was enough to make him stop and reconsider.

"I expected no less from you, Nat. Of course you told them. You're such a *good* girl." He smiled but there was no warmth that leached from his eyes. "But you see, you never went out with me." His hand moved upwards, away from the area between my legs and up over my stomach, circling the flesh there and leaving a trail of shame wherever it touched.

I looked at him and realised he'd already concocted an alibi. But of course it was his word against mine and surely no one would believe *him*? Perhaps my face reflected my incomprehension, perhaps he just wanted to impress me with his master plan but he seemed determined to give me the full story.

His hand finished gliding over the flat surface of my stomach and rounded over my hips and down towards my buttocks, pressing the thin fabric of my dress into the crease as he went. "We had a tiff when we were trying to decide where to go and you let slip you had been asked out by someone else earlier today. You taunted me and said you wished you had gone out with him instead…and we had an argument…" he sounded so plausible; I couldn't help but stare at him.

"Ah, you didn't know that I knew about your other date!" He grinned. "It's a small town and news gets around. But back to my alibi!"

He applied a tone of hurt resentment. "You said you'd have a better time with him and that you'd changed your mind about going out with me." Lightning-quick his face changed to that of a cunning liar and he blew me an imaginary kiss. "Of course I was devastated and it was just luck that I met up with Suzie here and we spent the evening in her flat watching TV."

"I'll tell them the truth!" I declared.

Rather than answer me he put on his hurt voice again. "I'm so sorry Constable, Mr and Mrs Price… I've no idea where Natalie went after she left me. I don't know where she might be."

Where she might be? The blood froze in my veins, to run coldly and sluggishly to a stop. Legs which had no power in them only just held me up, and my lungs sucked at the air as if I were underwater. The full implication of what he'd said hit home. I would only be able to deny it if I were around to do so.

"You're going to kill me." It wasn't even an

exclamation.

He laughed. "Seriously? You think I would kill a fine piece of arse like you? Honestly, where have you *been*, Nat? There is a market for girls like you and I intend to make good use of it."

Somehow that fate was neither better nor worse than the prospect of death would have been. It was just a death of a slower variety. One last thing occurred to me, a fact that might work out in my favour.

"Suzie's babysitter will say that you were not there watching TV. Then everyone will know you're lying!"

This time it was Suzie's turn to laugh. "What babysitter?"

I couldn't see her face but I tried to imagine it when I spoke, tried to keep it in mind so that I spoke differently to her, appealed to her logic and her obvious love of her son.

"Jakey's sitter! Whoever she is, she'll say that you weren't there!"

"Jakey," she spat the word out as if it were an insult hearing it issue from my lips, "doesn't have a sitter. The boy sleeps right through the night, soon as his head touches the pillow. So your theory is wrong, Miss Prissy-Pants!"

There was no babysitter! No witnesses. And no hope! All that was left for me, was to beg. From the comfort of my sofa, I'd sat in judgement of horror movie directors when the characters had begged for their lives. Now I knew it was I who was naïve and not them. I knew then that I would do whatever it took to stay alive and to get some chance to escape.

I tried to angle my body further towards him but it was difficult with Suzie still holding my hair. "You were right, I do like that," I moved my hand on top of his and slid it further down my buttocks, making him cusp the curve of bottom to thigh. I groaned as if I couldn't help myself, as if the desire in me was too strong to be contained. "Get rid of Suzie...it's too embarrassing with her around. Besides she's jealous of me!" I even managed to make my voice suggestively petulant.

I licked my lips, slowly and deliberately. "Get rid of her and I can show you a good time!"

CHAPTER 14A

10:10 p.m.

"I promise to never hurt you," I said, leaning forward to kiss him.

"That wasn't what I meant. I'm worried about hurting you," he said quietly.

"I trust you," I said simply.

"Don't!" he said abruptly, pulling away from me and the kiss. I didn't know whether he meant not to kiss him or not to trust him. I felt inexplicably let down. He smiled but it was half-hearted. "I think we need to change the topic to one that's a little lighter."

I knew he was right but I still wanted his lips against mine, the feel of his warm breath on my face as we leant closer to one another, the sensation that we were caught in a bubble, out of time and step with the rest of the world. It was a sense of oneness that I had never before experienced. A feeling that a missing piece of the jigsaw that was my life had been suddenly slotted into place – both exhilarating and terrifying at the same time - assailed me.

"If you had the chance to live anywhere in the world, where would it be?"

It seemed such a random question that I wasn't sure at first how to answer it. "Do you mean when I'm older and living alone? Or now?"

"When you are older, I guess," he responded.

I thought for only a minute. "I wouldn't want to live too far from my family...so..."

He cut in. "Don't you dream of exploring new places? Of just being yourself, somewhere no one knows you. Where all people know of you is what you let them see?"

I was confused. "But earlier you said you were angry at having to move, to change schools..."

"Yes but that was because the decision was made *for* me. None of it was my choice. I want to explore the world, not just settle for where someone has put me!"

"Oh!" I was unaccountably sad, as though he were leaving me already. I had no hold over him, no right to ask him to stay and yet I felt crushed at the thought that he was prepared to leave me at some future date. I knew that it was ridiculous as there was nothing to say that we would still be together by then, but I felt a wedge had suddenly been driven between us – the threat that one day he would be gone. Even though he had earlier warned that there was a possibility that his family could be moved on again, according to the vagaries of his dad's work, this was infinitely different. This was a separation of *his* doing and the possibility of it cut me to the quick.

"Won't you miss your family?" 'and me?' I wanted to add but didn't. His jaw clenched a little before relaxing into a smile. "Maybe I could convince some pretty girl to come and keep me company. Of course she'd have to be a good bowler..." he teased.

I smiled at the obvious joke but shook my head sadly. I couldn't imagine not living close to my family.

"There's a big world out there, Natalie. Would be a crime to live a whole lifetime in just one corner of it."

I was stung by the idea that he thought me so provincial. "It's not that I don't want to see the world..." I floundered, unsure how to express myself.

"But you want the security of your family around you. I guess it's different for a girl." His voice took on a different tone, one that I couldn't quite interpret. "I guess women need the security of what's familiar."

But to be alone with him under warm skies lit with bright stars; to be adrift at sea with his arms around me, bound for exotic destinations, was an intoxicating idea. And at night, lying with our bodies entwined, holding and stroking and loving each other with every fibre of our souls...

"Where would we go first?" My eyes challenged his. "Italy?"

"Mmm, the pizzas," he drooled. "And ice-cream!"

"France – the Eiffel Tower…"

"Dauphinoise potatoes and-"

I cut in. "Philistine! You're only interested in the food!" I leaned forward and gave him a light whack on his arm.

"Oh, fair lady, you have mortally wounded me," he joked, pretending to fall off his stool in pain.

"You are so thick-skinned I doubt someone like me could ever wound you!" I laughed back at him.

He sat back down, face completely serious. "That's where you're so mistaken, Nat. You are the one person who just might be able to cut me so deeply that I would never recover."

His words were so heartfelt that they stole the breath from my throat. My head spun with the implications. How was it possible to feel so at one with someone on a first date? To *need* them - just to be able to continue living?

"So where then?" I asked.

"India."

"Why there?" I infinitely preferred my locations to his.

"Because it's real," he said. "Europe - it's all tourist stuff. Don't you want to see the *real* world, in the raw, when the veneer of civilisation is peeled back to show the depth of degradation or beauty below?"

I wasn't sure I had understood him correctly. "You're saying you want to see degradation?"

"No…" he struggled to explain himself more accurately. "I want to see real people leading real lives…not what politicians or the propaganda on the news tells us…I want to see the real thing with my own eyes."

"Hmm," I couldn't fault his logic and his passion. "I went to Knossos in Crete once." I watched him wait for me to elaborate.

"And?" he asked.

"And all that I remember was ruins of what had once been a palace. It was so hot the tour guide carried an umbrella and the place was crawling with people. It didn't feel like a real place." I looked into his eyes, suddenly realising exactly what he'd meant before.

"It felt like a film set. None of it felt like real, living breathing people had once lived there." I thought back to the feeling that had overcome me as I walked across the site. "And I had this feeling…a certainty that if I could just creep in there at night, when no one else was around, then maybe, just maybe, it would feel more real…"

"That's exactly what I'm talking about," he said breathlessly. I was relieved that once more we were at ease with one another. "I want to visit Africa, see the wildlife before it becomes extinct. I want to try to understand how people live with civil wars and guerrilla warfare raging around them. And if I can help…then I want to do exactly that!"

"How would you be able to help? With money?"

"Not necessarily. Money can smooth things along but it doesn't help in itself."

Now I *did* feel provincial. "But those people are so poor…"

He leaned back on his stool, withdrawing a little from me and I wondered if it was because of my lack of understanding. "They need other things more than they need money. Like peace, for a start. And that's something I already know about," he said cryptically.

"What do you know about making peace?" I playfully poked him in the abdomen.

I wasn't prepared for the consequences.

He doubled over in pain, face paling to the colour of parchment. A cold, hard fear bit into my heart, stealing the warmth from my bones and chilling me to the core. "What's wrong? What did I do?" I stuttered, terrified, as I watched him catch his breath and attempt to straighten up.

"*You* didn't do anything." There were too many things implied in his words to ignore. His hands were held protectively over the area I had prodded. Gently I lifted them away and pulled up his top, just a little.

A large, livid bruise extended across his abdomen. Still black in places, the outer edges had already lightened to a pale green. But what caught my attention were the gnarled little scars that flanked the bruise, some of them still the bright red of recent wounds.

"What happened to you?" I exclaimed. I wanted to run my fingers over his skin; to absorb the pain and scars into my own body, taking the hurt away from him.

He wrenched his top down, hiding the wounds from me and perhaps himself. "My dad happened to me," he said slowly, reluctantly.

"Your dad did that?" my voice was too high, incomprehension and disbelief raising it an octave.

The pain in his eyes was profound. "Is that such an alien idea to you, Natalie? That someone who is supposed to love and protect you, could do such a thing?" His eyes challenged me not to understand. Suddenly I was reminded of his earlier edginess, his claim that he could not protect those he loved.

"Doesn't your mum stop him?" Immediately I knew it was the wrong thing to have said.

"Mum's the reason I have these in the first place," he said.

CHAPTER 14B

10:10 p.m.

"Get rid of her and I can show you a good time!" I tried not to let any notes of desperation leech into my voice.

"Yeah, like you would even know what that meant!" Suzie yelped indignantly behind me.

Determined to do my utmost to save my skin I reached both hands forward and grabbed his buttocks, trailing my hands around his sides and onto his crotch. The heat of his body burned through the fabric and into my palms and I wondered if I survived this, whether any amount of washing would ever make me feel clean again. He had been hard already but grew even more so as he felt my fingertips brush across him. A thin sweat broke out on his upper lip and he seemed to be debating inwardly what he should do.

"SHUT UP! Both of you!" There was a curious look on his face as if against his own reasoning he was beginning to believe me. I guess I had surprised him.

"Let's go back to your place," he said, talking around me to Suzie.

"No!"

"No!" Suzie and I spoke the same word simultaneously but for differing reasons.

"I don't want to share you with her," I lied.

"I don't want her fingerprints round my place, just in case..." she said.

I didn't know which of these arguments would persuade him against the idea but from his next comment I understood it had to be Suzie's.

"Yeah, you are right, no point in leaving evidence unnecessarily. We can take her to Shaun's place."

Shaking with terror, I remembered then that there were three of them and that was not counting the other guys we had arrived with. I had been so intent on getting away, I had forgotten that I had more than one pursuer.

As if she were reading my mind, Suzie supplied the answer to the unspoken question of where Shaun was. "He's getting us some more supplies," she stated cryptically.

What supplies? Drugs? Alcohol? Something else I hadn't even thought of yet?

My hands had frozen in place on his crotch as I realised my ploy hadn't worked. For a moment I wondered what would happen if I squeezed hard or punched him there? But Suzie still held me by the hair and I could think of no way of getting her to relinquish that hold. Not without scalping myself in the process.

For the second time in a row, they seemed to

be reading my mind. Suzie gave a quick tug on my hair, straining the strands at their follicles and watched as he pushed my hands away from him.

"Nice try, Nat. And I have to say you almost had me fooled there," he said.

"That's only 'cos you think with your dick!" Suzie stated, wrenching on my hair once more, perhaps to punish me for touching him.

They forced me down to the end of the street, walking either side of me, him with his arms wrapped around me like a loving date, her with her arm casually slung over my shoulders, concealing the hand in which she had secured my hair.

We reached the bottom of the deserted street and Suzie pulled out her phone. "Where are you and what's taking so long?" she spoke into it, frowning as she received the response. "Well, bloody hurry, up! We're on the corner, waiting."

I seized what might be my last chance to get him alone as Suzie gave Shaun directions to get to where we were. "It would be more fun if I wanted it too...if we were alone," I whispered to him whilst she was distracted.

"It's gonna be a whole lot of fun anyway, Nat... well, for me..." he leered.

I thought about those movies again, the ones where the victims begged to be set free. "Please let me go. I'm begging you. Nothing has happened yet...I could just go home...I swear I'll never say a word about tonight…I won't tell anyone…" Fat teardrops slalomed down my cheeks and ran into the corners of my mouth. I could taste the saltiness of them, the brininess which reminded me of the sea and the fact that I might never see it again. Whatever happened from this moment forward, nothing in my past had prepared me for it, that much I now understood.

"Even if I wanted to do that, which I don't, there would be no guarantee that you would keep your pretty little mouth shut." He left me in no doubt that he was not prepared to release me.

"My dad has money…not a lot but he will give you it all, if you let me go…" I tried another tack.

"So he's just going to empty his bank account for the guy who kidnapped and assaulted his daughter? I don't think so!"

"No, not like that. That was a stupid idea of mine…" I racked my brains. "I promise I won't say a word, I'll just get the money for you…"

"Aw! Isn't that sweet! Miss Prissy-Pants is so desperate not to have your sweaty hands on her pure lily-white flesh, that she'll steal all her daddy's money to buy you off!" Suzie deliberately put her own slant on it, deftly ensuring that my pleas and promises could not sway him.

"Is she right, Nat?" he held his head to one side as if regarding me in depth. "I'm hurt that you think so little of me!" But he didn't look in the least bit hurt.

Before anything else could be said, a large red car pulled up in front of us and Shaun leaned across from the driver's seat to push open the passenger door.

"When you said you'd pick us up a car, I never thought it would be something like this!" Suzie said admiringly, letting go of my hair as she prepared to climb into the front passenger seat.

"No you don't!" My captor on the other side kicked the door shut, denting the shiny metal and buckling the handle a little. "Stay on the other side of her so there's no problems," he ordered.

Suzie didn't look too happy at being ordered about, but she acquiesced anyway, climbing into the back and dragging me with her.

"Thought I'd told you before not to steal cars this expensive!" The comment was directed at Shaun but I felt Suzie cringe a little beside me and I wondered how much of the theft had been done at her instigation.

"Suzie said..." Shaun began and I knew that I was at least partly right.

"Never mind what Suzie says. Just do what *I* say!" There was a raw nerve being touched there, I was sure of it. I wondered how I could use it or even *if* I could use it to my advantage. "I told you before. The showier the car, the quicker it's more likely to be reported stolen. And the pigs will really be on a lookout for it, 'cos the owner will have flashed them some cash." It was said like it was a mantra, often repeated to the hapless Shaun.

"But I think it belongs to a woman! There's makeup in the glove compartment..."

"Jesus Christ! That's even worst. She'll be showing them her pussy just to get her car back..." he exclaimed. "Never mind, it's too late now. Just make sure that you wipe the car down when you abandon it, and I mean tonight, not tomorrow or next week sometime!"

Shaun was abashed. "OK. Sorry." I saw his eyes in the driver's mirror and Suzie's reflection there. If she gave any indication that she acknowledged his glance, I didn't witness it.

"Where to?" Shaun asked, driving around at random.

"Your place," Suzie responded, sounding like it had been her idea all along.

"Really?" Shaun beamed as if it were the greatest honour ever.

Perhaps his parents would be there! Perhaps I would be able to signal my distress to them... but the ludicrousness of that thinking didn't escape me. If there'd been any chance of someone else being there we wouldn't have been heading in that direction.

"Does Shaun live alone?" I asked in a small whisper, not even really hoping that someone would answer me.

"He does and he doesn't," Suzie teased, being deliberately evasive.

Was there a chance that there might be someone there who would come to my aid after all? But as soon as the next words fell out of her mouth, I knew that she had knowingly allowed me to build up my hopes a little, just so she could have even more fun, crashing them back down.

"He has a room in a house...the other guys that we came out with?" she turned it into a question as if we were having a normal conversation. "You know who I mean don't you? They have the other rooms."

She beamed at me.

CHAPTER 15A

10:20 p.m.

"I don't understand," I said, thinking that it was the biggest understatement I had ever uttered.

"No I guess you wouldn't." He was silent for a moment. "He gets stressed out. And then he takes it out on her... I try to stop him but..."

I swallowed the lump in my throat. "So then he turns on you." I'd seen enough TV shows to understand at least a little of his reality, a little of the fear and the feelings of inadequacy that must haunt him. "What were those other marks, the scars?"

He bit his lip nervously. "Cigarette burns. He likes to stub them out on me when he's feeling that particular way." The acid in his words burned through me in a horrible parody of his own tortured flesh. His eyes were far away, focusing on some inward sight.

I reached a hand out, but dared not touch him in case it was the wrong thing to do. Our budding romance seemed dangerously fragile and insubstantial under the weight of his confessions.

"The truth is that's why we had to move.

The constant rows, the knowing looks from the neighbours, the suspicions of the doctor whenever I had to visit him." His eyes swam back into focus. "After a while you run out of excuses...run out of time..."

"But the police..." I protested.

"We never get the police involved. Mum reckons it would only make things worse – make *him* worse."

I didn't know how to answer.

"The worst thing about it, is that I'm his son."

I nodded my understanding.

"Sorry Nat, you *don't* get it." He took both of my hands, forcing my eyes to meet his, "You know what they say - 'like father like son'. I even look like him, so why wouldn't I turn out the same? Every psychology book I've ever read, every case study I've pulled up on-line – *all* of them say that men generally end up imitating their fathers. Why should I be any different?"

His words horrified me, just the sheer thought that this caring, sensitive guy could ever think that about himself. I placed a hand gently on his abdomen, where the terrible hurts were concealed. "Because your body wouldn't look like this if you were like him. You got these scars from trying to defend your mother, from trying to defend yourself," I choked on the words. "You could never be like him. I promise you." I felt the words cleave themselves from my soul. "The very fact that you've read about it – tried to be different – that's the thing that *makes* you different. The fact that you see others' pain…you don't have to worry about turning out like him – you're already different!"

He nodded slowly and looked away, eyes bright with tears. "I can't be like him, Natalie. I can't hurt you the way he hurts my mum…"

"You won't," I said with certainty, taking one of his hands in mine as he continued to look away from me.

"You can't know that," he said slowly, trying to pull his hands free. "Guys who beat their wives and kids seem perfectly normal and reasonable to everyone else…they have a trick of appearing to be nice guys, right up to when they smash a bottle over your head…"

"Your mum didn't know what he was like when she married him, did she?"

He shook his head. "I'm not even sure *he* knew he was like that…that's why I…"

I cut him off. "No." I would not believe he could be like that and I wouldn't let him believe it either. "But if you truly have doubts, then you ought to hold back a little on the booze," I said, indicating his drink.

He surprised me by laughing. "The last few beers have been alcohol free. You didn't think I'd be boozing all night, did you? I'd never get myself into the position where I didn't know what I was doing."

I coloured slightly. That was *exactly* what I had been thinking. He smiled at my embarrassment, his face brighter than it had been all night. Perhaps some of it was a falseness, a need to move on from the recent disclosures but some of it was also relief at unburdening himself, I suspected. I squirrelled away my anxiety for him and strove to match his new elevated mood.

We smiled at one another tentatively, an unspoken agreement that whatever happened, we would face it together. Something passed between us – something invisible and indefinable and yet as solid and real as the stools we sat on.

He looked at the time on his phone and grimaced theatrically, eyes bulging slightly and mouth turning down towards his jaw. "It's nearly ten thirty and I feel like I've only just come out with you..." he placed his hand on my thigh where it seemed to burn through the material of my jeans, fusing into the skin below.

I too wondered where all the time had gone. I didn't want the night to end, for him to take his hand away, take his *body* away from mine.

"Maybe if they played that old Cher song, 'If I Could Turn Back time'..." I shrugged my shoulders at the music which was currently playing. There had been a constant soundtrack all evening but I hadn't really been aware of it until then. But if rewinding time had been at all possible, I knew instantly that I would have rolled it back to that very first time his father had lifted his hand in temper – and I would have been there – been there with whoever and whatever it took to stop it happening. I buried my thoughts deep in my head where he could not read them and plastered a smile on my face.

"You have given me an idea. Can you salsa?" He slid from his stool and performed a little movement to demonstrate. He winced only a little although the movement must have pained him.

I avoided his face, concentrating on admiring the way his hips swayed and his sashaying style.

He was trying so hard to move the conversation on that I knew he'd revealed enough for one evening. There would be other times to try to get him to report his dad, other occasions to make him see that was the only way. I forced a gaiety I didn't feel into my voice. "I've never tried. Seen it in movies though."

"Well, do you wanna try it?" he smiled and suddenly the expression was much more real.

"With you?" I joked.

"With me!" he agreed emphatically. "Who better, after all?"

"Here?" I looked around. Surely people would stare?

"No not here. There's a bar around the corner, serves a mean chilli and plays salsa music all night...we could go..?" he asked, his eyes pleading.

I couldn't refuse. "No to the chilli, thanks, but ...um...yes to the dancing!" I wondered how the new shoes would fare on a shiny wooden dance floor. But if I found it hard to keep my footing he would just have to keep a firmer, closer hold on me. Perhaps it would do us both a world of good, to have that closeness, that reliance on one another. I held my hand out to him.

We walked holding hands, a comfortable silence resting between us.

"We won't be able to stay long but we can at least have one dance," he watched me take a look around the salsa bar. "Used to be a little rough here but the new owners have cleaned the place up." Not even letting me put my bag down at one of the small wooden tables, he whirled me onto the dance floor. The revelations between us had brought a new intimacy to the fledgling relationship, a deep intensity which burned between us, almost demanding consummation.

Unprepared for the speed of the dance, my torso slammed painfully into his. "Oh God, I'm so sorry!" I apologised, watching him wince and raise a hard to his stomach.

"You'll have to make that up to me," he grimaced, face chalky with pain under the soft lighting.

"Do you want to stop?" I asked concerned.

He grinned a little shakily. "I think I'd suffer any amount of pain to be able to hold you like this," he said in such a way that I wasn't sure if it was a joke or not. He drew me in closer, sharing the warmth and the hardness of himself with me, leaving me feeling dizzier than any number of spins could have done. We were as one, lost in that moment, inseparable physically as well as emotionally, and I relinquished all hold of my sense of individuality, merging with him so that we seemed to inhabit one heart, one mind.

Hip to hip, he swayed me backwards and led me forwards once more, keeping us constantly on the move, intensifying the throbbing desire between us, ignoring his hurts.

"Keep your thigh next to mine and follow my lead," he stated, apparently unaware that I had already abandoned the power and the will to separate myself from him.

"OK, now just hold that stance for a minute," he pushed away from me, holding one of my arms above my head so that the underside was exposed. Sidling around me, he trailed his hand down the length of that exposed skin, across my stomach and then into the small of my back, before he clasped me to him once more, this time from behind. I felt the heat of his injured abdomen on my back. I could almost feel the whorled skin against me as if it brushed my own, seeking to fuse with my flesh and become whole once more.

Of its own accord my arm dropped down and lingered on the back of his neck. His hips swayed tantalisingly against me and I could feel the pressure of blood rushing through my veins. The music was slow and suggestive and reminiscent of balmy Latin-American lands where the passion was as hot as the local delicacies.

With the palm of my hand on the back of his neck, I pressed him closer to me and felt the soft caress of his lips against my neck. I breathed in the warm aroma of him and knew that it had been the perfect first date. We swayed until the track had finished and was replaced by something faster.

Reluctantly I felt him gently push me away but a moment later he was in front of me once more. Grasping my hands in his, he manoeuvred me whichever way I was supposed to go. The room and the other dancers became a whirl of merging colours as I spun around and across him before being drawn back into his embrace and then thrust out again.

Not having to worry about the steps as he propelled me where I had to be, I focused on adding a little panache where I could – a raised hand flourish, a whipping of my hair across my head – anything and everything to make it more authentic and more provocatively sexy.

The tempo of the tracks was ramped up and

the crowd went with the intensified rhythm. Couples whirled around the floor, moving away from one another and then back again and I could almost smell the pheromones they gave off. The sexually charged air was palpable. My breath came short and hard in my throat and it wasn't all to do with the frenetic dancing.

"I think it's time I got you home," he murmured into my ear on a close turn. My spirits fell and like a child I fought against the idea. "Just one more dance," I begged.

He shook his head. "There's no time. I have to get you back by eleven. That was the deal, wasn't it?"

I nodded my head sadly. "Yes. I have to be in by eleven." I tried not to think about what he was returning home to.

We left the bar as we had entered it, arms linked with one another. I took one last lingering look at the dancers who owned the dance floor, wishing we were still part of them.

"We can come again. If you want to, that is," he said, holding the door open for me to exit first.

I nodded eagerly. "Where did you learn to dance like that?" I asked, reluctant to think about what might happen once I left him.

"I just picked it up," he murmured, holding my hand as we headed towards my house, our steps perfectly matched.

"You just 'picked it up'?" I raised my eyebrows.

He relented. "Actually, I like those dance films. Pretty much everything from *Flashdance* to *StepUp*, I've seen about a million times," he admitted sheepishly.

"Ok, so Mr Show-me-the-real-people, Mr Keep-It-Real, is a big *Flashdance* fan?" I couldn't help but giggle. "Bet you even love *Dirty Dancing*!" I guffawed, because even though I loved it too, I'd never thought a guy could be a fan. The ability and opportunity to laugh after the intensity of the evening made me almost delirious with relief.

He grinned. "Man, that Patrick Swayze could dance!"

"Hey, you're not secretly gay are you?" I teased.

In answer he pulled me close once more and I could tell by the proximity of his body and the reaction of it to mine, that he was most definitely was not.

That kiss was the best of the night. His mouth covered mine and demanded a response that arose not just from my lips but from the very depths of my soul.

Reluctantly we parted and carried on walking, content to be quiet for a while.

The evening had been perfect...no, not merely perfect, it had been magical and other than the awful things he'd been forced to reveal to me, I wouldn't have changed anything for the world.

"I've had a really great-"

Rough hands grasped me from behind, encircling my waist and whirling me around, catching me unawares and knocking me a little off-balance. Rancid beer fumes assaulted me as hot, stale breath was exhaled into my face, making me gag and retch. The coarse hands pinched a little tighter, deliberately sliding upwards, grubby fingers splaying across my ribcage and towards my breasts.

"Save some for your old man!" the drunk leered, wild bloodshot eyes probing the depths of my cleavage, a thin line of drool clinging to his lower lip. He staggered with me in his arms but somehow kept his footing.

The line of saliva lengthened impossibly, elongated and stretched, seeming for one precarious moment to draw back upwards towards his mouth before it fell, detaching itself and landing on the ground at my feet.

"DAD, PLEASE!" I heard my date plead through a veil of disgust, eyes riveted on the excuse for a human being who stood behind me, his crotch jammed into the seat of my jeans. "Let her go, she's done nothing to you."

"Now that's not very friendly, keeping a sweet young thing like this for yourself..." his father slid one hand higher, attempting to cup my breast. I tried to pull away but I was held tight.

"My, you're a feisty girl!" the drunk slurred almost admiringly, as I tore at his hands with my own, clawing and drawing blood. He laughed at my efforts, refusing to let go, gripping tighter so that every breath I took was constricted and forced.

I didn't see the punch which landed on his chin but I felt its force as he was catapulted away from me, staggering backwards in a comical drunken dance, refusing to fall. When he came back again, reeling towards me as if attached by an elastic rope, there was a new purpose in his face and a growing animosity in his eyes. He was a force to be reckoned with and I knew what I was seeing was the real him; the truth behind the mask he usually presented in public.

"Like that, is it? She's too good for the likes of me, is that it?" He rammed himself into me, grinding his crotch sickeningly against me, vile, sour breath hot on my cleavage.

The punch that felled him was straight and true, landing squarely on his temple. With a crash, he fell to the hard ground with nothing to cushion his fall. I felt no pity for his hard landing.

Shivering through fear and emotions I could not fully identify, but some which felt wickedly primal, I watched as Nathan bent awkwardly down to his father. "Damn right she's too good for you," he said, so softly I almost didn't hear.

One after another he searched his dad's pockets, whilst the drunk man tried ineffectively to slap his hands away. His father seemed barely able to hold onto his consciousness and drifted rapidly in and out of awareness. Finding what he was looking for, Nathan held the item high and waited until his father's eyes registered the sight before speaking.

"You won't be needing these anymore." Light glimmered dully on the bunch of keys. "Don't bother going home. You aren't welcome there anymore." He pocketed the keys. "And if you do turn up there, I'll make sure you get a reception you won't ever forget!"

Something flickered in the drunk's eyes, some understanding that the line had finally been crossed. His eyelids closed once, twice and then ever-so-slowly his eyeballs rolled to the back of his head.

"Is he...dead?" I asked, terrified of that he might be, terrified that he might not.

"Nah," Nathan prodded him with the toe of his shoe. "Just blind drunk and unconscious. I've seen him like this before. He'll be out of it for hours, if not until the morning."

"Did you mean that?" I asked.

He patted his pocket where the keys resided. "Yes, every word. Tonight, with your support, Nat, I managed to admit to myself that things had to change. That I had to *make* them change. Make my mother stop denying what goes on and face up to it. It's the only way to move forward."

I nodded. "So what happens now?" I asked anxiously.

"Well, I guess I go home and I phone the police and tell them everything."

He put his arm around me and we began to walk again but the air seemed colder than before and I couldn't stop myself from shivering.

As we rounded the last corner which would bring my house into view, I prepared to pull him close for a final kiss. But instead of one or two lights on at home, as I had expected there to be, the whole house was lit up, every room illuminated against the night sky.

CHAPTER 15B

10:20 p.m.

My face still stung from where Rhys had slapped me but I was less concerned about that than about what the rest of the night held in store. Riding in a stolen car, with a driver who was probably over the limit before he even got in behind the wheel, to a destination that filled me with terror, I had never been so desperate in my life to see a police car. But luck, elusive and evasive all night, continued to hide her face from me.

We twisted in and out of streets, going first one way and then another so that I was unable to get my bearings accurately.

"You don't need to try to confuse her with where we're going," Rhys instructed brusquely.

"Don't want her to be able to tell anyone where I live. You know, after you're done," Shaun answered.

"You know what Shaun, you do the driving and I'll do the thinking. She won't be able to tell anyone where she's been when I'm done with her anyway," Rhys sniggered ominously, not even bothering to glance at me.

The car sped onwards by a more direct route,

only minutes passing before we pulled up at a run-down house in an equally run-down neighbourhood. I could have been two miles from home or twenty; I'd so completely lost my bearings.

Rhys pulled me roughly out of the car and up the steps towards the front door which he unlocked with a key that Shaun handed him. The smell inside the place was a mix of dampness and unwashed clothing, overlayed with the foul tang of dirty crockery.

"Welcome home, honey!" Rhys mocked as he pushed me through the door and turned to lock it behind me. It seemed of great significance to me that I remembered the layout. If the chance came to escape, I would need to know how. I tried to take everything in without really looking.

It wasn't a particularly big house and the doors downstairs opened into a central corridor. I didn't know if that was good or bad. There was a kitchen and a bathroom and then other rooms which looked to be largely unfurnished other than mattresses laid on the bare floors.

I huddled in the hallway, desperate for a means of escape. But there was none.

"Shaun, hand over the shit." Rhys held out his hand to receive the small package that was dropped into it. He examined the contents appreciatively. "Seems like good stuff." He handed it back. "Set us all up with some; think it'll help my *date* relax a little into the atmosphere."

He turned back to me. "Sorry I can't offer you the level of accommodation you've been used to, but the services will make up for it, I imagine."

I wanted to rip the leer off his face but I figured my best chance for survival was to remain impassive. I let him push me towards one of the mattresses. "Bring me some blow but other than that, don't disturb us," he called to Shaun, as if we were a honeymooning couple.

"Lie down!" he ordered.

The mattress was covered in stained, dirty linen and I didn't want to think who had lain there before, let alone whether or not they had been willing participants. A small window faced the makeshift bed and I wondered if it were locked and if I would get a chance to find out. I remained standing. Whilst I would do nothing to overtly anger him, I wasn't going to just comply with his demands.

"I said, LIE DOWN!" he said louder and more aggressively.

I remained standing but avoided all eye contact. Wasn't that what you were supposed to do with vicious dogs? Perhaps it would work with vicious guys too.

He strode over and grasping me by the shoulders, threw me onto the soiled bed. I couldn't help myself, my stomach heaved and I gagged but instead of being sympathetic or concerned, he just laughed.

"My, you are a princess, aren't you, Nat?"

I tried one last shot at getting him to remember the Rhys he used to be before whatever it was that had happened, had turned him into this monster. "Remember how we used to be, Rhys? Remember how we used to play ball games and sit and talk..."

He cut me short. "That was before, Nat. And I was dumb then..."

"No, Rhys, you weren't dumb, you were sweet..."

"Sweet gets you nothing you want in life!" he spat harshly. "Sweet gets you pushed around by others until..." he was interrupted by the door swinging open and Shaun entering with a joint held out to Rhys.

"Great! Now get out and shut the door behind you!" Rhys grinned, taking a long drag of the smoke and holding it in as if savouring it. "Come on, Nat, try it. You'll like it," he said, offering it to me.

"No, thank you," I said politely, as if I had the luxury of refusing.

He laughed and just as I thought that perhaps he would not force me, he slid onto the bed, joint held between the finger and thumb of one hand. Without warning he used his other hand to push me backwards so that I was flat on the mattress.

I felt the greasiness of the pillow under my

head as he climbed into a sitting position on top of me and pinned my arms down with his legs. I tried to twist away but he caught my face, pinching my nostrils to keep me still and making me open my mouth to breathe. Gasping hard, I struggled against his hold and with my tongue tried to eject the joint he thrust into my open mouth.

"Smoke it, bitch!" he ordered. Something inside me snapped. Nothing I had done or said up until that time had had any effect, nor was it likely to, I realised. I was all out of plans and defences.

"FUCK OFF! YOU FUCKING ASSHOLE!" I yelled in a voice that didn't sound remotely like my own.

"You know, if you'd shown a little bit more spirit, I might not have chosen you in the first place," he laughed.

I was too far gone to care what my actions resulted in. "GO FUCK YOURSELF!"

Calmly he took another huge drag of the joint. But instead of holding it in, he leaned over me and brought his mouth to mine. Still holding my nose closed, he covered my mouth completely with his, so that I couldn't breathe.

For a long moment I held my breath, refusing to inhale the smoke he held in readiness for me but I couldn't hold back forever. It was breathe or die and I wasn't ready to let go of life without a fight.

Drugged smoke was pushed from his mouth to mine and wound its sinuous way to my lungs. Desperate for oxygen, I drank the laden air and gasped for more. He removed his mouth from mine only long enough to take another drag which he then forced into my mouth.

By the fifth or sixth time, I was no longer concerned about *anything*. It was the strangest feeling I'd ever had. Like intoxication, it provoked a languor that ensured that whilst I was vaguely aware of what was going on, I no longer had the strength or presence of mind to do anything about it.

My head juddered to the mattress as he pulled the pillow from under it. The mattress seemed to be floating inside the room – a little island on which he and I alone existed. I felt his hands on my pants, dragging them roughly down and discarding them somewhere beyond the island.

Rough hands moved my legs but I had no energy to keep them in position.

I was wrong, it wasn't an island, it was a *boat*. And there were other people, other boats around me. Suzie's face looked down on me from above but when she laughed, the sound was like a seagull's caw. Not surprising, since she was hovering in the sky above me...

My head spun painfully and my throat was dry. The nursery song *Row, Row, Row Your Boat*, filled my head, the tune spiralling me away into a blessed oblivion.

CHAPTER 16A

11.00 p.m.

"Something's wrong!" The incongruity of the situation brought butterflies of unease to my stomach even before my brain had time to mull over the significance of Stacey's dad standing on my doorstep. A jolt of concern made me falter in my steps.

"I'm not late, am I?" I asked anxiously. If I had been, I was sure that under the circumstances, once I explained everything to my dad, I wouldn't be in trouble. In fact my dad would probably insist on driving Nathan home and waiting with him until the police arrived to take his statement about the attacks his father had made on Nathan and his mum.

Nathan shook his head. "It's only just gone eleven."

Why should Stacey's dad be at my house when I'd gone out on a date? He couldn't be collecting her because she wasn't there. It wasn't as if he and my dad were friends, they only vaguely knew each other. And that was through mine and Stacey's friendship.

"I'll come over with you, if you like," Nathan

said, recognising that whatever was going on was out of the ordinary and unexpected.

"Thanks, I would appreciate that," I responded.

We had walked to my house with our arms around one another, but now we separated and walked apart. I wondered if he relinquished his hold on me for my sake or for his own. Was he worried how my dad would react if he saw a boy with his arm around me? Was I worried about it? I really didn't know. All I knew for sure at that precise moment, was that nothing was as it should have been.

My father's eyes swept over me as I approached. Worried that I was in trouble for some misdemeanour I didn't even know about, I felt my shoulders tense, but when his gaze washed over me towards Nathan and yet did not linger there, I knew that something far, far worse was going on.

"Hi, Mr Papadopoulos." I smiled briefly. "Dad, this is Nathan, my date." The words came out almost shyly but they were immediately disregarded by the two men.

"Natalie, I am so relieved you're home. Stacey has gone missing. And her father is looking for her," my dad cut straight to the point. His eyes flicked briefly over Nathan but there was no other acknowledgement. His face was blanched with concern and there was a clipped, hurried tone to his voice I wasn't used to hearing.

"Gone missing?" I repeated stupidly, looking from one face to another as if I could find some explanation there. "Gone missing where?"

"That's what I hoped you could shed some light on," my father said.

"She say she going do homework at your house tonight! She say 'no come before eleven pm Papa'. Too much homework she say! No get finished before eleven pm. But she lie! She no here!" Stacey's dad was beside himself with worry. His normally cheery face was pulled tight with fear and apprehension.

"Here with me?" I couldn't seem to stop myself from repeating what was being said no matter how hard I tried. "But she knew I was going on a date..." Which meant that she had never actually intended to come here. She had deliberately lied for her own secret purposes. What had she been up to? And why? And how had she thought she'd get away with it?

My dad frowned. "I already told Mr and Mrs Papadopoulos that...but they were adamant that's what she said..."

"Stacey's mum is here too?" This was turning into a circus. I silently cursed Stacey for her stupidity. Her parents would never trust her again.

My dad nodded. "Your mother has given her some brandy to steady the poor woman's nerves." Dad looked like he thought they could all do with some.

"Perhaps she is on her way home now," Nathan supplied from where he stood behind me, reminding me that he was still around.

"Stacey's not allowed to walk home on her own. So wherever she went, she must have been intending to be around here at eleven. She would have waited outside for her dad and no one would have known she hadn't been here all evening!" The explanation came to me whole and clear on a blast of intuition.

My father seemed to become properly aware of Nathan for the first time. "Thank you for bringing my daughter home safely, Nathan. I guess you had best be off home now before your parents worry too."

It was such an innocent remark and completely wrong under the circumstances that I almost blurted everything out. At the very last moment I managed to hold my words back and let Nathan respond how he felt he should. He surprised me with his answer. "If you don't mind, I'd like to stay and try to help. I can give my mum a call now and explain the situation."

I signalled with my eyes that it was unnecessary. Nathan had his own problems to deal with but he dismissed them with a subtle shake of the head. All I could do was grab a chance to speak to him alone, as soon as I could.

My dad nodded. "That's very good of you. I

don't know how or if you can help but it's appreciated."

I watched this exchange dumbfounded. Either my father had taken an instant liking to Nathan or the situation was so serious that it required all other considerations to be put aside. I decided on the latter.

"Do you know where she could be?" Mr Papadopoulos turned his distraught face towards me and I could have wrung Stacey's neck for putting him through this. I racked my brains for the answer. We had several other friends, although not as close as the two of us, but there would be no reason for Stace to lie about being with me if she were seeing one of them. The only reason would be…

"Rhys asked me out today," I didn't know how to end without embarrassing Nathan in the process. "I would probably have gone but then Nathan asked me out…" I cringed at how it sounded but it was after all, the truth. And didn't someone once say that the truth could set you free?

"Stacey knew that they had both asked me out and she was…" I struggled to find the right word, "not jealous but…" there was no choice but to be completely honest, "but I know she wished she had been asked out too."

Three pairs of eyes watched and waited for me to continue. "I think maybe…maybe she took my place and went out with Rhys." My dad and Stacey's looked at me dumbly. Only Nathan caught my meaning.

"She took your place on the date," he said and as the words fell from his lips, I knew they were right. I nodded.

"Rhys from around the block?" my dad asked.

I nodded again. "We were friends before his family moved away - guess we still are – but I just don't think of him in that way..." I tried to explain for Nathan's benefit. "If she has gone out with him, she'll be fine though!" I said, feeling certain that all would end well. But in my head I wondered why she hadn't told me she was going to call him after I cancelled our date. Why had she not said anything to me? Had she been embarrassed? Or was there a slyness in her that I had never seen before? Suddenly I felt cold all over.

"You know where this Rhys lives?" Stacey's dad asked.

"Yes," I replied simply. "They live not far away. I can take you there."

"But if she is not back yet, then shouldn't we wait here or we might miss them?" Nathan asked logically.

I had a thought. "What if Stace goes home while we are all looking for her?"

"Her brother, he is at home and he phone me as soon as she appear!" There was a distinct sense of an unspoken clause to Mr Papadopoulos's sentence. There was an unvoiced 'if' and none of us dared express it. And yet I couldn't help but think that we were all overreacting.

The dads went inside the house to collect car keys and to update the women. Left outside with Nathan I didn't want to follow them inside, nor did I wish to eavesdrop on his call home to explain the situation. But I was worried. "Your dad..." I began.

"I told you, he will be passed out for hours yet, and by then I will be home."

"And you'll call the police straight away?" I made sure.

"Yes," he promised. "To be honest, this gives me a little time to think, to clear my head and find the words to explain everything to my mum, to make her see that we have to keep him away."

I guessed it made sense. While he called, I wandered over to the car, waiting for everyone to be ready to go. Why Stacey had lied was now obvious. She had desperately wanted to be asked on a date and had made it plain she thought Rhys was nice. She also knew that her father and older brother wouldn't let her go unchaperoned and she'd seen how to use my absence to her advantage.

But a part of me ached at her deceit, not just to her family but also to me. Why had she not said what she was planning to do? It wasn't that I would have wanted her to ask my permission as such, but it was a rather weird situation and even thought I hadn't chosen Rhys for myself, I wasn't sure how happy I was that he would be going out with my best friend instead. Was I so easily replaceable? And did Stacey think so little of our friendship that she was prepared to jeopardise it over a boy?

It certainly looked that way on all counts.

Having finished his call, Nathan came towards me. "I just told my mum what was going on here. She understood and said to call her as soon as there's any news," he stated. "I didn't mention my dad. Him not coming home tonight won't strike her as unusual anyway."

I nodded, not trusting myself to speak.

"You are quite cut up about this, aren't you?" he asked perceptively.

I nodded once more but refrained from speaking lest my voice gave away the full depth of my feelings. It felt rather shallow of me to be so upset at Stace's duplicity after what I had witnessed Nathan go through with his dad.

"Why were you angry?" he asked. "Is it because she involved you or because she went out with the guy who could have been your date tonight?" he asked quietly.

"Both, I guess," I answered truthfully, a little ashamed and hoping that he understood even though I did not fully understand it myself.

"I think the only thing you need to worry about is that she's alright...which I'm sure she is," he amended quickly. "They probably just forgot the time, like we nearly did!"

But of course this implied that they had been having such a good date that they *could* forget the time and perhaps only made things worse!

He smiled shyly. "Don't feel bad about being a little put out. I'm just glad that you chose me and I hope you still feel the same, especially after everything you saw."

Before the men came out of the house and caught us, I planted a kiss on his lips. "So am I, Nathan, so am I." I smiled a little shakily. "There's no truth in that old saying, you know."

He regarded me with a lack of comprehension, forcing me to spell it out.

"There's no truth in the saying, 'like father, like son'. None at all."

CHAPTER 16B

11.00 p.m.

The drug-induced fog had begun to clear from my brain. I took note of my surroundings.

I had been half conscious during it all; enough to realize I was being raped, and raped again; aware of the grinning faces above me but unable to lift a limb in resistance. I knew that at some point I had screamed, perhaps even more than once - and that every protest had been in vain.

I was limp, unable to move; though my body ached as though it had been torn in two. Helplessly I peered at the perpetrators: Rhys, Shaun, and Suzie, who had been present throughout. No mask-wearing psychopath could have inspired more terror in me, than did their three remorseless faces.

They stood tight together in a huddle. I could only dimly make out what they said, as though they were far away and distant, talking though some invisible tunnel.

"We have to get rid of her!" Shaun said, face contorted in anger.

Suzie pulled on her clothes whilst she spoke. "Shaun's right. Get rid of her, she's trouble!" she warned. "We don't need her!"

"It's more risky to dump her, than to keep her," Rhys retorted, pushing Suzie away from him as if bored with her. I didn't know if they knew I could hear them or whether they just didn't care.

"You're not leaving her here...no way am I taking the rap for this if it all goes wrong..." The rest of Shaun's words were cut off as Rhys grabbed him by the throat.

"Nothing's gonna go wrong. You are going to drop me and Suzie off, then take her to Big Max's place. Big Max knows how to take care of girls like her."

My head and body pounded in pain but an image of my fate came sharp and clear to my mind. Somehow - between Rhys and Suzie being dropped off and me being delivered to this new destination - I would have to take my chance to escape. I might have failed so far. I couldn't afford to fail again.

Hoping that they would think I was still in the drugged state I'd been in previously, I lay still and motionless. Suzie finished dressing and came right up to my face to look into my eyes. I struggled to keep my gaze unfocused and blank.

"She's still out of it," she pronounced, pulling my pants back on and straightening my clothes. I let her haul me around, feeling the pants hiked uncomfortably against me but stifling any protest.

"Don't know why you are bothering with that," Shaun laughed. "Big Max will have a queue lined up to take them off again!"

I wanted to be sick, both because of what they were implying and because of what they'd already done to me, but I held it down. The time for self-pity would come later, when it was safe to grieve for my lost innocence. For my lost belief that I would always be alright.

"It's easier to send her out of here with them on, than to try to get rid of them without incriminating us," she explained in a slow voice. "They are evidence..."

"She's right!" Rhys nodded slowly, seemingly reluctant to concede any victory to her.

"Then what about everything in here, everything she touched?" Shaun's voice had an edge of mounting panic.

"Wash the bedclothes she was lying on and your own clothes..." Suzie stopped when Shaun shook his head, face white and drawn.

"What? You don't have a machine?" her voice struck me as strangely incredulous given the state of the place. "For God's sake, you're hopeless, Shaun!" Suzie turned to Rhys. "Did she touch anything other than the bed when she came in?"

"No. Nothing." He didn't even need to think about it.

"Right then since you two seem incapable of thinking without using your dicks, here's what we're going to do." Suzie looked at them both as she spoke. "We get her in the car. Then we get the bedclothes into a bundle and put them in too. When Shaun gets rid of her he can come back to mine, shower and I'll wash his clothes and the bedclothes, just to be sure."

"Barry, the guy at the cinema, won't say any-thing if questioned ..." Rhys almost spoke to him-self and appeared to be trying to run the scenario through his head. "Shaun, you're going to have to wipe the car down after, and abandon it...it'd be best if it could be burnt out..."

Shaun nodded.

I held my breath. What if Rhys's next thought was that it would be easier to kill me and leave me in the car *whilst* it burnt out? Seconds of my life ticked past in a kaleidoscope of memories, good and bad. I saw the faces of my family and an image of my old dog, Jess, even though she'd died years before. Was this how it felt, to know you had reached the end of your life, whether by nat-ural causes or not?

Insanely, Rhys featured in some of the happy memories...the old Rhys - before he became this monster I didn't know.

Put together like this, I realised what had never occurred to me before – that my life had been particularly charmed. I saw how many people loved me and were loved by me in return. I saw such depth of feelings and realised that some people never even had that from one person, let alone so many. And yet…and yet I was not prepared for death. More precisely, I was not prepared to be robbed of life… not by these scum…

I worked hard to stay immobile when what I really wanted was to leap up and attack them. Not sure if I were capable of even the leap up, an attack would be pointless against all three of them. My best chance was in continuing to appear defenceless… and yet it went against every principle I had. I let my eyelids droop as if they were too heavy and relaxed my throbbing body as much as possible.

But the more the drugs wore off, the more my humiliation and violated body became apparent. Even lying still, the pain in my groin was almost unbearable. I wanted to draw my legs up, curl myself into a ball and howl in agony and bitter grief. Yet I could do none of those things.

Letting them roughly pick me up, was hard. I wanted to lash out at them, kick and bite and tear but instead I lay slumped in their hands, a dead weight of trash that they needed to dispose of. Between them, they half-carried, half-dragged me back to the car and bundled me into the back seat, the stained and soiled bed clothes sprawled in my lap. Keeping all the trash together.

The indignity of it was armour against them if they but knew it. Silently I vowed to myself that they would not go unpunished, that I would not die or be secreted away as they planned. I would escape and I would see them rot in jail for the rest of their natural lives.

I thought Suzie was in the back with me but couldn't be sure unless I turned my head. I remained slumped against the car window, eyes only half open...trying to keep alert without *looking* alert. My head really hurt and it was too warm in the car. Rounding corners, I swayed in the backseat and it was so dark and quiet I could almost have been lulled to sleep if it were not for the pain and the very real fear for my life.

A nice neighbourhood came into view... the clean-looking well-kept houses standing tall and straight in the dark like sentinels; the nicely mown front gardens a testament to the homeowners' attention to detail...none of these people would ever know that a drugged and raped girl sat in a stolen car, only yards from where their own children slept soundly in their beds.

I had once been one of those people, those children. I too had believed that I was protected from harm, wrapped up in my safe home with my loving parents. But danger had only been an arm's reach away. How many other girls had been lured by that innocence? That ignorance?

My house wasn't far from here. Only a few more minutes' drive. Shaun wouldn't go that close, I reasoned. But if he had? What would

I have seen? My parents outside? Worrying and waiting for me, but assuming I'd just forgotten the time? A police car? What? Perhaps I would never know.

"Let me out here. No point in risking going any further!" Rhys ordered. I was right; he had been in the front seat. Would Suzie now get in the front and leave me alone in the back? I stayed slumped and unmoving. The car stopped and I guess Rhys got out but there was only the sound of one car door opening and closing. Suzie apparently had thought it best to stay put.

"OK, drop me off as quick as you can," she ordered Shaun and the car turned around and sped away. Without looking, I saw Rhys cross the road and walk briskly towards his home. I wondered what would happen when he got there.

Would his mother kiss him on the cheek and enquire how his night had been? Would he smile sweetly and tell her that he had molested, drugged and then raped me? Would he tell her that the girl who used to sit at his mother's kitchen table was now drugged and beaten in the back of a stolen car, on the way to 'Big Max's'? Would he tell his mum that the girl had been raped so violently that she suspected the wetness which continued to seep through her pants and dress was not just semen - but blood? Would he tell her any of these things?

Of course not! He would tell some other tale,

that she hadn't shown up or something…and he would shrug his shoulders and probably even get a cuddle from his mum, words of sympathy and love. I had to stifle a sob for the self-pity which descended upon me.

The scene from the window had changed dramatically whilst I had been reflecting on my thoughts. This new neighbourhood we drove through was nothing like my own. Here the houses were run-down, paint peeling, walls cracked and in need of repair. The front gardens, where there were any, were overgrown and had lacked attention for at least a decade. I guessed this was where Suzie resided.

The car stopped and someone got out. Once more we sped off into the darkness. Now there was only Shaun and me.

CHAPTER 17A

11.15 p.m.

We climbed into the car, my dad and Stacey's in the front, and Nathan and I in the back. It was strange to be sitting in dad's car with Nathan, but then again, what hadn't been strange and unusual about the evening?

What would happen to Stacey when her dad got hold of her? Would he ground her for a week, a month…forever? I wondered if she had told him the truth, whether his reaction would have been as bad as she'd feared. Certainly by staying out late and lying to him she had escalated his response in a way that I was sure he would never let her forget. But if she'd told him calmly, asked his permission, would he have relented? Whatever the outcome, it would have been better than what was about to go down now.

And what would happen when we all turned up? Not just her dad and mine but me and Nathan too! A veritable crowd of people! Would she be ashamed? Or just angry? If anyone had the right to be angry then surely it was me? She had stolen my date.

OK, that wasn't strictly true as I had chosen

Nathan and not Rhys, but couldn't she have found someone completely different? Did she have to rub my face in it like that? What if I'd had a terrible night out with Nathan and wanted to apologise to Rhys and go out with him instead on another night? She had taken that away from me and I wasn't sure if I could so easily forgive her.

It didn't take long for the car to pull up outside Rhys's house. Different to the house the family had had before they moved out of town, it was similar enough to be confused as the same one, transposed to a different plot.

Lights blazed from a few of the windows, so someone was awake. What would I say if I saw her here? How would I feel, knowing that I had spent many afternoons sitting at that same kitchen table chatting with Rhys, even if it had been in a different house?

"Stay in the car," my dad ordered as he and Stacey's dad got out, shutting the car doors quietly behind them. I looked at Nathan as we sat alone in the car, and then without even consciously thinking about it, I opened my door and got out, waiting for him to do the same.

"Your dad said to stay here," he said, unmoving.

I stood with my door open, challenging him. "Yes, he did. But I have to see this for myself." I didn't normally go against my dad's wishes, but tonight was different. Tonight everything had been different...like something carried on the wind had brought a real and irreversible change to the land, an unyielding change to *me*.

I'd been drinking alcohol and had experienced my first real grown-up kiss. I'd been assaulted by my boyfriend's dad and I'd learned things about human nature I had no wish to dwell upon. Perhaps because of all that, I felt older and less inclined to be told what to do. A line from the old *Dirty Dancing* film came into my head. I looked him clearly in the eye. "Nobody puts Baby in the corner!" I said, knowing he would instantly get my reference.

Neither of us laughed. It seemed somehow too significant, as if there was a drawing and tying of the two, parallels between the film and the intensity of how this evening had turned out and was continuing to turn out. He got out of the car from my side and I shut the door quietly.

The front door to the house was open and we looked at each other before we stepped over the threshold and closed it softly behind us. Raised voices came from the kitchen and it was to there we headed directly, not even glancing into any of the rooms we passed on the way.

My dad and Stacey's stood opposite Rhys's parents like opponents in a boxing ring. As Rhys's mum noticed me with Nathan at my side, I saw her gaze flicker once to her husband and then back to Rhys, instantly dismissing me. Shame flared hot and red in my face. Like it or not, I was a part of this horrible situation, and so now, was Nathan.

"Where is my Stacey?" Mr Papadopoulos thundered, near hysteria making his voice reverberate off the kitchen walls.

"I told you, I don't know!" Rhys tried to look perplexed and failed. My heart sank as he looked from Nathan to me and back again, seeming to take in every detail of how we stood together. His gaze seared me to the core.

I had hurt him! I'd never even thought about how he would feel to be confronted with the reason I hadn't gone out with him! I'd been so intent on seeing Stacey and letting her have some of my hurt at what I saw as her betrayal, I hadn't spared a thought for poor Rhys and how he would feel! I felt my face deepening in colour as my shame and embarrassment intensified.

Rhys's mum seemed confused. "You told me you were going out with Natalie!" she said. "But that clearly wasn't true!" I squirmed in my shoes at the thought that everyone would hear how I had accepted a date from him, then cancelled it to go out with Nathan instead.

"No, Mum, I told you I had *asked* Natalie out," he explained. "But she said no." His voice was flat and without intonation but I could tell he'd been wounded by my rejection. I wondered what his mother thought of me now.

"So where does Stacey come into it?" Rhys's mother asked, still confused.

"Well, see, after Nat cancelled on me, I got another call. It was Stacey. She said…" he paused and I held my breath. What exactly *had* she said? How had she phrased it? Had she put it like he hadn't been good enough for me? Like he was better off without me? Neither of those things sounded like the Stacey I knew. Then again going out with the guy who had asked me out first, didn't sound like the Stacey I knew either. Perhaps I didn't know her at all!

"Well?" his father pushed.

"She said that Nat had been asked out by another guy and was going out with him instead." Rhys cast an angry look at Nathan as he spoke, a fire smouldering in his eyes. It was blunt but at least it was true, I thought. "She said that seeing as how I was obviously at a loose end and she had nothing to do tonight, why didn't we hook up together."

"So you *did* go out with her?" It was my father who asked the question but all eyes were riveted on Rhys.

"Yes and no."

"Which is it, yes or no?" his father asked impatiently.

There was a strange atmosphere in the room, a tension that hadn't quite been there a minute before. I couldn't make up my mind if Rhys was deliberately confounding us all by the half answers he had given, or if he was confused as to why we were all there.

"Mr Papadopoulos's daughter hasn't come home, Rhys, so you had better tell him everything you know!" There was some warning or threat implied in Rhys's dad's voice, which I only half-recognised. I figured that my dad and Stacey's must have explained the situation when they arrived and yet Rhys didn't seem to have understood the full implications. If he'd gone out with Stacey, she should have been home by now.

And if he hadn't gone out with Stacey then where *had* she gone? And was she still there, wherever that was? No call from Theo had been received and I'd seen Mr Papadopoulos check the signal and battery on his phone several times.

"I only got back a few minutes ago myself," Rhys looked at his mother who confirmed the statement by nodding, "and I only saw Stacey briefly so…"

"How briefly?" I hadn't mean to butt in, hadn't been aware that the words were forming in my mind, sitting on the tip of my tongue. But suddenly there they were.

Rhys tried not to look at me but when he did, I saw anger in the tightness of his mouth and eyes. No wonder, I berated myself. First I accept then dump him, then I turn up at his house accusing him of betraying me! I vowed that once he'd answered me, I would remain silent afterwards.

"I met her as she wanted,[cc4] at seven-thirty. But then I saw some friends who suggested we go with them...and...and..." he floundered. I felt awful for having put him on the spot. "And I don't know why, but Stacey suddenly changed her mind." He shrugged his shoulders. In silence we waited for him to continue.

But before he could elaborate, his dad asked a question. "Who exactly were these friends?" His eyes fixed hard on his son and I got the distinct impression that his thoughts had moved away from the whereabouts of the missing girl - the reason we were all there.

"Well...um...Shaun was one of them..." Rhys stuttered, casting his eyes to the floor as if the names were printed on the polished tiles.

"And?" his dad asked expectantly.

"And Suzie was another of them," Rhys admitted reluctantly.

"I told you to stay away from that girl!" his mum cried, hands pulled up to her face and over her mouth, only managing to partially cover her shock and fear. None of it made sense to me.

"Suzie?" I asked, thinking that the only Suzie I knew was from the shoe shop. An image flickered through my head. Rhys in town. Loitering by the shops. Hanging around...

"Suzie from the shoe shop?" My voice seemed to have gone up an octave since I used it last.

"Suzie from our school who had the kid?" Perhaps I wasn't phrasing it the best way ever, but surprise had overtaken my ability to communicate eloquently.

Rhys's dad's face was almost unrecognisable as he answered my questions, lips pulled back in a snarl and eyes filled with pain. "Yes, Suzie from the shoe shop! Suzie who had a kid! *His* kid! *Our* grandchild!" He spat the words out with venom, as if all of it was my fault. I recoiled from him, astounded by the force of his words as much as their meaning.

Were they true? I had no cause to doubt them, coming from his dad as they did - but even so - Rhys and Suzie? I would never have guessed in a million years!

"Really?" I turned to Rhys for confirmation.

A slight smirk flitted over his mouth and trailed across his eyes. I wondered how I'd ever thought I knew him. "It was you?" I couldn't hide my shock. "It was *you* who got Suzie pregnant?"

"So *she* says," he said, neither denying nor confirming it. I thought back to the little I'd known of Suzie from before. Before she got pregnant. She hadn't seemed all that different to Stacey and me. Not then anyway. Now of course, it was a different matter.

But even so…Rhys? I couldn't get my head around it. Rhys had always just been a sweet, dependable kind of guy…

"So your sleazy friends turned up and Stacey made off?" Rhys's dad cut through my thoughts and directly to the point of why we were there. But it seemed that his mother was not so easily put off her own worries.

"I told you not to hang about with those people anymore, Rhys. They get you in trouble-"

"Mum..." Rhys sighed, talking over her.

"JUST TELL ME WHERE MY STACEY IS!" Mr Papadopoulos bellowed, cutting through the other voices. "I no care who fathered who's baby. I just want my daughter home and safe. Please just tell me where she is!"

CHAPTER 17B

11.15 p.m.

I was finally alone in the car with Shaun. The irony of it didn't escape me. Like an expectant lover I'd yearned to be alone with him but rather than passion, it was escape which was on my mind.

I had no idea how far or close Big Max's place was, so therefore no idea how long I had. All I knew was that time was of the essence. I was in pain and still rather groggy but worked on getting myself more alert without obviously doing so.

"Where's everybody gone?" I slurred as if I had only just noticed. "We goin' 'nother party?" I giggled as if I was actually enjoying myself, enjoying the degradation they had put me through. Mentally I ran through times tables then silently recited the alphabet backwards. It helped clarify my mind but I held on to the feeling of being doped up. I'd never excelled in drama at school but then again my life had never before depended on my ability to completely fool someone.

I thrust the foul-smelling bed linen off my lap. I wanted to run a hand between my legs and look at what came away. Was there blood as I suspected? In a way it was of no relevance. If there had not yet been enough damage done to have caused me internal bleeding, there soon would be. I could be sure of that.

I considered my options. I could throw open the door and push myself out. The car was travelling fast and I would either be injured in the stunt or possibly killed by another oncoming car. Even if I escaped either of those two things, there was nothing to prevent him from stopping the car and catching me. In the state I was in, it was unlikely that I would get far before he caught up with me.

I could throw the bed linen over his head, effectively blindfolding him and more than likely causing him to crash the car. It was anyone's guess whether either of us would survive that. As unbothered as I was about causing his death, I was not unbothered about causing my own!

What other options were there? Could I get into the front, somehow open his driver's door as we were moving, push him out and then take control of the steering wheel? Only if this was a movie and I was the heroine, I decided, moving onto the theorem of Pythagoras in my head before deciding that I had thought enough. It was time for action.

There was only one thing *to* do and it was the

same thing that women had done for millennia –
I had to use what I had.

"I liked what you were doing to me back
there…" I forced myself to touch the back of his
neck in what I hoped felt like a warm caress. His
skin was tacky and cold and I had to suppress the
shiver that ran down my spine at having to lay a
finger on him. Bile rose in my throat but I swallowed it back down, relishing the taste of it for it
helped me to feel real. This might be a game I was
playing but the consequences were genuine, and
they were deadly.

"Coulda fooled me! You bit me! Bitch!" he said
angrily. Vaguely I remembered sinking my teeth
into his palm as he held it over my mouth. I su-
pressed a shudder at the memory.

Perhaps this wouldn't work but it was all I
had. I gave it my best shot. "Oh, but I thought you
wanted it a little rough. What's the matter? Don't
you like me, Shaunie?" I put a note of petulance in
my voice, trying to copy how Susie spoke to him.

"You bit me!" he repeated as if I'd hacked off
his arm with a chainsaw. And God help me, if I'd
had a chainsaw to hand, I would have done that
very thing! And I wouldn't have stopped with his
filthy hands either.

I tried to pull myself a little more upright and
something inside me protested. Pain shot out
from the deepest centre of me, radiating across
my abdomen to wring out its final victory in the

nerve endings in my arms and legs. I needed a shotgun, a hospital and a miracle, in that order. Wetness flooded down my legs and I wondered how much time I had before I blacked out from pain and blood loss.

Clenching my teeth, I folded my upper body to the roof of the car and painfully swung one leg over the back of the front seat. Repeating the procedure for the second leg, I managed to get in the passenger seat without him stopping me.

The upholstery was sticky from my blood but I didn't care. I slumped into its deep padding. I would lose a whole lot more blood if I failed to pull this off.

"What are you doing?" he asked, seemingly genuinely confused.

"We could have some fun now that we're alone!" I stated, in what I hoped was a seductive voice.

"Rhys said I have to take you to Big Max's!" He sounded undecided though.

"I don't know who Big Max is but I know a *Big* Shaun!" I wanted to heave at having to say the words and forcing myself to lay a hand on his crotch almost made me retch.

He groaned and for a moment shut his eyes. The car slowed imperceptibly but not enough that I could safely leap out and make a run for it.

"Let's stop for a while. Rhys will never even know..." I urged. Perhaps that was the wrong thing to say because his eyes shot open at once.

"You don't want me at all...you are just trying to get away from me..." he said slowly as if voicing a dawning revelation.

"No! No that's not true!" I stuttered.

He laughed and I wasn't sure if it was because he was playing me at my own game, ensuring that I tried harder, or whether it was genuine.

"I...I just want to ...." I searched for the right thing to say under the circumstances, "to make you happy." I finished with what I hoped was a sad smile.

He was still driving, still heading for Big Max's and I had to get him to stop, had to get him to turn the engine off before we got any closer or he changed his mind. I thought about how I'd seen Suzie act. Maybe if I could emulate her it would be more realistic and he would be more likely to believe me.

"You feel so good," I murmured, thrusting out my chest as if I couldn't help myself. Back arched, I felt the throbbing pain start up again in my groin as too much of my weight was put on it. I tried to change the angle at which I sat, taking the strain off my injured body but it was impossible to get anywhere near being comfortable. I settled for less pain rather than no pain. "We could have so much more fun if you stopped the car..." I tried to make it sound like a suggestion, a good idea that he should act upon and not an escape plan.

"Well-" He never got any further before something hit the front of the car and bounced off the windscreen, smashing it into a thousand fragmented pieces.

CHAPTER 18A

11.30 p.m.

I'd almost become so caught up in the idea of Suzie and Rhys that I'd forgotten why we were there in the first place. Stacey's dad's shouted demand brought us back to the present with a bump.

"I DON'T KNOW WHERE SHE WENT!" Rhys shouted back, flecks of spittle flying outwards from the corners of his mouth. The volume and anger directed at the distraught man seemed strangely out of context. Was it because Rhys felt he was being accused of something he hadn't done, or was there an element of guilt there too? Did he feel that in some way he'd betrayed me? I rankled at the thought of him and Suzie…it was right under my nose and I'd never even suspected.

"Why does everyone think I've had something to do with her not going home?" He stormed over to where a large crate of beers stood on the kitchen counter and pulled one free of the packaging, rummaging in a drawer to find the bottle opener.

As if we were encased within the most delicate of glass globes which would shatter with the slightest of movements, no one spoke. In the short time that it took him to locate the opener, use it and swallow a swig of beer, I felt as if the illumination in the room had changed.

The bulb which hung from the light fixture no doubt gave off the same amount of light that it had mere minutes before, but the quality of that light appeared somehow redefined, as if it no longer illuminated everything and everyone equally, but sought instead to amplify some things and reduce others, bending around them in a way that should have been impossible.

Shadows on the wall seemed larger and more lifelike and the angle at which the light was reflected off the numerous stainless-steel appliances and utensils seemed more acute. It felt like all the light in the room was focused on Rhys. As if it were a sentient being, compelled to wait for his answer.

"I think you'd better tell us what you *do* know," his father said sternly.

"I don't know any-"

"Stop it, Rhys!" Normally a quietly spoken woman, his mother's voice shook with fear and recrimination. "Stop it!" She moaned softly, dragging out a chair and sitting down with the weariness of a woman twice her age. We stood above her; with her and yet distanced from her.

"I can't stand any more of this, Rhys. I can't do it any longer!"

"Sarah – honey?" Rhys's dad looked from his wife to his son and back again uncomprehendingly.

"I tried to keep it from you, Frank, God help me I tried. But I can't stand it anymore...all the lies and the guilt." Sarah gave her husband a deeply apologetic look but when she turned back to Rhys the look was gone and had been replaced by one of revulsion.

"Look I do'on know what is goin'on here," Stacey's dad gestured around, eyes wide and a little unfocused. "And I do'on wanna know neither. I just want my Stacey back!"

"Mr Papadopoulos...I'm so sorry about this! But I think we'd better get this all out before we get much further." Sarah turned from Stacey's dad but she didn't look at Rhys. Averting her eyes as if she could not bear to look at her son, she pleaded, "Rhys, *please* tell him where his daughter went!"

"I don't KNOW where she went!" Rhys shouted, face pulled into a scowl.

Bolting upright and thrusting the chair away from her, Sarah was at Rhys's side in an instant, her fingers knotting into the material of his shirt, pulling at the thin fabric, her face fraught with fear. Rhys tried to pull away from her, tried to shrug her off, but she held on tight. The bottle jerked in his hand and then slipped away, spinning through the air, discharging its contents over the clean floor and landing with a clang.

"Tell him where his daughter went, Rhys and I'll help you as much as I can. I promise." She closed her eyes for a second and I saw her throat swallow. "I'll do what I can for you." Her eyes bulged and a rapid pulse beat against her temple, marking time with her words. I stood rooted to the spot, mesmerised by what she'd said and what might be implied within the words. It felt like I was in a Jerry Springer show. Perhaps any minute now, Stacey would come bounding in and renounce me for being a bad friend and Rhys as a bad date.

"I swear I don't know!" Rhys shook his head at his mother, discharging thick tears which fell unheeded. In spite of what I'd learned about him and Suzie, my heart bled for him. To be treated so humiliatingly and in front of us all, was just too embarrassing.

"Sarah, what the hell's going on here?" Frank dragged his wife off of his son and held them at arm's distance apart from one another. But Sarah wasn't finished.

"You swear it, do you Rhys? Like the time you swore you weren't sleeping with Suzie? Then like the time you swore that the baby wasn't yours, couldn't be yours?" Her voice was strange, laced with accusation and blame. And something else I couldn't quite put my finger on.

"We've been over and over this, Sarah. It's

done, can't be undone! The boy's learned his lesson. He knows it was a mistake…"

His wife rounded on his wife. "Learned his lesson? *His* mistake? What about *our* mistake? What about our mistake in ever trusting him again? Because now he has brought some other mess to our door!" Her face contorted and blackened in disgust. She turned to her son. "Tell them."

Rhys's only answer was a strangulated sound, neither intelligible nor recognisable.

"You never did have the guts to own up to anything did you, Rhys?" Frank said slowly. "I haven't got a clue how this all fits with this girl's disappearance but since my son is clearly somehow involved, I guess you have a right to know about him." He spoke directly to Stacey's dad.

"We moved away, not because of my job - that was just a story we told everyone. We moved away to get him away from her," he gestured vaguely, meaning I assumed, the absent Suzie. He took a step away from Rhys, resting his hands on the back of the empty chair.

"We thought he was mixing with a bad crowd so we moved. But do you know the irony? I lost my new job and we ended up having to come back here anyway." He shoved the kitchen chair back into place so hard that it clattered against the table, knocking over the salt cellar and spilling it in the centre of the wood.

"But it didn't matter whether we had stayed away or come back because even in a new town where he knew no one, Rhys had managed to find the lowest of low-life scum to hang out with, just as he did here..." He turned his attention to his wife. "So what else do you know? What do you know that you haven't told me? What other skeletons are you hiding for him?"

"Nothing!" she whispered, refusing to meet his eyes, fingers picking at the fallen grains of salt as if she intended to put them back in the cellar.

Frank leaned forward and stilled her hands. "That's not what you said a minute ago. How bad can it be? It can't be worse than finding out about Suzie!" He took a deep breath. "For the boy's own good you have to tell us what you know. Keeping things hidden for him will only make it worse..."

Sarah looked at their joined hands on the table. Saying nothing, she slowly withdrew her hands from under her husband's.

"Mum, don't," Rhys begged. Sarah didn't look at him.

"Don't what, Rhys? What is it that you don't want her to say?" Frank demanded.

Rhys lowered his head under his father's withering stare.

"Let these people go, Frank, let them get on with their search," Sarah smiled vaguely at us, as if finding Stacey was not her primary concern.

"I want to know what you're hiding for him,

Sarah. I want to know what *you* know." Frank held his wife's gaze unwaveringly.

"He didn't know what would happen...he couldn't have..." Sarah stuttered. The tension in the room, already heavy, seemed to concentrate further so that the air felt gloopy and dense.

"Mum! Please!" Rhys begged frantically. "Please! No!"

I held my breath, afraid that if I let it loose, it would change everything, shatter it beyond recognition.

"What are you talking about?" Frank said quietly, but when he got no answer he took a step closer to his son, focusing on the boy's face. "What's your mother talking about, Rhys?"

Rhys didn't answer. Tears washed down his face and he seemed to have forgotten that we were in the room. He held his arms out as if in supplication or entreaty but neither his mother nor father moved forward into the embrace.

Sarah held a hand to her mouth and for a moment I thought she was going to be sick but instead she spoke through her fingers. "I'm doing this for you, Rhys! Just like I've done everything, your whole life! Tried to protect you...I thought I was helping...but now I see..." she trailed off. The hand that had been slack at her side rose up to clasp the other hand. Fingers interlaced, she held them before her as if in prayer.

"The weekend you were away, a few months

ago, sorting out that big account, do you remember?" Sarah asked her husband. He nodded silently. "And when you came back I said that Rhys was unwell, that he had a bug of some sort?"

Again he nodded. "You kept him off school."

"Yes, I did, God forgive me. It wasn't a bug! It was a hangover! And whiplash from the impact."

"Whiplash?" Frank asked incredulously. "From a car accident?"

Sarah nodded. "He had a bruise all the way across his chest from the seatbelt. From here to here." She ran a hand diagonally across herself, from one shoulder to the opposite hip.

I wondered why the exact location of the bruise was significant but Nathan had grasped it more immediately.

"He was sitting on the driver's side," he breathed softly.

Without turning in our direction, Sarah picked up on the remark. "Not just on the driver's *side* but in the driver's seat!"

"But he can't drive!" Now it was Rhys's dad's turn to pull out a chair and sit down.

"Mum! *No!*" Rhys begged, his arms still held out to his mother. I tried frantically to piece together this new information; to realise what the whole picture was.

Sarah shook her head but held herself back. "We have to get this out, Rhys. The guilt is killing me!" She looked her husband directly in the eyes as she spoke, but her voice was directed at all of us.

"He didn't see the other car. It wasn't his fault...she was driving fast and there was a bend and she had her full beam on and..." Sarah spread her hands helplessly, then clutched them together, pulled them into her lap. She looked like she was about to pray.

At the side of the wall, Rhys sank to his knees but I could feel no sorrow or pity for him. All I could feel was shock. I remembered the man in the bar. The one whose wife had been killed in a hit-and-run. Was it his wife they were discussing?

"She died, didn't she?" my dad said in a half-whisper, as if he had never meant to say it out loud. Even so, it found its way to each and every one of us who stood in that kitchen, watching as Rhys's parents' lives fell apart.

"She died," he said, answering his own question. "And they never got the kids who did it but they found the car. It'd been stolen and was a burned-out wreck by the time they got it. All the evidence was either gone or contaminated..."

While he spoke, everyone's attention was riveted on my dad but then it swung back to Rhys and his parents as if that brief hiatus had been necessary to allow us to comprehend the full complexity and scale of the confession.

"And *you knew!*" Frank spat at his wife with loathing as if it had been her who had killed the woman. "You knew all this time and you covered up for him!"

Sarah was crying freely, mucus running down her nose and mingling with the tears. "I didn't know until the next morning when I caught him coming out of the bathroom. The diagonal bruise was fresh, as was the smell of drink on him. Then when I heard the news report, I put two and two together." She wiped her hands roughly across her face.

"The reporter said the woman was dead; killed instantly they thought. It wasn't like admitting it was Rhys was going to save her..." she implored. "He still had his whole life ahead of him, Frank. It was just one little mistake. And she was driving fast, too fast..."

Going down on one knee before his son, Frank looked like he intended to either lock him in an embrace or pray for his soul. So when he grasped Rhys by the throat and dragged him up so that they were both standing, I was shocked.

No one stepped in to intervene. Rhys stood pinned against the wall by his father, shaking in terror, his eyes as wide as a cornered animal's. Frank drew back his right arm as if he meant to punch the boy in the face but at the very last minute he diverted his aim, striking the wall to the right of the boy's head. The plaster cracked in a spider-web design. It must have hurt but Frank didn't make a sound. He dropped his hands from Rhys and took a step back, as if reluctant to be in such close proximity to his son. Not once did Rhys lift a hand in his own defence. Instead, he continued to cry loudly, fat tears rolling unchecked down his face.

Bringing my own hands to my face as if I could shield myself from the horror of the revelations, I realised that I too was weeping. Hot stinging tears bled from me. They fell for the unknown woman and her husband who I had met earlier. They fell too for Frank, and for Stacey and her parents, and perhaps even a little for Sarah, Rhys's mum. But not for Rhys. Not a single tear.

Without looking, I felt for Nathan's hand and knew that he was crying too.

As if he no longer regarded him as his son, Frank managed to quell the fire and disgust in his eyes long enough to bring his face close to his son's. "YOU TELL THIS MAN WHERE HIS DAUGHTER IS, OR I WILL KILL YOU WITH MY BARE HANDS!"

Rhys shook his head, snot flying in all directions. The action was like a red flag to a bull. Frank seized Rhys again in one hand, wrapping long fingers around the boy's throat, pinning him back to the wall. With the other hand, he slapped his son across the face. "TELL HIM WHERE SHE IS!"

CHAPTER 18B

11.30 p.m.

Whatever had hit the car, it had been big enough to cause damage. My mind raced while my gaze focused on the blood smeared on the shattered windscreen.

Luckily, I'd fixed my seatbelt when I'd climbed in the front. Unluckily, Shaun was similarly strapped in. But I'd still been slammed up hard against the dash, banging my head and making my nose bleed. There was pain in my shoulders and neck too. Almost as much pain as there was in my abdomen and groin and I wondered if I had broken a rib or shoulder. I could move my head, that much I already knew, because I'd turned it in the hope that Shaun would no longer be in the car. Whether he would be dead at the side of the road, having passed through the shattered but still fitted windscreen, or out of the car examining what he had hit, I really didn't care, although given the choice, the first would certainly have been preferable to the last.

But he was still in the driver's seat next to me looking dazed but unhurt.

"We hit something!" he said stupidly, looking down at his lap. "Are you hurt?" he asked.

It was a dumb question under the circumstances. I had been hurt even before the accident and a lot of that was his doing but I realised the question was more automatic than anything else – a reaction to the shock of the impact.

"A little, I think, but not much," I responded, wondering how this new turn of events would affect things. Would it have been better to have implied that I was badly wounded, that I needed a doctor? A hospital? Or would that have panicked him more? Would he have phoned Rhys or even Big Max? No, perhaps I had given the best answer I could have. "Are you alright?"

He nodded and my heart fell. After all the lectures we had in school about safety when driving...and here he was fuelled by alcohol, drugged up and yet still fine after an accident! There was truly no justice in the world.

"What did we hit?" I asked, hoping he would feel inclined to investigate.

He shrugged his shoulders. "Don't actually know if we hit it, or it hit us, but something happened."

Yes, something had happened. Somewhere out there, beyond the confines of this car, someone lay bleeding or dead. There were no other cars around and there had been no noise that I could remember, nothing to indicate that another car had been involved. We were surrounded by fields on a straight road that held no bends another car could have suddenly appeared from.

"Was it someone on a bike?" I asked as if he knew, trying to remember if I had noticed anyone. He shrugged once more. "You should go and see," I suggested, hoping that he would get out the car but leave the keys in the ignition.

He nodded, surprising me by taking my suggestion as an order. Then again it had looked like he was used to taking orders, either from Suzie or from Rhys. He opened his door and swung one leg out, leaving the keys untouched. My heart hammered so loudly I feared he would hear it. I tried not to think about my plan.

I could move across, start the engine and drive off! Except for two things, my brain unhelpfully supplied. The first was that I didn't know how to drive. But if numbskulls like Shaun could drive, whether legally or not, how hard could it be?

The other thought was more gruesome. If whoever we'd hit now lay on the road in front of the car, I would have to drive *over* them to get away. If they were alive I would effectively be killing them and if they were already dead, I would be desecrating their body. Even if I knew how to reverse, the problem would not be solved. The injured person could just as easily be at the back of the car as the front!

Whilst these considerations ate at my conscience, survival instinct battling moral dilemma, Shaun removed the quandary for me by reaching over and snatching the keys at the very last moment. Now my only hope of getting away was to follow him out of the car.

I climbed out of my side and resisted the urge to immediately run away. The best thing to do was to assess the situation. Perhaps if someone were injured, Shaun could be convinced to take them to a hospital and I could make my escape there. I walked around the front of the car. A body lay there, perfectly still and completely impassive. My spit turned to a foul paste in my mouth and my stomach heaved. There was a thin coppery smell to the air which combined with the stench of burned rubber to make me feel lightheaded and queasy. I bent down towards the body.

Light brown hair flecked with its own blood, its fur matted and filthy, it was not a person at all. It was a painfully thin, unkempt dog. A stray that had seen only misery and misfortune in its life and that had now had the saddest demise ever.

"Is it dead?" I asked, bending down, full of pity for the poor creature whose fate had become so entwined with my own. The lost and broken empathising with the equally lost and broken, I felt a kindred-ship with the dog that was in direct

271

contrast to how I felt about the human next to me.

To my horror he booted the poor thing as it lay there, injured and defenceless. It gave out a thin yelp but did nothing to shield itself. And in that moment I hated him so completely I would have buried a knife in his belly if I'd had one to hand. I would have twisted it cruelly and with malicious intent have withdrawn it, only so that I could reinsert it deeper into him.

"If it's not dead yet it soon will be! Fucking thing nearly scared the life out of me!" he said angrily and without the slightest shred of compassion. He pulled his leg backwards as if preparing to strike it once more. I hauled my agonised body upwards, ignoring the pain, focusing on his leg and putting myself between him and the dog.

For a moment he seemed inclined to move around and past me to the creature or alternatively just to kick me instead. I held his gaze, challenging him without words. He dropped his eyes from mine and backed off slightly.

"You think it's hurt that badly?" I asked, managing to keep my voice even, my compassion hidden. He was probably right, I told myself. The fact that it still hadn't moved probably proved that.

"Well, if it isn't yet, it will be by the time I drive over its sorry carcass." There was a not-quite-laugh in his voice. The word sorry, often used to invoke pity, was used for an altogether different purpose.

I couldn't let him kill the dog. If I stood by and let that happen, I would deserve every bad thing that happened to me. To save myself, I had to first save the dog. I thought fast. "Rhys will go mad if he hears that you left more evidence. If you run over this dog, there will be all sorts of tyre tracks and things…"

I wasn't sure of my facts but figured that his fear of Rhys was my one weapon. Perhaps it didn't matter that the car was stolen and he had been ordered to burn it out. If he did what he said, he would be leaving evidence on the road and he knew it.

"S'only a dog, for fuck's sake!" he said, annoyed at my logic but unable to entirely dismiss it.

"Exactly!" I worked more logic on him. "It's only a dog, so just let it be. We can move it to the bushes at the side of the road there," I pointed only a little way off, where at least the dog would be safe from other cars. "Probably no one will ever find it…and then we can park somewhere and get on with what we'd planned." My stomach recoiled at the thought of him laying his hands on me.

"OK!" he said reluctantly, grabbing the creature's back legs and leaving me with its head and upper body.

Placing my hands under the dog's coat, I

could feel the papery skin covering its bones and how it shook in fear and shock at our touch. I tried to be extra gentle to compensate for Shaun's roughness but I saw the pain reflected in its eyes as it looked up at me pitifully. A thin whine issued from it wheezily and for a moment I thought it had breathed its last as its cheeks puffed up and down and then became still. But its breathing must have regulated because it blinked suddenly. *Stay alive,* I thought at it, hoping that what they said about dogs being intuitive was true.

Tenderly, I placed the dog's head and upper body on the ground under the bush. Shaun tried to throw it down, but as I was supporting most of its weight he didn't achieve the impact he had hoped for. It was trembling, lungs now bellowing laboriously and I worried that the cold air would worsen its condition. I had no clothing to cover it with and nothing soft to lay under it. If only Shaun would agree to put the bed linen around it...but I knew without even asking that he wouldn't.

I'm coming back for you, I promise! I made the silent vow to the dog, running my hand softly over its head, feeling its fear and distress and pain magnify my own perilous situation, amplify the desperation I felt.

"Leave it...let's go," said Shaun, straightening up. I pulled myself slowly upright. Terrible pain and fear made acting unnecessary in attempting to look as if I truly could move at no quicker speed. But as he took his first few steps away from me and the dog, I plunged through the bramble of the bush and into the open field beyond. And I ran.

Pain streaking through me like a hot flame, I ran.

CHAPTER 19A

11.45 p.m.

"TELL HIM WHERE STACEY IS!"

Rhys snivelled, trying to pull free of his father, but Frank held him fast. His top was crumpled where the material had been balled and there was a slight tear across one of the seams. I fastened my attention on those few undone stitches, on the thread which hung loose and free, its duty to bind the material together, abandoned. Part of me was surprised at the ease with which the garment was unravelling, unveiling its fixings in a way that had never been meant to happen.

Only gradually did I realise that my father had slipped his arm around me protectively and that I was still crying. I wasn't alone. Of all of us in the room, only Rhys's father was dry-eyed, his face as arid as dust. Perhaps his tears had been shocked into submission; perhaps they would come later. Or perhaps not at all. Maybe they never would. Shock, I realised, is like grief - personal and brooding.

"Where is my girl? I beg you..." Mr Papadopoulos took a step towards Rhys. His face had a grey tinge which sat under his normal olive complexion like a dark angel awaiting its moment to strike. He had aged ten years in the short time since the afternoon and his eyes were rimmed with black shadows. Tears coursed down his cheeks and ran off his face in rivulets. But never once did his gaze waiver from Rhys.

Rhys cowered under his father's hands. A livid red handprint still marked his cheek where he had been slapped and it stood out in contrast to his otherwise pale skin. I swallowed hard, fighting the emotion down inside of me and focused on the red stain.

"Frank, let him go," Sarah implored, clutching at her husband's hands, trying to wrench them from her son. Frank shook her off easily and her hands fell once more to her sides before trembling and fluttering up into the air like small birds hunted by a larger one. They had almost taken on a life of their own and she struggled to contain them, finally clasping them together, bringing them once more to her face in a parody of prayer.

Shoving Rhys away from himself, Frank wiped his hands down his jeans, as if trying to remove the feel of the boy's skin under them. Rhys raised his hands to rub at his throat which already looked bruised, but still said nothing, refusing to divulge any information he had.

His eyes were wide and yet they maintained a guarded look. His mouth remained resolutely closed.

"We have to call the police," my father said, pulling out his phone and already beginning to key in the number. I half expected one or both of Rhys's parents to object, but to my surprise it was Stacey's father who stopped him.

"Not yet," he said, placing his hand over the phone and holding it there, preventing my father from continuing the call.

"Please, *please* don't mention the car accident," Sarah begged. "It's got nothing to do with your daughter being missing…"

"Have you learned *nothing* from this?" Frank asked his wife. "Are you still prepared to cover up for him and what he's done?" He turned to my dad. "Call the police, it's our best bet to find the girl quickly."

Stacey's dad shook his head. "No. This boy is our best bet." He looked at Rhys with obvious contempt. "Get my daughter back safe and I make this easier for you."

I wondered if he knew what he was promising, wondered what part he thought that Rhys had played in Stacey's disappearance. Sarah nodded desperately, eager for her son to accept the deal. Her eyes were too bright, too shiny. They conveyed only desperation.

Rhys looked at his mother for a few moments

before he found his voice at last. "I won't have to go to jail?" There was something different about his voice that I couldn't put my finger on, some cunning that I hadn't heard previously. It made me even more uneasy than before.

The adults looked around at one another as if seeking a consensus of opinion. Every face had its own version of resignation written large upon it, as if the truth were something that they recognised as being often hard-won and frequently a bitter pill to swallow. Sarah reached for the support of her husband but her questing hand was left empty.

Although I hadn't been aware of him moving, Frank stood as far away from his wife and son as the conformities of the room would allow. I think we were all waiting for him to respond with words of reassurance but he seemed completely impassive. The silence stretched out into an interminably long minute until finally it was my dad who spoke.

"I think that decision will ultimately be up to the courts...but if Mr Papadopoulos speaks up for you and tells them that he got his daughter back safe and sound, it'll go a long way..."

"She's at Big Max's house," Rhys blurted out, eyes cast down towards the floor.

"Where's that?" my dad asked.

Rhys shrugged. "It's on the other side of town."

"Give us the address!" My father and Stacey's spoke simultaneously but it was Sarah who cut through their words.

"Is Stacey alright?" she asked Rhys slowly and frighteningly quietly, as if she would've done anything rather than voice the question. Or hear its answer.

The question surprised me. How was Rhys supposed to know that, if Stace had gone off alone...and then the implication dawned on me. She hadn't gone off on her own as he had stated. It was *all* a lie!

I felt Nathan squeeze my hand but I couldn't remove my gaze from Rhys who remained where he was but let his eyes travel the room, allowing them only to halt when they alighted once more on his mother.

Even before he opened his mouth I knew that things could never be the same again – that *I* would never be the same again.

"She was teasing me, Mum, saying how Nat had stood me up...and she was so pretty and she smelled so good..." his attention was focused solely on his mother, as if no one else existed. Sarah's hands slid down from her face and without their support her expression crumpled. She raised her hand to her ears as if trying to ward off the words but the confession continued, hammering stones into the place where her heart used to reside. I knew that because it was exactly how I felt.

"She wanted it as much as I did…but then she pulled away…" little-boy tone delivering the rapists' mantra. Every feature in his face shouted out his belief in his right to take what he wanted.

Stacey's father sank in slow motion to his knees. The air seemed to have a breathless quality to it, like the vacuum of space. Mr Papadopoulos's face was a horror mask, lips pulled back in a soundless grimace, cheeks hollowed out by the elongated O. I could see his chest pulsate once, twice, three times before becoming still. For a long moment he held the pose – a rigid marionette – before crashing to the floor.

My dad redialled on his phone. "We need an ambulance at…" he looked at me for the address but my mind whirled with everything but the right answer.

"What's the address here?" he shouted, frustration and fear leaking from his voice. Rhys' father held his hand out for the phone and my dad passed it to him. Through a dense mist I heard him talking to the controller.

"Yes we need an ambulance and police officers…"

I guess he gave the address but there were too many other things going on for me to notice. My dad knelt on the floor pounding on Stacey's dad's chest. Nathan helped him, holding Mr Papadopoulos's head and counting out loud.

But my attention was riveted on Rhys and his mother. Sarah had moved close to him again and for a moment seemed undecided how to react. In the stark light of the kitchen, her eyes were pools of infinite sorrow; playgrounds where the dust of dead children played hide and seek with the wind. And as she held her arms out to her only child - her son - I saw the true depth of her misery. A faint groan escaped her, a sound of the most complete wretchedness and desolation, that it seemed to have stemmed from her very soul.

That sound burned into me like no other and I swear that if I live to be a hundred I shall never ever forget its desperate and anguished arabesque.

Taller than her by some way, in her arms Rhys looked like the little boy he had once been and less of the monster that I realised he had become.

I looked at the face I knew so well - the boy I had virtually grown up with. Where had that boy gone? And who was this stranger that I saw before me? What had happened to him, to have turned him into this?

"Why?" I asked, as if any answer could ever deliver us from this pain, could even go any way to making this right, justifying his actions.

Glassy-eyed, he regarded me as if he had only noticed me for the very first time.

"Why what?" he asked me stupidly. Did he think that the confession absolved him of his sins?

"Why did you rape her? Because that's what you're telling us you did, isn't it, you bastard! You *raped* her!" My voice had risen and broken with the accusation. Without being aware that I had moved closer, I beat my fists on his back, pummelled him wherever I could reach.

Strong hands dragged me off. My father still attended to Mr Papadopoulos, pumping on his chest and breathing into his mouth. Nathan still helped him. That left Rhys's dad who I assumed was the person holding me back. I fought against the restraining hands.

"Leave him, he's not worth it!" I didn't know if Frank was talking to me or his wife, or both of us, but before I could figure it out, my dad was at my side once more.

"He's going to be alright, I think," he said, nodding in Mr Papadopoulos's direction. "I know the ambulance and police are on their way…" Distantly I could hear approaching sirens. "But it will take a while to fully explain the situation to them, time Stacey might not have…"

He never got to finish the sentence.

Frank cut in. "Rhys, you are going to take us to that girl and we are going to get her back!" Grasping his son by the sleeve, he dragged him away from Sarah who crumbled to the hard, cold floor, arms empty and eyes vacant. I noticed how Frank seemed reluctant to touch Rhys's bare skin where it showed below the bunched-up sleeve, pulling on the fabric of the shirt instead. He handled him as if he were a venomous snake instead of his own flesh and blood.

"Natalie and Nathan, you stay here with Sarah and Mr Papadopoulos…" my dad started to say but stopped when he saw the distraught look I cast him. He cast a quick look at the two prostrate people on the floor. Neither of them would be any help to anyone, nor would they benefit from anything other than the most intensive medical care.

"Look honey, Stacey might be in a bad state – it's not something I want you to have to see… And this house where she is…well, there might be…anything going on there," he explained. "And someone needs to stay here until the paramedics arrive."

"Dad, it could have been me instead of Stacey! I have to see her! I have to be there for her! She will be so scared…" whatever betrayal I had felt at Stace stepping into my shoes on the date had evaporated. No matter how badly she'd acted, she didn't deserve this! No one deserved this.

"Sarah's made her bed, guess she's the one will be lying in it!" Frank said, not even willing to look in his wife's direction.

My dad looked at Nathan who still knelt by Mr Papadopoulos. "Can you stay and fill the police and paramedics in?" he asked.

Nathan's eyes met mine, silently searching for the answer I wanted him to give. Without words I implored him to stay just until the ambulance arrived and to understand that I could not. He nodded and in that moment I knew that he would always put me first.

"Once he's in the ambulance, go home," I urged him, knowing how important that was. We smiled grimly at one another. The night, already full of unanticipated events seemed to be spiralling uncontrollably away from us, whilst a yawning pit opened at our feet. I had a horrible feeling that it was only the start.

Whilst Rhys's dad made him scrawl down the address we would be heading to, I used the time to deliver a quick kiss to Nathan's cheek. It was as natural and as right under the circumstances as anything else I'd done and I was neither embarrassed nor uncomfortable about showing the affection in front of my dad.

Everything had changed. The rules of our world had been smashed and it was a cold dark universe that we prepared to enter. If I could not have Nathan with me in person, I would be taking him in spirit. I hoped that he held some vestige of me in him, to give comfort and support. What lay ahead for him in the unfolding blackness of the night would be as daunting and life changing as what awaited me.

"Just stay safe!" he whispered to me.

"And you," I whispered back.

We were both about to embark on rescue missions we were thoroughly unprepared for. Anything could happen and even though the police would not be far behind either of us, I knew that there was still a huge element of risk. But that was outweighed by the very real danger that we now knew Stacey to be in. Every second counted. Every single second.

We flew out of the door leaving it swinging open behind us.

CHAPTER 19B

11.45 p.m.

The field was dry and firm. And my feet were bare, devoid of the heels I'd worn earlier. But that was where the good luck ended. The land had been ploughed recently and there were ruts and furrows that seemed to swallow up my steps, making progress slower than I would have liked.

Running as fast as I could, I was aware that it resembled more of a speedy lurch than a smooth glide and whist I was in no way concerned with the aesthetics of my actions, I *was* concerned about the consequences. I was also concerned about where I could run *to.*

Other than the road I'd escaped from, the field was bordered on all sides by other fields, flat land which allowed no hiding places, no source of rescue. No hope. The only way of getting away from Shaun here was to outrun him; in bare, bruised feet and with possible internal injuries that was less than impossible.

And yet he didn't seem to be in pursuit! I stopped in my tracks for a moment to listen. Was he sneaking in from another angle, somewhere ahead of me, planning to cut me off in my path? I looked back the way I'd come. For a moment there was nothing and then suddenly the scene darkened as the headlights of the car were switched off.

Had he realised that if he left them on, some passer-by, some Good Samaritan might stop and then he would be found out? Possibly. Or maybe he was just ensuring that he would save the car battery.

But perhaps I was far enough away that the night would shroud me in its darkness? There were no streets and therefore no streetlighting. Only the moon illuminated the land below. Perhaps if I continued cautiously, making as little noise as possible, I could get far enough away that he would never find me. Then I could make my way back to the road at a higher point than I'd entered the field and find some nearby houses at which to beg for help. It seemed like the only plan available.

A spindly tree in the distance was the sole thing which alerted me to the fallacy of the plan. If I could see the tree as it stood in its stark aloneness in the field, picked out darkly by the overhead moon like a silhouette, an artist's impression of a tree rather than the real thing, then surely I too could be picked out just as easily?

I waited for him to whisper insidiously in my ear as if the moon colluded with him and not me, obscuring him in the darkness like an evil cloak whilst I was illuminated by its bright countenance. But still he did not appear. Undecided what to do for the best, I hesitated. Where I stood I could run in any direction. Therefore logic said that regardless of the direction in which he approached, there would be three clear other directions available for escape. But for how long?

How long would he wait before he called for reinforcements? Ten minutes? More? Less?

With a start I realised that I was shaking. I had assumed at first it was the natural response to my imminent danger and the necessity of flight. But my breathing had slowed to an almost normal pace, my lungs were no longer fit to burst and yet I trembled like an octogenarian. Coldness seeped thought to the marrow of my bones and my vision was distorted. The blackness of the night seemed to have a texture to it that I hadn't noticed before, as well as an earthy coppery smell. But most frightening of all was that the night seemed to throb, appeared to eddy and well, before my eyes as if I stood on the threshold of a vortex.

I realised that I was in dire trouble. If I stayed where I was I would either be recaptured or die of blood loss. My blood pressure was lowering with every trickle of blood that seeped from me and if I didn't get help soon it would be too late. As if to underline the realisation, my vision dimmed dramatically as my body tried to shut down to save itself. I struggled to stay conscious and focused.

If I passed out it would be the end of me! And somewhere out there Shaun hunted me. It was just a matter of time!

Pain washed over me as I forced myself to take a single step forward. Perhaps adrenaline had got me this far, had masked my nerve endings and covered my pain receptors allowing me the luxury of pushing myself beyond my physical limits - but it had either run out or no longer worked. I was racked by pain so intensely that I almost wished I could die. Unbidden, my eyelids fluttered shut and my body folded to the hard, compacted earth below...and then imprinted on the back of my eyelids, I saw something which made me gasp for breath.

I saw a booted foot make contact with a soft and broken furry body. In my mind's eye I relived the moment that Shaun had kicked the injured dog. That precise second when he had discarded the very last shreds of his humanity, even more so than during what had been done to me...

If I lay down and died, I would be letting him get away with that. And not only would *I* die but the dog would too, and hadn't I vowed to it that I would come back for it? That I would *save* it?

Perhaps it was silly but it was that thought which drove me onwards and as the seconds pooled into minutes, other thoughts and images entered my head. I used every one of them mercilessly, placing one foot in front of the other, heading back towards the road at a higher point than I had left it. I saw the image of my mother as if she were bent over my coffin, her face pale and lined with grief. I took a step forward.

I lifted my foot once more and thrust myself onwards as I saw my father place a hand on her shoulder, his face filled with unvoiced anguish. I moved my weight to the other side of my body and stepped again, using the resultant pain to fill out the image in my head of my friends at school gathered around my graveside, of Stacey bereft without her best friend...I edged forward and this time I saw Rhys standing at my grave, crocodile tears flowing freely down his face.

Like a presentiment of doom I felt the vision meant something. Was there something I was missing? Something I had failed to take into consideration? Why had Shaun not yet come after me?

Because he was watching from where he stood, hidden in the bushes! Whichever way I went he could see me clearly and merely had to wait for me to arrive! I stopped dead in my tracks.

It was then that for the first time that night, I felt fate take pity on me. Perhaps luck is a sentient thing after all, perhaps it lies in wait to see how far someone will go to help themselves before it decides whether or not to intervene. Or perhaps it is as inert as we generally think it to be, but at that moment it arrived in the shape of a dark puddle of mud.

I had taken one step into the slime before I was even aware of it. Smooth and slippery, it stole my footing and plunged me into its filthy mire. Thick sludge covered me head to toe, sticking my clothes to me and pasting my entire body in its filth. Under my breath I cursed this new development but the expletives died on my lips as I hauled myself from the shallow bog.

Where before the moonlight had held me encased in its beams, now the faint light seemed to glance off me, to bend around me as if I were but a figment of the imagination. Covered in mud I was invisible in the night sky. I was camouflaged!

But my course had already been plotted before this most recent development and I would have been foolhardy to have continued blithely onwards to where Shaun already no doubt waited for me to emerge.

Desperately tired and aching and only just managing to hold onto consciousness, I fell to my knees and crawled back in the direction from which I'd come. If I was wrong and he waited there for me then I would have lost - but somehow I felt that finally my luck had turned. I was aiming for a little way past the spot where I had entered the field. A little way up and even further from where he presumably waited.

Painstakingly slowly, I continued to crawl

until the bushes were just ahead, their thick foliage obscuring the road beyond and anything that waited there.

It was then that I saw the approaching headlights.

CHAPTER 20A

MIDNIGHT

I got in the backseat of the car with Rhys's dad whilst my dad climbed back behind the wheel and Rhys got in the front passenger side. The clunk of doors closing and seatbelts being strapped in was the only noise before the engine revved back into life.

Rhys had stopped snivelling, for the moment anyway. He seemed to be tensely coiled as if waiting for something to happen. I wondered what thoughts raced through his head. It was impossible to know but more than likely he was afraid for his future. I certainly hoped he was. I hoped that he worried he'd be locked away in a dark cell for the rest of his life and I also hoped his fears were well founded and became reality!

"Which way?" my dad turned to him as the car began to roll forward.

Rhys leaned towards my dad and pointed. "Go..." and in an instant he had released his seatbelt - or perhaps he had never connected it in the first place, flung open the door and launched himself out of it, rolling onto the hard tarmac. Immediately he picked himself up and sprinted up the road ahead of us, disappearing through a hedge.

"Drive!" Frank barked, diving out of the rear door in determined pursuit of his son.

My dad floored the pedal and without even taking the time to close either of the doors, sped up the road. The doors clunked open and half-shut a few times, straining the hinges and I worried that one or both would catch the side of the parked cars we passed, sending us into a spin and eventually a crash but he skilfully avoided all obstacles and soon our sheer speed forced the doors to slam shut.

Confined to the car, we twisted and turned through the narrow residential streets, following by road as closely as we could. Every so often we would catch a glimpse of either Rhys or Frank but it was as much guesswork as it was deduction where they would emerge.

"You ever heard of this Big Max?" Dad asked as the car slewed around yet another tight corner. Even strapped in I was sliding around on the back seat, only just managing to keep my balance. I shook my head 'no' before realising that he was too focused on the road to see me in the rear-view mirror.

"No. Never."

"Then we have nothing else to go on, except for Rhys!" Dad commented worriedly. "Did you see the address he wrote down?" he asked hopefully.

"No. But we'll find her, won't we, Dad?" I knew that he couldn't actually say any words of reassurance but I needed to hear them anyway. The night was so dark and the circumstances so strange that it had an other-worldly feel to it – I couldn't quite believe what was going on.

"We *have* to find her!" he said at once. It wasn't the reassurance that I had hoped for. Instead it was a confirmation of the urgency of our task which left me with a dry mouth and writhing snakes in the pit of my stomach.

I scanned the velvet night outside the side window. "There! Over there!"

The car screeched around another corner in the direction I had indicated. It was a dead end! A large brick wall stood at the head of a cul-de-sac and my heart sank. We had lost Rhys! But as the car beams straightened up, Rhys and his dad were picked out in glorious technicolour!

Unable to scale the wall, Rhys panicked and turned in the direction of the beams, seeking another escape route. But any way out necessitated him passing the car and he had hesitated a fraction too long.

Not even seeing Frank as he emerged from the gloom, Rhys was caught by the throat and thrown by his father up against the wall. There was a brief struggle but Rhys was no physical match for the older man. Frank drew back his arm before thrusting it forward, his fist connecting with the side of Rhys's jaw.

There was an audible thud which I heard even over the noise of the idling engine as Rhys's head flew backwards into the brick. A thin trickle of blood spurted from his lip and he seemed dazed. Gasping for breath from the chase, Frank seemed less concerned about getting his breath back than on punishing his son. He drew back his elbow a second time. Abandoning the car with the engine running and the lights on, my dad threw himself from the car, laying a restraining arm on Frank before he could release another punch.

"This isn't getting the girl back!" he said quietly.

The look that Frank turned on my dad was equally split between rage and despair. My dad didn't back down. I saw Frank's mouth open and close but no words came out. Perhaps he was out of breath, perhaps it was just that whatever he felt, words were not strong enough to convey. A look of purest contempt filled his face as he looked back at Rhys but he nevertheless relinquished his hold on him and threw him towards my father.

I watched my dad take hold of Rhys and drag him to the back of the car where I sat alone. Opening the door he placed a hand reluctantly on Rhys's head, bending him and forcing him into the back, next to me.

Thinking that I would be required to get in the front I opened my door and prepared to step out. "Stay there, Natalie!" my dad instructed as Frank climbed in too, so that Rhys was sandwiched between us.

My flesh crawled at the close proximity of him, pushed into the side of me as he was. Up close he reeked of alcohol and stale sweat and other smells I couldn't quite define. In the overhead interior light which flickered on above my door his eyes appeared bloodshot, his pupils dilated to extreme proportions.

He was snivelling. There was a cut just above one of his eyebrows and blood and tears ran down his face together. Sweat had spiked up his hair in places and dampened it down in others and dirt was streaked across one cheek. He reminded me a little of how the hero tended to look in action movies but the irony that he was the villain, not the hero, didn't escape me.

He ran the back of one hand under his nose, wiping a thin smear of blood and mucus across the already dirty cheek and leaving a thick trail of bloodied snot across his hand. I recoiled from his presence, pushing myself against the door as much as possible so that no part of me came into contact with any part of him.

"You pull a stunt like that again...or send us in the wrong direction, and so help me," Frank's voice quivered with suppressed emotion, "I *will* kill you!"

In any other circumstances the words might have been an empty threat, an exaggeration at worst. Then and there we all recognised the truth of them.

"But you don't understand...Max will have me killed for telling...Stacey might not be the only girl there..." Rhys snivelled.

There was a moment of shocked silence while we all digested his words and what they implied.

"Right now at this very moment," Frank looked at his son as if seeing him for the very first time, "I don't care if he does." It was said with such dispassion that even I gasped.

"Dad, you don't mean that!" Rhys protested.

Frank ignored the plea. "Which way, Rhys?" he demanded as my dad pointed the car out of the cul-de-sac.

"DAD! SAY YOU DON'T MEAN IT!" Rhys bellowed, turning towards his father as much as the tight confines would allow.

"I don't *have* a son anymore!" Frank said with a calmness I wondered at. And then his voice rose in a crescendo of emotion that blew us all away. "But if you don't point us in the right direction for that girl, I will strangle you with my *own fucking hands* right this VERY MINUTE!"

Between thick gulping sobs Rhys pointed out the way.

CHAPTER 20B

MIDNIGHT

Headlights approached from the direction in which we'd been travelling. I would have preferred that they had been going the opposite way, back towards home…but it was better than nothing.

As far as I was aware there had been no cars passing through this stretch of road since Shaun had driven us along it, so this approaching car might be my only chance to escape. I couldn't afford to miss it.

And yet…what if it was Shaun? Perhaps he thought he could lure me out like this? Perhaps he thought that it would be easier to have me flag him down, than to try to search for me.

Would I be able to see the driver before he or she got close enough to see me? It was a risk. If I waited too long before revealing myself, he or she might not see me and then I would have revealed my position to Shaun without any means of escape! But I couldn't just assume that the driver was someone other than Shaun either!

The car came closer and I strained my eyes to see the figure behind the wheel as well as the shape and size of the vehicle itself. Whatever its colour, it appeared to have a more metallic sheen to it than the one Shaun had stolen and yet I couldn't be completely sure. Perhaps the sheen was an effect of the moonlight rather than the car paint.

Nor could I tell from the angle at which it approached whether it was a different size or shape! The windscreen! The car we'd been travelling in had had its windscreen shattered...but perhaps Shaun had merely kicked the broken glass from the frame?

I held my breath knowing that whatever decision I made would have consequences beyond the immediate. Salvation or surrender...which did the car and its driver represent?

A thin smell of diesel came to me but I didn't know if it was real or a figment of my imagination once more. And then suddenly another miracle occurred. The interior car light flickered on and stayed on, as if the driver needed illumination for some reason. Perhaps he or she searched for something with one free hand and couldn't find it in the dark? It was irrelevant for that one dim beam called to me like a beacon.

The driver was a woman! I could tell that by the long flowing hair which fell freely around her face. It wasn't Shaun! My heart bounded into my throat and I found I couldn't swallow. I prepared to leap out into the road ahead...and then one tiny, insidious thought slithered its way across my brain.

I was alone on a country road, covered head to toe in mud. The woman would take one swift look at me and speed faster on her way! How likely was it that she would stop for a stranger at this time of night and in this location? And that was before I took my appearance into consideration.

She would only stop if forced to... A dangerous idea sprang into my mind. There was a risk I would be killed but there again that risk had been around all evening and yet here I was, still alive! Maybe it was a chance I had to take!

The car was not close enough that its beams picked out the tarmac of the road by the side of where I crouched. The woman had either forgotten that the interior light was on or preferred to alleviate the darkness because she continued to drive towards me fully illuminated.

I positioned myself on the road ahead of her, sprawled out and looking as much like the victim of a hit-and-run as I could manage. I shut my eyes and held my breath. The noise of the approaching car grew closer and closer and I kept my eyes closed for fear that I would open them in the instant before the wheels ran over my prostrate body.

There was the faint sound of music played too high through low quality speakers, a sort of tinny warble to the notes. The car was seconds away and I prayed it would be able to stop in time.

Even through closed eyelids I felt the beam of the headlights as they discovered me on the road ahead. I counted silently, one, two, three... the wheels continued to turn, continued to bear down upon me...until suddenly there was a screech of brakes and a smell of burned rubber and the car skidded to a halt a hair's width away from crushing me to death.

"Oh my Lord!" the woman gasped, coming to stand over me. "Are you hurt, dear?" she asked. Her breath had a sugary scent to it as if she had been sucking a sweet and I wondered if that had been what she'd been searching for with the light on.

I worried about how to play it. I couldn't afford to scare her off but neither could I give Shaun enough time to catch us up. "I...I ..." I muttered as if coming round in unfamiliar circumstances.

"Oh my Lord!" she repeated, bending down to get a closer look.

I fluttered my eyelids open to find the most repulsive looking angel I have ever seen. Little piggy eyes looked down on me from a face that was too lardy and too heavily made up to ever be considered attractive.

"Can you walk, dearie?" she asked, seeming to

have enough problems heaving her own considerable bulk back up without trying to help me too. My brain appeared to have accepted the brief stillness as an indication that I was safe and that adrenaline was no longer needed to block my pain receptors. No acting was required as I held onto my abdomen and bent over my own hands as I got to my feet and stumbled forward.

Soreness lacquered my every movement with a sheen of agony and sweat.

"Best get you to a hospital I think!" my rescuer stated, holding onto one of my elbows and leading me towards the passenger door of her car. For a moment I hesitated. I was covered in thick mud and bleeding and would ruin the interior of the vehicle. Even in the state I was in it seemed churlish to just assume the woman wouldn't mind. I turned to her.

"I'm covered in mud…" I said as if she was unaware of the fact.

"That doesn't matter, dearie," she said helping me into my seat and then moving back, preparing to shut the door, "we need to get you safe."

Something about the way she said the word 'safe'; something about the flicker of her eyes towards the foot well, in the back seat, alerted me to my mistake even before she finished the sentence. "Don't we, Shaun?"

I felt him leap up from where he had been hiding, a thick rope held taught between both hands.

I tried to fight him off as he wrapped the rope across my throat, pulling it tight and hauling me towards the back of the seat, crushing my windpipe and asphyxiating me.

I grappled at the rope, tried to get my fingers under it as blackness began to descend over me for real this time. At the very last moment the rope loosened and I drew in a huge whooping breath.

Like controlling a dog on a lead, Shaun drew me out of the front seat and into the back, beside him.

"Natalie" he said in a conversational tone which was completely out of context with the situation, "meet Maxine."

CHAPTER 21A

Sunday April 28th 12:22 a.m.

The clock on the dashboard showed that Stacey had been missing for nearly five hours. I tried not to think of what might have happened to her in that space of time.

"Are you sure you're taking us on the most direct route?" my dad asked.

"There are a few different ways to get there but this is the one I know best," Rhys answered.

"That had better be the truth," his dad muttered menacingly.

"It is, I promise!" Rhys exclaimed with the innocence of a choirboy. I heard his words but kept my head turned away from him so that I didn't have to be repulsed by his evil face.

I felt as if we had been in the car for hours and had covered hundreds of miles and yet I knew that we were less than a half hour's drive from home. Initially I had recognised the roads we travelled along but after several twists and turns my sense of direction was fading fast.

Fields flanked the road on both sides, vast expanses of flat land that in the daytime most probably looked unremarkable, but at night and under this witnessing moon looked dark and so devoid of life that we could have been on the moon itself.

"Just up here, there is a track…" Rhys said, pointing it out as we approached.

If he'd not been with us, guiding our way, we would most surely have missed the dirt trail that led up the side of one of the fields. Without even bothering to indicate or slow down to change gear, my dad jolted us from the road and onto the narrow track. As the car began to straighten up we could see that there was a building some way ahead. It didn't look like anything other than an ordinary farmhouse. The car slowed to a crawl.

"Is that it?" Dad asked.

Rhys nodded and my dad turned the car headlights off. "Just so that we don't alert them that we are here," he said.

Only one light seemed to be lit in the whole of the house, a downstairs room which appeared to have no curtains or other covering across the bare window. I wondered if it was a kitchen.

The car crept forward. Our painfully slow progress up the dark track was in such stark contrast to the earlier race against time that I began to feel disassociated with what was going on around me. It was almost like this was some huge hoax, a prank with which to show me the perils of the big bad world, so that I would take note and strive never to be a victim…

But it wasn't. The situation was as real as I was. And I wasn't the victim, Stacey was.

"Who lives here?" Frank asked quietly, looking at the deserted area around the house. I realised that there were no parked cars, no signs of occupancy at all.

"Just Max, I think!" Rhys started to shrug his shoulders as if the question and its answer were irrelevant to him and then thought better of it. I heard him turn to me in the darkness. "You shouldn't have stood me up, Nat."

Like all this was my doing! He said the words as if Stacey would have been fine if only *I* had gone out with him instead of her! I drew my breath in sharply but before I could utter a word, I was thrown a little forward as my dad slammed on the brakes.

Rhys never even saw the fist which connected with the bridge of his nose, splintering the cartilage and spraying us all with droplets of blood. My dad pulled himself back down into the driver's seat.

"I'm sorry, Frank, but I couldn't let him just get away with that! None of this is Natalie's fault!" he said softly but with a steely edge to his voice that would not carry outside the confines of the car.

"It's OK. If you hadn't done that, I would've been forced to have done the same thing myself," Frank responded as if the two men were merely discussing something as mundane as emptying the bins.

"You broke my fucking nose!" Rhys snorted through the blood and mucus which streamed down his face.

"Any more sound out of you and I'll break your fucking neck as well!" my dad promised.

I'd never heard him swear before. An air of real menace emanated from him and I knew that he meant every word he spoke. So apparently did Rhys, for he shut up instantly, contenting himself with holding his ruined nose and rocking back and forth on the seat.

"We're going to have to get in there!" Frank said as if there were no doubt in the matter.

"Shouldn't we wait for the police?" I asked. They couldn't be far behind us and were trained for this sort of situation.

Dad and Frank passed a knowing look between them. "It might take the police a while to locate this place even with the address. It's rather remote..."

It dawned on me that it was down to us to save Stacey. If every second really did count, then by the time the police got here, it might actually be too late. An idea occurred to me. "Let's phone the police. We can tell them where we are and find out how far away they are!"

Dad passed me the phone. "Go ahead, Nat."

I understood then that no one would prevent

my dad from trying to rescue Stacey as soon as he possibly could. I watched Frank flick the interior light switches off so that they would not come on when the car doors were opened.

"Dad! Be careful!" I whispered as the two men crept out of the car, leaving me alone with Rhys in the back. I wasn't scared of him though; my revulsion was too strong for any other emotion to top it.

I shuffled as far from him as I could. He had gone into a sulk and sat with his head bent and both hands wrapped around his nose. I thought that if he gave me any trouble it would be easy enough to haul on the distorted flesh of his nostrils and reduce him to a whimpering heap.

I dialled the police and was rapidly patched through. "What is your name and location, caller?" I was asked. I ignored the question.

"A girl has been abducted. Her name is Stacey Papadopoulos..."

"Caller, we are already investigating the incident and a car has been dispatched..."

I interrupted immediately, cutting the assured voice off mid-track, "No you don't understand! We're at the house she was taken to ..."

I could see my dad and Frank peering through the kitchen window before looking through the other ground floor windows. I couldn't tell if they had seen anything of significance.

"Caller, DO NOT enter the property! Give me

your location and wait..."

"My dad and another man are about to go in..." I said desperately, not thinking to give the address, too caught up in the immediacy of the situation.

"What is your location?" her voice was sharp and concise.

I watched my dad try the door and discover it was locked.

"I don't...exactly...know...but..." my words were punctuated by each kick that the two men delivered to the large wooden door. I gave the controller as much of a description of the place as I could and as much as I knew of its location. My voice felt far away, my ability to control it reduced to ashes. I never thought to ask Rhys for directions, or to torture him until he supplied them.

"Hurry!" I breathed into the phone, as on the final kick the door swung inwards and my father and Frank disappeared from sight.

CHAPTER 21B

Sunday April 28th 12:22 a.m.

Between them, they forced me onto the back seat. "Don't worry about trying to get too comfortable, we're not going far, fortunately," Max said to Shaun's amusement.

"You're a woman!" I stuttered in disbelief. I had assumed all along that Max would be a man, a natural assumption to have made perhaps but one which had inevitably hastened my downfall.

"My, you're a sharp one!" Maxine mocked. "Shh! Don't tell anyone," she raised a sharply manicured talon to her mouth, bright red nail polish set against luridly painted lips. I thought she must be as ugly inside as she was on the outside.

"How can you do this? You are a woman – you're supposed to protect your own kind!" I wasn't making this any better for myself but I had come to the conclusion that all hope was gone. And if that truly were the case I would not go quietly. Of that I was determined.

"My own kind?" she snorted. "And who might that be, then?" she asked, climbing behind the wheel with some difficulty and starting the car.

Because of her bulk she needed the driver's seat pushed back as far as it could go. Shaun pushed me down into the narrow gap between front and back seats on the driver's side.

"Keep her head down!" Max instructed. Shaun pushed my face into the upholstery at his side and I was at least grateful that he hadn't thought of any other way to keep me silent and hidden.

"My own kind...?" Maxine mused as if to herself but I knew from the tone it was delivered in that it was meant for my ears. "Fat ugly women who never get a second glance from anyone? Is that my own kind?" she laughed harshly and for a moment Shaun joined in before apparently thinking better of it and shutting up.

"It certainly isn't pretty, slim little slips of girls like you, is it? That's not my kind at all. Lithe little things who think the world owes them a favour just because daddy loves them and they have mommy's looks and a winning smile..."

I breathed squalid air as filtered through the seat cushion, got a lungful of dust-tainted breath and coughed frantically.

"Hey Shaun, let up on her a little. She's no good to us dead!" I heard her say. My head was yanked up and I gasped at the air.

The car made a sharp turn to the left.

CHAPTER 22A

12:30 a.m.

I couldn't just sit and wait for them to re-appear and the idea of being alone in the car for an extended time with Rhys didn't appeal either. I checked that the keys hadn't been left in the ig-nition and then I too climbed out of the car.

Rhys showed no inclination to move and I wasn't worried he would escape with me gone. My sole concern was to find Stacey and get out of there with all of us alive.

As there was no longer any need for stealth, I slammed shut the car door and was rewarded when Rhys jumped in his seat. I wished I had taken a moment to put his head in the jam before I closed it.

There was no sound other than the faint noise I made on the gravel path which led to the door my father and Frank had disappeared through. On the way, I passed the lighted window which showed an empty kitchen, as neat and organ-ised as my own back home. It seemed strangely out of place, as if a sink full of dirty crockery would have been more fitting. A small table with two chairs pushed under it sat in the middle of the floor space. Covered by a red checked table-cloth, it too seemed strangely incongruous and I couldn't help staring at it as I passed.

Was that where Big Max sat and listened to the screams emanating from the bedrooms? Or was it where he sat afterwards? Where he sat with Rhys or whoever else had delivered a fresh girl? The thought chilled me to the bone. I reached the doorway. Darkness bloomed beyond that small entrance into a world that I had thought myself unlikely to ever enter. I shuddered but gathered up my courage. My dad and Frank were already in there somewhere. Stacey too.

Although I had not shut the car door quietly, I felt a sudden need for stealth in progressing further. I tiptoed inside.

CHAPTER 22B

12:30 a.m.

The car swung first one way and then another, following a twisted route, perhaps a shortcut. I tried to think of ways I could escape, but there were none which came to mind. None which didn't involve supernatural powers or strokes of good fortune.

"Lots of men will pay lots of money for a pretty little thing like you," Max said. Her words tore into my heart like knives. Were there that many bad people around? Or was it just that where one was, they all congregated, like blood-hounds on the scent of a victim?

I wished that they had not seen me on the road; that the tyres had rolled over me before they'd even noticed I was there. Awful as the pain might have been, it would have been a quicker and cleaner death than the slow torturous life set out before me now. And then I remembered the dog, the one I had promised to save.

It was doomed and so was I.

I had no idea what time it was, but I knew that my dad would have phoned the police when I didn't arrive home on time. Would he have believed Rhys's account of things? Would he have believed that I had gone off somewhere without phoning home to explain the situation? Or would Rhys have convinced him that I was so hurt, so ashamed to be effectively dumped on a first date, that Dad would think it true? Would he have phoned around all of my friends trying to establish where I had gone? Losing vital time in which he could have been searching for me?

I thought of how Rhys had looked when I had bumped into him outside the shoe shop. His clean-cut good looks, the bright white teeth... would Dad be taken in by all of it, just as I had?

"Nearly there, poppet..." Max said as if I was a young child desperate to reach our destination. I felt bile rise in my throat and rather than swallow it back down, I spat it out, right into Shaun's lap.

"Ew! Bitch has just sicked-up all over me!" he cried, pushing me away from him roughly.

In the second that my head snapped up, I caught a glimpse of the open road ahead and the time as displayed on the dashboard clock. It was 12:40.

CHAPTER 23A

12:40 a.m.

Heavy footsteps pounded above my head and I knew that my dad was up there with Frank. Ignoring the other rooms on the ground floor, I made my way to the stairs with no caution at all. Taking the steps two at a time, I was soon at the top.

Six doors were ajar. All of the rooms were lit up. I guessed that my father and Frank had switched on the lights as they searched, not bothering to turn them off afterwards. Presumably, they hadn't bothered with the downstairs as they had looked through the windows from the outside and found nothing.

Choosing the nearest doorway, I barged through to find that I had entered a bedroom. The room was not particularly large and contained only a bed. But it was no ordinary bed and looked as if it were comprised of two double mattresses pushed together. It was unmade and dark stains fouled the surface of the sheets. I wrinkled my nose in disgust and closed the door firmly behind me.

Five other doors stood ajar but before I could

choose to enter any of them, my dad and Frank emerged.

"Nat, you were supposed to stay in the car," my dad said but it was not an admonishment. He was in too much shock for that. Light glowed from the room behind making a silhouette of him as he stood there in the semi-darkness.

"Have you found her?" I asked, urgency forcing my voice out in a rapid stream.

He shook his head but barged past him anyway, to see for myself.

"Nat, no!" he warned, but it was too late. I sidestepped him into the room.

CHAPTER 23B

12:40 a.m.

"I'm sure you'll think of a way to get your own back, Shaun!" Max sniggered, making the seat in front of me judder.

Even though I had largely purged the contents of my stomach I still felt queasy and likely to throw up again. I tried to raise a hand to my mouth to wipe away the drool that lingered there but Shaun yanked hard on the rope around my neck.

"Don't try anything funny," he warned. I kept my hands still lest he considered the move to be aggressive.

"Five more minutes and you'll be at your new home!" Max laughed again, making me want to smash her ugly face into the steering column and tell her that was *its* new home.

"Course it won't be your home for long. Not once I've found a buyer for you, that is," she seemed to realise that she had spoken out of turn and bit her words off sharply.

"And how much do I get for bringing her?" Shaun said boldly.

Max laughed. "How much do *you* get? That's a

good one!"

"I brought her to you, didn't I?" he said angrily. I could feel the heat of his temper from the way he tightened the rope around my throat. I kept as still as I could.

"What you brought me was a load of grief, that's what!" I could hear the temper in her voice too now. "Stray girls are ten-a-penny. They're everywhere – sleeping rough in doorways, on park benches...they're easy to pick up and to keep hold of. No one's looking for them. No one even knows they're missing!"

"Yeah, and?" Shaun seemed not to be getting the point and Max became exasperated.

"And I don't normally take in girls like this one. She'll be missed...people will be looking for her and therefore she's a risk." She clearly wasn't sure she had made her point. "So if anyone ought to be getting paid, it's me, not you! In fact you're lucky I don't charge you for disposing of her..."

CHAPTER 24A

12:45 a.m.

I pushed past him and into the room beyond. Another large bed furnished the room, this one adorned with a pink bedspread with hearts and flowers appliquéd on the cover. Three white teddy bears sat on a plump pillow and there was a white dressing table opposite the bed.

But that was where the resemblance to a normal girl's bedroom ended. On a hook above the dressing table hung a set of handcuffs. Not plastic play ones, these ones appeared to be made of stainless steel and cruelly fashioned. On the dressing table, besides the lipstick and cheap bottles of perfume stood a whip and other things whose function and use I could only guess at. But really didn't want to. All of the items had only one thing in common. They looked to me like instruments of torture. My stomach flipped and I wished that I'd heeded my dad's warning.

"She's not here," Frank said from another room, as I stumbled back through the doorway and into my father's arms.

"Wish you hadn't had to see that, Natalie," my dad said, cradling me as hot tears fell from my eyes.

"The house is empty?" I asked and both men nodded. "So what do we do now?" I dried my eyes with the back of my hand. It didn't seem right to just give up.

"Rhys said there were other ways to get here. We could drive around and see if we can find them. But we have to face the possibility that they have already moved her on…" My dad's words pounded through my head.

"We have to find her…we HAVE TO!"

My dad and Frank nodded but there was a look which passed between them which said they thought it was a lost cause. I ignored the look, dismissed it as irrelevant. They would not stop looking because I wouldn't let them. Silently we made our way out of the house.

"Shouldn't we turn off the lights so they don't know we were here?" I asked.

"No point. The fact that the door is kicked in will alert them to that fact! Anyway the police will be here soon enough," Frank said, but my dad disagreed.

"Nat's right. This Max will know nothing until he gets to the door…there's no sense in giving the game away early…"

We turned off the lights and shut the front door as much as it would close.

Wearily we climbed back into the car. Rhys hadn't moved and still sat bent over himself as if in self-protection. As my father started the engine and turned the car back onto the long drive which led to the main road, the clock on the dash read 12:49.

CHAPTER 24B

12:49 a.m.

"Home sweet home!" Max sighed, as if genuinely pleased or relieved to be safely back.

The car slowed down in preparation of a sharp turn but did not make the turn. Instead it continued moving forward, going straight on. Ahead, where I thought Max had been intending to turn, there was another car emerging from a long driveway, edging out of it and appearing to hesitate as to which way it should go. My heart leapt as I saw the registration and knew who sat behind the wheel.

It was my dad!

My dad had found me! But I didn't even have a chance to get him to notice me before my head was jerked roughly down once more and Max sped up again as if she'd never been intending to take the turn.

"Who was that?" she barked at Shaun who seemed suddenly terrified into silence.

Foolhardy as it was, I could not miss my chance to goad her as she'd goaded me. Perhaps she'd lose her nerve, perhaps she'd crash us into a tree but the opportunity for revenge was too sweet to ignore.

I fought against the restrictive rope which still bit into my flesh. "That was my dad, that's who. And he's coming for me!" And just in case they did not realise the implications, I spelt it out clearly for them.

"And he'll be coming for both of you, too!" I crowed.

CHAPTER 25A

12:50 a.m.

Another car had approaching, slowing down as if about to take the turn but when the driver saw us, it had sped up once more and carried on with its journey. Was it possible that it had just been someone who was lost? That the driver had no connection to us or the situation? One look at Rhys told me otherwise. There was a look of utter panic on his face – an expression of sheer terror that I hadn't seen before.

And I wasn't alone in noticing it.

"WHO WAS THAT? WAS THAT HIM? WAS THAT MAX?" Frank shouted at Rhys who had lifted his head just as we were about to turn onto the main road.

Stuck in the back, my view of the car had been hampered. I didn't even know if there was only one person in the car or many. My dad cut in, unaware of the change in Rhys. "The only person I could see was a woman...a rather obese woman but certainly not a man..."

Rhys spoke as if my father had never spoken. "Yes, that was Maxine," he confirmed before adding, "and now she's going to kill me!"

CHAPTER 25B

12:50 a.m.

"Fuck! How did they find me?" It was Maxine's turn to be shook up and I savoured every minute of it. The car had gained speed and now we hurtled along the road.

I was far from safe but knowing that my dad had been so close to finding me, gave me some hope at least. I couldn't see out of the rear windscreen but somehow I knew that he followed behind. I knew that *he* knew it was me in the car.

"Get rid of her!" Maxine demanded.

"What?" said Shaun stupidly as if he couldn't understand what was being asked of him.

"GET RID OF HER!" Maxine spat the words out.

"How?" Shaun seemed to be at a loss to know what he should do. I kept my mouth shut in fear that one wrong word would be the end of me.

"Throw her out the car," Maxine said as if disposing of me meant nothing to her. "They won't be able to stop in time and they'll run her over. It solves the problem of her testifying against us and it'll slow them down!"

"You mean kill her?" Shaun seemed to be reluctant to go that far, I was relieved to see.

"No, I mean send her on a *fucking holiday*!" Max shouted exasperated. "There's nothing at the moment to prove that she didn't choose to be with you. To have sex with you, is there?" Maxine reasoned, taking the bends as if she were a rally driver. I hoped my dad was being as careful as he could. He was my only chance of survival.

"She's pretty roughed-up," he said slowly as if thinking it through.

"So she liked it rough! They can't prove you raped her! And if she's dead she can't protest her innocence!"

There was a horrible logic there that almost defied my ability to counter it. The time to speak had come and I knew everything depended on what I said.

"Shaun, listen to me," I appealed to him. "As it stands, you raped me...you'll serve a few years at most...but if you do as she says, you will be a premeditated murderer. She might be telling you to do it, but she won't do the time for it – *you will*, Shaun. You'll get life and they'll lock you up and throw away the key!"

"Don't listen to her! She's trying to fool you with her words!" Max cried from the front.

"Shaun, listen to me! Not her! If you murder me, your life will be over! But if you help the police, tell them what you know about her and the men who use her house, the judge will go lightly on you..."

"DON'T LISTEN TO HER, YOU FUCKING IDIOT!" Maxine bellowed.

"SHUT THE FUCK UP! BOTH OF YOU, FUCK-ING BITCHES! JUST SHUT UP!" Shaun yelled back.

Realising that he would not just do as she bid, Max tried to reach a hand behind herself to feel for the handle of my door. Afraid that she would reach it and that she would take the next bend so fast that I would automatically tumble out of the open door, I caught her hand in mine and brought it to my mouth. I bit down hard.

The last thing I remembered was the sensa-tion of spinning. Then the world went blissfully quiet.

CHAPTER 26

1:05 a.m.

The car we were following spun suddenly across the road as if the driver had lost all control. It crashed into the barrier to one side but instead of coming to rest, it tilted forwards and upwards, desperately seeking the road once more.

For a breath-taking second it hung almost vertically in the air: a metal new-age ballet dancer performing a stunning pirouette, before majestically tossing its heavy metal body to the ground once more, upside down and on its roof.

Like watching a carousel going round, spinning faster than the eye can follow, the vision produced a sympathetic feeling of motion sickness in the pit of my stomach. And yet there was a terrifyingly beautiful aspect to the scene too.

Ten, twenty times the car spun full circle – there were no hiccups in the spin, no pauses where one end spun faster than the other, no imbalances and no deviation from the centre – the car spun perfectly within its circle.

Illuminated by our own headlights as we stood in front of our car we were washed by alternate headlights and taillights of the other car, bathing us in a seeming bloodbath before washing us clean with purifying white.

From the occupants of the other car there was no sound. Stacey was in there – alive, dead or somewhere in between. In that instant, I thought of Schrödinger's cat, that philosophical conundrum we had discussed only recently in school. I had at the time been a little unable to get my head around the thought experiment; now the simplicity of it cut through me like a knife. I no longer knew whether Stacey was alive or already dead but one thing was certain…unlike the fabled Schrödinger I would not metaphorically hang about until the inevitable happened!

I started forward but was halted by the two men at my side.

"Not until it stops spinning! You will be hit and hurt, possibly even killed if you get close before then," Frank said.

We watched the car, big wheels rotating in the night sky as it slowed to a stop.

"Rhys?" I asked Frank. I don't know whether I was asking whether he would help or if he was alright, it was more a reaction to the situation than anything else.

"He won't get out the car," Frank's mouth was downturned as if he could not be more disgusted with his son if he tried. I wondered what the future for this family would be. Would Frank ever forgive his wife for covering up for Rhys? Would he ever forgive himself for not noticing and acting upon the change in his son? They were questions that were too big for the night and for me to even contemplate. I pushed them out of my head.

The car gave a final slow spin and ground to a halt.

Filled with trepidation, I edged forward.

"She'll be in the back," my dad said to Frank who nodded in agreement.

The front and rear windscreens were intact and as far as I could see, they were the most likely means of escape the occupants had. Landing on its roof, the car had sustained some structural damage from the weight of the undercarriage bearing down and the doorframes looked buckled and warped. It was unlikely they would open freely. I tugged on one just in case.

The door was lodged tight in its bent frame but just beyond it I could see Stacey, curled into a ball and seemingly unconscious.

"She's here!" I cried, tears springing immediately to my eyes at the sight of her. Distraught as I had been up until then, the full horror of the situation only just hit me. This was my best friend and on one night she had lived through enough horrors to fill a book...at least I hoped that she'd lived through them.

A sickening thought played on my mind. Even when the car had passed us we hadn't seen any sight of her in it. Had she already been dead? Had they been about to dispose of her body when they came face-to-face with us, at the end of the driveway?

There was a metallic taste in my mouth and it took a moment to realise that I'd bitten though my lip.

"Stand back!" Frank said as he aimed a large rock at the rear windscreen, holding it and preventing it from being flung into the interior of the car. The rock smashed the window with ease but as he withdrew his hands I realised that they were bloodied and ripped from the impact with the glass.

"Get her out!" he ordered as he went around to the front of the car, presumably to repeat his actions.

Between us, Dad and I hauled Stacey out. She was filthy and covered in mud and dried blood but she was warm under my hands, a sure sign that life had not entirely left her body.

"Help me get her over there," Dad nodded towards the grass verge beyond our car.

We placed her down gently and I moved her head so that I was sure she had no obstruction to her breathing. Her chest rose and fell in short, shallow breaths - she didn't seem to be in obvious pain. She kind of looked like she was sleeping.

"We still have to get the others out," Dad said, already starting forward.

"We have to get the others out?" I looked at

him as if he had gone mad.

"This car could explode...and there are people inside..." he said calmly.

I looked at him in surprise. "But Dad those people..." I couldn't even find the words to express what I wanted to say. I tried again. "They are not worthy to be saved..."

I expected him to nod and walk away but he didn't. "I know how you feel, honey, but we have to save them if we can!"

I pulled away from his restraining arms, not wanting to agree, not needing to listen. His eyes bored into my back as I turned away from the sound of his voice. "We have to save them for *us*, not for them!" he explained.

I turned around. "For us?"

"Because it's the right thing to do. Let the law and the courts and the prisons sort out their fate. Tomorrow or the next day. But for today, for this moment in time, it is not our right to be judge, jury and executioner!"

"But Dad, look at what they did to Stacey!" I pointed with shaking hands to the prone figure on the grass. "They could've killed her...they might have even been planning that..."

"And we'll make sure that the courts know that!" he nodded, his voice level and reasoned even in the face of my impassioned stance. "But if we wilfully stand and watch them die, we'll be no better than them!"

"But we are! That's why we are doing the world a favour if we let them just burn to death in that car..." Whether it was the words I had chosen or the images they evoked, I suddenly realised what he meant. To stand by and watch that happen would somehow diminish my own humanity, lessen it to some extent. The means *did not* justify the end. These people, and that included Rhys, had to be punished but it was not my role.

I nodded and without another word of protest followed him to the rear of the upturned car. A young man was trapped there, hanging upside down, still held tightly by his seatbelt.

"I'll get him out." Smaller than my dad, it was easier for me to climb inside and depress the button to release him. He fell straight and hard to the new floor of the car and lay there lifeless. Was he dead? In the cramped confines of the car, it would have been difficult to have felt for a pulse but I tried anyway.

Not knowing if I was doing it correctly, only copying what I had seen done on TV shows, I pressed my fingertips to his wrist. There seemed to be a vague beat but I couldn't be sure if it was his pulse I was feeling, or my own.

"Come on, Natalie, get out of there before this thing goes up!" my dad urged. There was a distinct smell of diesel although I couldn't tell how long it had been there. Perhaps I had only just noticed it or maybe it was stronger than before?

I tried to get my hands under his arms but his body was too twisted to allow me easy access. His head had flopped down onto his chest and hindered my every move. Without too much thought I yanked it forwards by the hair, feeling some of the strands tear out in my palm. The move allowed me access to his underarms, where I then placed my hands.

I might have saved your life, you unworthy scum, I thought at him, *but I sure as hell hope you have a banging headache!*

Backing out of the rear-view window, dragging him with me, I felt Dad's arms reach past me and grab the weigh from me, releasing me from my obligation. Out of breath and exhausted, I watched him haul the unknown guy to safety and place him a little distance from Stacey on the grass. To my gratification, he neither placed him down as gently as we had with Stacey, nor with any regard to his possible injuries.

"Where's Frank?" he asked coming over to me as I watched the car from a safe distance. Sparks flew from it as if it were kindling under a bonfire.

I had almost forgotten about Rhys's dad in all the activity. I looked at the back of our car. Rhys sat there alone. Frank was nowhere to be seen.

"The last time I saw him he…" I tried to think back, "he went round to the front of the car!" My eyes were drawn back to the scene ahead of us as the words tumbled out of me.

As if fate had been waiting for that revelation before racking up the tension, a larger spark lit up the night air, flaring into the sky like a messenger to the Gods.

"Oh my God!" Dad said, starting forward.

"DAD! PLEASE!" I begged, the urgency in my voice slicing through the rights and wrongs of the situation.

"I have to help Frank! Stay with Stacey, Natalie!" he ordered, racing around to the other side of the car. I could no longer see him and for a moment stood indecisive. And then I realised something. If he had been right about not standing by and watching Stacey's captors die, then it was surely doubly right that I should not stand back and watch him die?

Not bothering to skirt around the car using the grass verge, I ran more directly to the other side but the scene which met my eyes stopped me in my tracks.

Frank and my dad struggled to heave the largest woman I had ever seen, other than on TV documentaries, out of the windscreen. Easily twice as big as the space that she was effectively jammed in, they appeared to have managed to haul her only part way out before she got trapped by her own bulk.

"Help me!" she groaned, clawing at the empty air in front of her, sharp red fingernails seeking purchase on something and coming away empty.

I had the crazy thought that maybe if we stuck just a little shard of glass in one of those fingers that she might deflate like a balloon, allowing her to pass easily through the opening.

Frank and my dad redoubled their efforts, grunting and pulling on her arms so much, that at one point I swear I heard some faint popping sounds as if they were about to tear off at the sockets. Still she budged no further.

Sparks flew off the car in showers and I feared it was only a matter of time until the whole car went up, taking my dad and Frank with it.

"You can't save her!" I yelled at the two men. "The fire crew will get her out!" and then a thought sidled too late into my mind. What fire crew? Had any of us phoned them? I knew I hadn't and I was fairly sure that my dad hadn't either.

My dad looked at me with eyes wide and I knew he had read my thoughts.

"Stand clear of the car!" he called to both Frank and I, as he dashed back towards his own car.

Throwing himself into the driver's seat he surprised me by driving forward instead of backwards and away from the upside-down car. He collided with the other car, catching it on a slight angle and making it perform a half spin. The stuck woman looked like she was on a macabre carousel ride, long straggly hair billowing out behind her head.

Whilst the other car slowed to a halt he backed our car away to a safe distance and turned it around so that it was facing away from the wreck before he got out once more. But instead of returning to us, he foraged in the back for something, emerging with a rope slung over one arm.

Aware that time was fast running out, he ran back to the trapped woman who now dangled facing our car and slipped the rope over as much of her body as he could, before tightening it.

"What are you doing? Get this off me!" She tried to fight him, slapping at his hands and arms.

"If you want to live, you will hold on tight to this!" I heard him say disparagingly but I couldn't for the life of me figure out what he was up to.

Frank however seemed to know exactly what my dad was doing. Without a word passing between them, he took up the slack of the rope, ran back to our car and tied it to the tow ball. Then he got behind the wheel.

My dad finished what he was doing and pulling me behind him, he shouted to Frank. "Go!"

Wheels spun and there was a smell of burning rubber and then suddenly the whole frame of the windscreen was pulled from the old car, the woman still stuck fast inside. She was dragged a few yards before the car stopped but other than light grazing she didn't seem particularly hurt. But she wasn't finished. "I'll get that bastard, Rhys, for ratting on me like this," she said, not even aware that one of the men who stood before her was his dad.

"Perhaps you will. But you will more than likely be locked up for the rest of your life, as will all the men whose names you'll give to the police!" Frank said. "And as for Rhys..." his face clouded with sadness, "I hope that he'll also get his just rewards for his actions."

I understood the bigger picture then. In saving this one rotten, worthless life, my father and Frank had ensured that everyone who had played a part in the rape and abduction of girls like Stacey, would be reprimanded and charged. If they had let this excuse for a woman die, much of the evidence would have died with her!

Even so, I could not bear to bring myself to look upon that wicked face. Dazed and emotionally drained, I dragged myself over to where Stacey lay unmoving. Sitting next to her on the grass verge I cradled her head in my lap as I called the emergency services.

"They will be here soon," I told the unconscious girl who lay so still. "The paramedics will come and they will fix you up, Stacey..." I hoped my words were getting through to her, but there was no sign she heard at all.

Tears fell hot and heavy from my face onto hers, washing away the grime from her skin to expose the pallor beneath her olive complexion.

"Stace, I hope you can hear me," I sobbed. "I

know what happened. I know what they did to you. Don't let them win..." Had it been my imagination or had her eyelids flickered for just an instant?

I spoke louder and with more determination. "Stacey Papadopoulos...do you hear me? You had better wake up, 'cos I need my best friend right now!" This time I was sure that I saw a flicker!

Neon lights bathed me in their fluorescent glow as, just like in the movies, it was at that point that the police cars and the paramedics turned up. When everything had been done and the bad guys caught.

I watched them rush around. "Over here!" I called to the paramedics but my voice came out in a hoarse whisper. "Over..." and then I felt something grasp my hand weakly.

"There's something I need you to do, Nat..." Stacey said in a voice that was weak and fragile and tore at my heart.

I bent my head and listened to her instructions, not once interrupting or asking for clarification.

"Promise me?" she said as the paramedics gently lifted her onto a stretcher.

"I promise!" I said, hand on heart like we used to do when we were still kids.

She smiled faintly.

I watched them load her into the ambulance and close the doors.

"Where's Rhys?" I asked Frank unthinkingly. He turned a traumatised face towards me. "Where he deserves to be..." his eyes flickered over to one of the police cars.

I nodded. "You did the right thing," I said. He nodded slowly back at me, a broken man who in one night, had lost everything worth living for.

I found my dad and kissed him on the cheek. "Go home. Tell Mum I'm fine and that I'll be back as soon as I can!"

My dad was clearly worried.

"You have to trust me," I said quietly, waiting until he nodded, giving him time for the fear to subside from his eyes.

"Where are you going?" he called after me as I hurried away.

"I have one last thing to do," I called back over my shoulder, not meaning to be evasive but realising the urgency of my task. I ran up to one of the police officers who stood guarding the suspects.

"Officer, I need your help!"

CHAPTER 27

2 a.m.

It was easier to find than I had feared - the abandoned car which still contained the evidence of Stacey's rape and abduction. But the car was not my priority. The police would take statements from her and would have found the car with no problem anyway.

My priority was keeping her promise for her. She was in no fit state to do it herself, so I was her surrogate. It struck me as more than coincidental, more than fitting. She had already been my stand-in after all.

During the short drive in the police car, I had only half been looking for the road she had described. The policeman was much better at that than I could ever be, so I let him look whilst I thought. Would Rhys have raped me if I had gone on that date instead of Stacey? Would I have been subjected to everything the way she had? There was no definite answer to the questions but my head assured me that everything that had happened would have happened, regardless of the victim.

I thought too about why I'd chosen to commandeer a police officer rather than ask my dad to drive me out here. The obvious answer was that I was bringing the police to the evidence, the stolen car and stained bed sheets, but I knew that was not my real reason.

I wasn't even totally aware of what my real reason was, other than some desire to do this part on my own, without my dad trying to shield me from the pain of truth, or having to look in his eyes and know that he too realised it could so easily have been me.

But more than anything else I left my dad behind because I had to. This was the last part of our swap, that strange thing which had passed between Stacey and me without us really being aware of it...and that meant I had to do it alone.

I left the policeman standing at the side of the abandoned, stolen car, radioing for a forensics team and I scanned the bushes at the side of the road.

Just as Stacey had said, half hidden under the foliage lay the dog that they had hit. It was deeper under the bush than I'd expected it to be and I suspected that it had dragged itself under to die.

I held my breath and crouched down. There was a horrible coppery smell and instinctively I recognised that as a bad sign.

For a moment I thought that I was too late, but a soft quivering of the leaves which camouflaged it, indicated that it was still alive, if only just. I parted the branches, trying to gauge how best to pick it up without causing it unnecessary pain. Seeing me, it whimpered and shrank backwards, further into the foliage. I reached out a trembling hand to soothe it.

Large brown eyes regarded me with fear and dread and the poor thing tried again to heave its broken body away from my questing fingers. Heart breaking just by looking at it, I knew that I could not fail it. I had to uphold the promise I'd made to Stace and keep the promise she had made to it. Gently, I took it into my arms, all matted fur - skin and bones with no substance - and held its rapidly beating heart close to my own.

I couldn't tell how badly injured it was. Couldn't tell whether it was male or female or even what colour it was under the dirty matted fur. None of that mattered. All that mattered was that it was alive. And that it remained that way.

The police officer wanted to take me directly home but I begged him to take me instead to the nearest 24-hour vets. He radioed for directions and I could have kissed him when he put the flashing lights on and drove like his life depended on it.

Lights blazing and siren howling, I guess the racket woke the on-duty vet, or perhaps the police had informed him we were already on our way. He was groggy and dishevelled, but as soon as he saw what I held in my arms, he took on the professionalism of a top surgeon.

"I need to be with him when you operate," my voice was shaky.

The vet shook his head. "It's a sterile environment and he'll be asleep, he won't know if you are there or not," he argued.

"Then you had better get me one of those gown things you wear, because I'm not leaving this dog's side." I put my heart into the words, making them emerge as if carved on steel.

The vet huffed and puffed but he went off to fetch a theatre gown for me.

"Can you let my dad know where I am and that I'll call him when I'm ready to come home."

The policeman looked surprised. "Are you sure you want to stay here?" he asked.

I nodded. I thought about giving him a message for my dad to pass on to Nathan but it seemed overly complicated. I held his gaze. "I need to know if my boyfriend has reported his dad to you."

"That's confidential information," he said. "You could phone him and ask him yourself," he suggested.

I knew that I could but I wanted the assurance from the police direct. I looked away.

"If you give me his name and address I could tell you whether there have been any reports come in, but I can't tell you what it was about…"

I gave him the information and listened while

he radioed in. Nathan had made a report. He was safe. I exhaled and watched the policeman leave.

In those few moments I stood alone in the consultation room, I knew that what had happened this one night, would stay with me for the rest of my life. I knew too that the promises I had made, were not for one night's duration only... but a lifetime.

The vet returned and I held the dog's head, stroking it and murmuring soft words, whilst he administered a general anaesthetic. Then I scrubbed up like I was shown and donned the theatre gown. It was way too big and reached almost to my ankles but that didn't matter.

"He's a she, by the way," the vet said as he made a small incision around one of the animal's wounds. Somehow the fact that the dog was a girl made her condition all the sadder.

"She's got multiple cuts and grazes and a broken leg. She's thin and emaciated but there's no reason that with good love and care, she can't get back to health," he said, pinning the bone and pushing it back into place.

"Can I take her home as soon as she comes round?" I asked anxiously.

The vet frowned. "If she's a stray she may have once been someone's pet. I'll have to check if she has a microchip embedded under her skin first." He pulled the needle and thread he was using to stitch up the wounds once more through the skin and tied it off.

Pulling off his gloves, he reached for an instrument I didn't recognise. He ran the instrument over the dog's sleeping body.

"There doesn't seem to be a microchip in her. So I guess she's yours now. If you want her. But she ought to stay here for a few days on a drip, until she gets her strength back," he cautioned.

"No. What medical attention she can get by staying here will be undone by her feeling of abandonment," I argued. "She will heal just as well at home with me and she'll be loved." I let him hear the break in my voice so that he understood my mind was made up. He nodded slowly.

"While she's still asleep can I use your phone to call my dad to get him to pick us up?" I asked.

"Phone's in the office, first door on your left," he said.

I left him bandaging my dog and as I shrugged out of the operating gown, I made my call. Dad answered on the first ring.

"Where are you?" his voice, unusually sharp, echoed out of my phone and around the empty office.

"I'm still at the vet's," I said, knowing that it was not the ideal time to give him the full explanation but having to give him something. "Stacey made me promise to fetch a stray dog that got hit by the car she was in." It wasn't the full story but there would be time enough for

349

that later.

"Is it alive?"

I nodded, even though I knew he could not see me. I needed the movement to emphasis the words. "Yes. And she's coming home with me." I almost heard him nod in return, as I knew he would.

Now that I had dealt with my promise I felt a burden removed from my shoulders and with no need to be strong for a while, I broke down.

"Daddy, can you come fetch me?" I asked through sobs which racked my whole body. I heard him answer a strangulated 'yes' and knew that he was crying too. We hung up. I hadn't asked if he knew how Stacey was, or even whether her dad would pull through. Those were things I knew he would rather tell me and I would rather hear, in person.

The office was too empty to remain there alone. Beyond the large plate glass windows, shadows leapt and pranced about in the night. I couldn't decide if I was less afraid now that I knew what evil the world was capable of, or more afraid, and I was relieved for my own sake to get back into the room where the dog was just starting to come round.

My heart bled when I saw how it tried to wag its tail on seeing me, as if it recognised that I would love and look after it from this day forward. And maybe, indeed it did. People say dogs know things like that. I hope it's true.

"She's younger than she looks," the vet said, running a hand over the dog's matted hair. "Maybe only eighteen months to two years. She's never had puppies but I reckon she's been a stray a long time to have got this thin."

I nodded and found that I was crying again. Or perhaps I just hadn't stopped. I bent my head down to the dog who favoured me with a lick from a rasping tongue.

"I have given her an antibiotic injection and painkillers. There are tablets here to put in her food, one three times a day for seven days and I want to see her again tomorrow." He corrected himself, remembering that it was the early hours of the morning still, "Bring her into either the Sunday evening surgery or Monday morning, so I can examine her again. And build her food portions up slowly as her stomach will be shrunken. Little amounts frequently, rather than two big meals."

I nodded and he left me alone with her for a while, busying himself with cleaning up the theatre and clearing away the surgical instruments.

"Going to have to think of a name for you, girl," I told the dog as fresh tears fell from my face. I hoped that Stace and her dad would both be okay but it was up to fate.

"Your dad has arrived," the vet said, coming back into the room. He helped me lift my dog and carry her to the car, placing her gently on my knees. "Now you two take care of each other." He smiled at the dog and then at me, before closing the door.

The car journey back was quiet. Mum had come out with Dad and refused to sit anywhere but in the back with me. For some reason I was embarrassed to talk about what had happened to Stacey with her. Stace had taken my place...it could have been me instead of her who was now hospitalised.

"The doctors say that it's early days but Stacey will be fine," Mum volunteered, stroking the dog's head slowly, careful not to spook it.

"And her dad?" I asked fearfully, worried that he hadn't been mentioned.

Mum shot Dad a look in the rear-view mirror. "Turns out it wasn't his first heart attack, just his biggest one. The others were smaller and he wasn't even aware of them. They think he'll be okay, but he has to go on a strict diet and exercise regime."

No more chips, chips, chips for him then, I thought. I quelled the crazy, hysterical laughter that threatened to swallow me up. "Can I visit them?" I asked. "Stacey and her dad, I mean?"

Mum patted the dog's hair and mine simultaneously. "I'll take you to the hospital this afternoon, once you've had a rest." She paused as if unsure whether to continue. "I know you feel terrible right now. But your dad and I are so relieved that you're safe..." her voice was halting and hesitant. "You have probably forgotten, but it's your birthday today...and we just wanted to let you know that we love you so much..." she pressed something cold and hard into my hand. "It isn't your main present but it was going to be a significant one."

I opened my palm. There on a pink diamanté keyring was my very own front door key, the one I had been promised when my parents considered me grown-up enough.

"Natalie, your dad and I have always done all we can to protect you, and we always will," tears streamed down her face. "This is a dangerous but wonderful world and tonight more than ever, you've shown that you are the sensible, brave, clever girl, we always knew you'd be. We are so proud of you!"

Suddenly the key didn't seem the shining icon I had always thought it to be. In the warm darkness of the car interior within the safety of the people I loved, I finally let the tears run free.

EPILOGUE

Sunday April 28th 2 p.m.

"I'm so sorry!" Stacey croaked when she saw me. Drip lines fed from the back of one hand up to a stand at the side of the bed. She tried to sit up, grimacing as she did, turning her face away in shame.

I plumped up her pillows and sat down on the chair next to the bed. I wanted to reach across the divide between us; across the gap that was as emotional as it was physical. I settled for stretching my hand towards hers on the pristine white of the bed linen.

"You've nothing to be sorry about," I said, sad that my hand still lay empty whilst hers clutched at the sheet below it. I watched her fingers turn as pale as the sheets so that I could barely tell where one ended and the other began.

"I should have asked if you were OK about it. I shouldn't have gone behind your back!" Her eyes filled with tears and I knew that she was genuinely remorseful. In a way, what had happened to her was irrelevant to the relationship she had with me...what she was trying to apologise for was not considering my feelings. I knew I had to put her straight.

I took her unresisting hand in mine, feeling the fingers uncurl and warm against my own. "I chose Nathan, Stacey, so it was fine that you wanted to go out with Rhys. But you're right, you should have told me and you should have told your parents too. What you did was stupid!" I didn't mean to but couldn't keep the anger from my voice. I felt her hand go rigid and I wanted to kick myself.

She hung her head in shame. "I guess I paid the price though."

Now it was my turn to hang my head. There was an awkward silence. She tried to pull her hand away but I held it fast. I was not giving up on our friendship and I would not let her do so either.

"I've given a statement to the police...and apparently Max is co-operating, giving them a list of men who..." she trailed off but we both knew what she meant.

I nodded. There would be time in the coming days and weeks to follow the progress of the case, to discuss how many would be brought to prosecution. For now it was enough that the doctors had said there would be no permanent damage to Stace and that in the future she could still have children if she wanted to.

"They'll go to prison for a very, very long

time," I assured her.

She nodded, eyes bright with tears. With difficulty I swallowed the lump which lay in my throat and tried to move on, tried to move us *both* on.

"Your dad is doing well. I just popped in to see him," I offered.

She laughed. "Yes. He's already talking about introducing healthier options into the shop and including salads free with all main meals."

I grinned. "Ever the salesman, your dad." We laughed together and it felt as good as it always had. Things had changed and yet they had stayed the same.

"How did it go with Nathan? And will you see him again?" she asked quietly, almost shyly.

It felt strange hearing her ask that question after all that had happened to her. I looked at her for a moment without answering. She nodded slowly. "He took my body without my permission and he almost took my life…" she said, and I knew she was talking about Rhys, "I won't let him take any more from me! He will not take my emotions, my feelings. He will not take our friendship and he will never, *ever* take my soul."

I smiled. "No. And he will never take your courage either," I added.

Stacey smiled back. "So now we are agreed on that, will you tell me how it went with Nathan?" she asked, her eyes imploring me to let things be how they'd always been between us.

"He's great...yes, I think we will be to-gether..." I stuttered, hoping that was not too much information too soon. I left out all the stuff about his dad. That was Nathan's story to tell and his choice to whom he told it.

"I spoke to him this morning. It's just him and his mum now – his dad's gone." I censored the in-formation, leaving out the fact that his dad had been arrested and that even now lawyers were or-ganising the placing of restrictive orders on him, so that he would never be able to be with striking distance of his wife or son, ever again. I smiled. "It looks like Nathan will be staying at our school and not moving again."

She smiled, genuinely pleased. "I'm happy for you, Nat. I really am." Her mouth turned down suddenly and huge sobs racked her broken body. I wanted to hold her, to tell her things would be okay but I knew now that it was an empty prom-ise. Not everything would always be okay in the end.

"Right, this young lady needs more medica-tion and some rest, so I'm afraid that I'm going to have to ask you to leave!" a brusque nurse bustled over and virtually lifted me out of the chair.

Stacey reached a drip-connected arm out to me, preventing me from leaving.

"The dog?" she asked, eyes fearful, and I knew suddenly it was the information she had been dreading most.

"She's fine and resting at home with my dad while I'm here. She had a broken leg but she'll be fine." I smiled. "Just like you and your dad." I bent down and gave her a peck on the forehead. "Just like our friendship. We will be fine." And with that I saw my smile returned. Her eyes flickered closed and I realised how exhausted and frail she was. I turned to walk away but two steps from the door, I was halted by her voice.

"Nat!" There was an urgency to her which chilled me to the core but when I turned to face her once more, I found her smiling softly. "I nearly forgot!" she grimaced as the nurse injected something into the Venflon in her hand. "It's your birthday today! Happy birthday!"

The words seemed anachronistic. Out of time and place with the events which had unfolded. But perhaps if we worked at normality enough…

"I'll be back to see you later! I'll bring you some birthday cake and maybe we can even watch *The Wizard* together, if that thing plays DVDs?" I pointed to the small TV that hung on a bracket from the opposite wall.

"I'd like that," she said sleepily as the nurse lowered her pillows, "always did have a thing for that Tin Man…"

I laughed but she was already asleep. And even though I knew she could not see me, I stopped and blew her a kiss before exiting through the swing doors, heading home to my family and my dog.

That year my best present was the gift of life.

———

ABOUT THE AUTHOR

Carmen Capuano

 Born into poverty in
Glasgow, Scotland, Car-
men Capuano moved to
England at the age of
eighteen. A full and var-
ied working life saw her
relocate from London to
Birmingham, and finally
to the small Worcester-
shire town of Broms-
grove, where she still
resides with her chil-
dren and dog.

A prolific writer, she has penned more than
twenty screenplays and as many novels in nine
years, covering every genre from rom-com to science fiction.

PRAISE FOR
AUTHOR

"The Owners, Volume I" is a page turner of a read. The structure of the novel, being a double narrative perspective, leap-frogging chapter by chapter, really hooks the reader.

I thought it was beautifully written with wonderful use of imagery. For example, 'The drone of an insect outside served to shatter the silence, its drum a seeming answer to the staccato drumbeat of his heart'. The musical term 'staccato' conveyed to the reader how fast the boy's heart was throbbing with fright.

This is a novel ideal for the young adult readership, as there were elements of peril interspersed with loving relationships and concepts of what makes us human. I thought there were many thought provoking elements such as making us think about our own relationships with our own pets. There is also the added fea-

ture of the mystery about the Eyons, who are they? Who controls them? And why? These questions leave the reader wanting to read the second volume, which is an excellent hook into the forthcoming series.

- GOODREADS

For me this is the Animal Farm, 1984, Atlas Shrugged book of the 21st Century. What has been put together here is a new vision of what could be from a totally different angle than what you and I had to read in High School English.

I was fascinated by this world that was all too possible, that this very talented author has created, takes it that one step further, like going from black and white TV to HD color in one fell swoop.

I am not going to tell you one thing about the two lead characters, other than the mind blowing reality of who they are slowly forms in your mind, but is never truly revealed until the end of this book, which incidentally, is only the start of their journey. I can't wait to review the second one, this is that good. We have a real winner here folks, a definite must buy, will be on your shelf for a lifetime and your kids as well, turning into compulsory reading in school if they have the traditional schools around that long. I give it a

4,999. The only reason it isn't a 5.0 is because of a few typos, so in reality 5.0. WOW

Brilliant and Brutal Coming-of-Age Story
Split Decision, essentially a coming-of-age novel, is both brilliant and brutal – brilliant in its execution and brutal in the sensitive subject matter it explores.

Such an innovative and imaginative read. I freaking adore this book

Thought-Provoking Dystopian Novel ~ 4 and a half stars
This is the first book that I have read by the author and I found it both page-turning and thought-provoking, which played on my emotions.

There were plenty of twists and turns. You will not be able to guess what the ending of the story is. I am eagerly awaiting the next book.

- GOODREADS

Fast paced and gripping, while vastly divergent from my normal fare, this story held my interest and kept me reading. The ambitious storyline tackled world-building and characters with equal success, providing references that were easy to relate to even as the plot seeks to carry you to places unknown.

- GOODREADS

Read this book over two nights. Well written, the characters drew me in - sent me back to my teenage years - the insecurities of growing up! It made uncomfortable reading in parts, simply because it was realistic and gritty. Will definitely read more books written by this author 5*

- AMAZON.CO.UK

BOOKS BY THIS AUTHOR

Future Imperfect

Future Perfect

In The Darness Between Worlds

Jigsaw Girl

The Plan

The Boy Who Rescues Pigeons

Ascension

Saving Grace

Invisible

The Owners Volume 1: Alone

The Owners Volume 2: Storm Clouds

The Owners Volume 3: Dark Side Of
The Sun

The Owners Volume 4: A New Epoch

Thre Owners Volume 5: Eyon Rising

The Owners Volume 6: Blood Sky

The Owners Volume 7: Hunter's Moon

And Many Many More...

Printed in Great Britain
by Amazon